MURDER AT THE
BRITISH MUSEUM

MURDER AT THE
BRITISH MUSEUM

JIM ELDRIDGE

Allison & Busby Limited
11 Wardour Mews
London W1F 8AN
allisonandbusby.com

First published in Great Britain by Allison & Busby in 2019.
This paperback edition published by Allison & Busby in 2019.

Copyright © 2019 by JIM ELDRIDGE

A CIP catalogue record for this book is available from
the British Library.

10 9 8 7 6 5 4 3 2 1

ISBN 978-0-7490-2396-6

Typeset in 10.5/15.5 pt Adobe Garamond Pro by
Allison & Busby Ltd.

The paper used for this Allison & Busby publication
has been produced from trees that have been legally sourced
from well-managed and credibly certified forests.

Printed and bound by
CPI Group (UK) Ltd, Croydon, CR0 4YY

To my wife, Lynne, my partner in every way

CHAPTER ONE

London, 1894

Daniel Wilson and Abigail Fenton walked through the high-barred black iron gateway in Great Russell Street that gave entrance to the British Museum, then strode across the wide piazza towards the long row of towering Doric columns that fronted the magnificent building. Atop the columns were ornately carved friezes, recreating the imposing architectural styles of ancient Greece and Rome to inform the visitor that within this building were the treasures of those great civilisations, along with every other form of erudition and wonder known to man since the dawn of time.

They climbed the wide steps, passing beneath the huge porticos into the main entrance.

'Murder at the British Museum,' said Abigail, still bemused. 'It's a place where many of the exhibits celebrate violent death, but I'd never have thought one would actually occur here.'

'Murder knows no boundaries,' said Daniel. 'A palace or a hovel, a desert or the most modern city in the world. It's nearly always about love, money, power or revenge, and that can happen anywhere.'

Abigail cast a look at Daniel and smiled. Daniel Wilson, private enquiry agent and her husband in all but name. She recalled the shocked expression on the face of her sister, Bella, when she'd told her.

'I am going to live with Mr Wilson,' she'd announced. 'When I am not engaged in travelling, doing my archaeological work.'

Bella had looked at her, bewildered.

'As a lodger?'

'As his lover.'

Bella's mouth had fallen open and she had stared at her elder sister, her eyes wide in shock.

'Will he not marry you?'

'In fact, Daniel has asked me to marry him on several occasions. It is I who have said no. I love him very much, but I'm not happy with the fact that once I marry, everything I own becomes the property of my husband. *I* would become the property of my husband.'

'But . . . but . . . to live in sin . . . !'

'It is not sin, not in our eyes. We love one another, we wish to be together, but I am not prepared to become a chattel of someone else.'

Perhaps one day she might marry Daniel, she thought as they mounted the steps. *He is everything I could want: kind, considerate, intelligent, resourceful, and – yes*, she thought to herself as she looked at him – *handsome, but in a slightly rugged, mature way*. His face looked attractively lived-in, not like some of the whey-faced narcissistic dandies she sometimes met when on an archaeological dig, who tried to impress her with their scholarship and knowledge. Daniel didn't try to impress her, he just did. A former detective inspector with Scotland Yard, one who'd worked closely with Inspector Abberline as part of his team of elite detectives, Daniel had left the police and set up as a private detective – or private enquiry agent, as he preferred. It was to Daniel that influential people turned when faced with a difficult case. His reputation for discretion, coupled with his success rate at solving crimes, meant people who hired him could trust him implicitly. Any secrets that were unearthed by him during an investigation would remain secret; at least, to the public. Reputations would be protected. Unless that reputation was a cover for a villain, in which case the villain would be ruthlessly exposed. Daniel would never be part of a cover-up, no matter what inducements might be offered to him.

He is the first person I ever met that I feel I can trust completely, thought Abigail. *And that is why I am bound to him.*

After the bright daylight of outside, made even brighter by the breadth of the piazza, the interior felt dark, even with the gaslight illumination of the lower floor, but the gloom was brightened by a huge poster, an illustration depicting a youthful King Arthur in armour accepting a sword from a woman's hand which had risen from a lake. Above the picture were the words 'The Age of King Arthur – Exhibition Now Open'.

'I thought Arthur removed Excalibur from a stone,' murmured Daniel.

'It depends which version you read,' said Abigail. 'The historical texts say nothing about a stone, or a Lady of the Lake, or even of Excalibur. But I believe this exhibition explores both the historical and the romantic. I shall be interested in examining it.'

'And I'm interested in the practical purpose of our visit,' said Daniel.

He strode to the reception desk and said to the smartly suited man on duty, 'Good morning. Mr Daniel Wilson and Miss Abigail Fenton to see Sir Jasper Stone. He is expecting us.'

The man took a thick diary from beneath his desk, opened it and consulted it.

'The entry for today only says that Daniel Wilson has an appointment with Sir Jasper,' he said. 'There is no mention of Miss Fenton attending.'

Daniel fixed the man with a firm look.

'The initial letter from Sir Jasper asked me to attend. I replied that I would be delighted to do so, and that Miss Fenton would be accompanying me. If her name is not in your book, then the oversight is on the museum's part. *We* are to see Sir Jasper.'

The man hesitated, then began in a superior sniffy tone, 'I'm sorry, sir, but . . .'

Politely, Daniel interrupted with, 'You will be sorrier still if Miss Fenton and I depart, and you have to explain to Sir Jasper that it was you who turned us away.'

The man returned Daniel's firm look, then swallowed and said, 'Of course, sir. I will arrange for someone to escort you to Sir Jasper's office.'

'Thank you,' said Daniel. 'But I know the way. I have met Sir Jasper before.'

As Daniel led the way from the desk towards the stairs, Abigail asked, 'Was that outburst of Stone Age masculinity done to impress me?'

Daniel shook his head. 'No. I encountered him before, on a previous case I did here for Sir Jasper involving a stolen Saxon jewel. The man was officiously annoying then, and he still is.'

'And you enjoy puncturing that sort of superior attitude.'

'I'm not sure if "enjoy" is the right word,' grunted Daniel. 'It's just that posture annoys me. It's an abuse of a tiny piece of power to "put people in their place", as they call it. That same man will kow-tow and give flattery to a lord or a lady.'

'It's fortunate you left the police,' commented Abigail drily. 'You must have been a thorn in the side of some of your superiors.'

Daniel grinned. 'I was once described by a superintendent as my own worst enemy,' he said.

He led the way down the wide stone stairs to a corridor adorned with statues from ancient Egypt along its length.

'You must feel at home with all these,' he commented as they walked along the corridor.

'Most of the exhibits along here are New Kingdom,' she said.

'How "new" is New Kingdom?' asked Daniel.

'1550BC to 1077BC,' replied Abigail. 'The later part is also known as the Ramesside period after the eleven pharaohs that took the name Ramesses.'

'How do you remember all this?' asked Daniel, impressed.

'The same way you seem to remember the name of every criminal you've ever arrested,' said Abigail. 'It's what we do.'

They reached the end of the corridor and then climbed a short flight of stairs to where two doors of dark brown oak faced one another. Daniel went to one and knocked on it, entering at the call from within.

A middle-aged lady was sitting at a desk, and she smiled as she recognised Daniel.

'Mr Wilson! Sir Jasper will be so glad to see you.'

'My pleasure, Mrs Swift,' said Daniel. He indicated Abigail. 'Allow me to introduce my colleague, Miss Abigail Fenton. Miss Fenton, Mrs Swift, Sir Jasper's secretary.'

The two women smiled and shook hands, and Mrs Swift asked tentatively, 'Excuse my asking, but are you by any chance related to *the* Abigail Fenton, the Egyptian scholar and archaeologist?'

Before Abigail could reply, Daniel cut in with a proud, 'In fact, she is that self-same Abigail Fenton.' He turned to Abigail, smiling, and said, 'I told you your name would be known here.'

'Indeed,' said Mrs Swift. 'Sir Jasper was recently in conversation with Hector Makepeace, who was singing your praises.'

'Exaggerated, I'm sure.' Abigail smiled modestly. To Daniel, she added, 'I assisted Hector Makepeace two years ago in a dig at Khufre's Pyramid at Giza.'

'Is Sir Jasper available to see us?' asked Daniel.

'I'm sure he is,' said Mrs Swift. 'I'll just go and tell him you're here.'

She scurried out of the office to the door opposite.

'Hector Makepeace?' enquired Daniel.

'A wonderful man,' said Abigail. 'In his seventies, but with the energy and enthusiasm of a ten-year-old. I learnt an awful lot from working with him.'

Mrs Swift reappeared.

'Sir Jasper will see you now,' she said.

Daniel thanked her, and he and Abigail crossed to the other door. A polite tap, then they opened the door and stepped into the very cluttered office of Sir Jasper Stone, Executive Curator-in-Charge at the museum.

Every available space seemed to be taken up with papers or books; every shelf, the surfaces of the two desks and most of the chairs were similarly groaning under the weight of paper, frequently with a carved ornament on top to stop them being disturbed by a draught and blown around when the door was opened. Two chairs, however, had been left cleared, ready for Daniel and Abigail.

Sir Jasper himself was a portly, benign figure who seemed to have modelled himself on the Prince of Wales, both in his style of dress and the shape of his beard and moustache. He stood up to greet them as they came in, shaking Daniel warmly by the hand.

'Mr Wilson, it's good to see you again, and thank you for coming at this difficult time.'

'My pleasure, Sir Jasper. Allow me to introduce my colleague, Miss Abigail Fenton.'

Sir Jasper shook Abigail's hand warmly as he said, 'Miss Fenton, it is a pleasure to meet you. I know of your work, of course, at the Fitzwilliam, and in Giza and other sites in Egypt. And I read that recently you've been involved in archaeological research along Hadrian's Wall.'

'Indeed,' said Abigail. 'I'm flattered that you're aware of me.'

'The world of museum curation is a small one, especially when it comes to archaeology,' said Sir Jasper. 'Word about good people spreads.' He smiled. 'And about bad people.' He gestured towards two chairs opposite his desk. 'Please, do sit.'

They sat, and Sir Jasper's face grew serious as he said, 'I take it you know why I've asked for your assistance.'

'A man was stabbed to death here a few days ago,' said Daniel.

'Professor Lance Pickering.' Sir Jasper nodded. 'His work on Ambrosius Aurelianus features heavily in "The Age of King Arthur"

13

exhibition we are currently staging. It's been hugely popular. On some days the queue to get in to see it has stretched right out onto Russell Street.

'On the day of the murder, Professor Pickering had not long arrived. He was here to help promote the exhibition by giving a talk on Ambrosius and his connection with Arthur. Not that the exhibition needed any promotion, but the arrangement to have Professor Pickering here had been made before we saw how successful the exhibition was.'

'I assume he was also here to promote his book on Ambrosius,' put in Abigail. 'I saw it on display at the entrance.'

'Yes, indeed,' said Sir Jasper. 'Again, that was an agreement made before the exhibition opened so successfully, but we agreed to honour our agreement with the professor, so his book has been on display both at the exhibition and in the museum shop.

'On the day in question, Professor Pickering handed in his hat and coat at the cloakroom, and then went to the gentlemen's convenience to freshen up before his talk. The staff on duty became worried when he didn't appear and the audience for him were waiting, so one of them went to investigate. The door of one of cubicles in the convenience was closed. In fact, it had to be broken down because it had been bolted from the inside. The body of Professor Pickering was discovered within. He'd been stabbed a number of times.'

'The rest of the convenience was empty?'

'Yes,' said Sir Jasper. 'That was the other puzzling thing; a notice saying "Out of Order" had been put on the door. But the person who escorted Professor Pickering to the convenience swears the sign was not on the door then.'

'So the killer put the sign there to stop anyone coming in and

14

perhaps preventing the murder,' said Daniel. 'This suggests the killing was planned and not a random act.'

'That was Inspector Feather's opinion as well,' said Sir Jasper.

'Inspector John Feather?' asked Daniel.

Sir Jasper nodded.

'A very good man,' said Daniel. 'If he's on the case I'm not sure you need me.'

Sir Jasper hesitated, then said awkwardly, 'Unfortunately, Inspector Feather is not in charge of the police investigation. His superior officer, Superintendent Armstrong, has taken charge, and he has different views on the case to Inspector Feather.'

'Yes, he would have,' said Daniel grimly. 'I'm guessing it's not just the murder you wish us to investigate, Sir Jasper?'

Sir Jasper gave a wry smile. 'Very perceptive of you, Mr Wilson, as always. No, the murder is one thing. My main concern is the reputation of the museum. If the reason for Professor Pickering's murder might in any way adversely affect the museum . . .'

'I understand,' said Daniel. 'Leave it with us, Sir Jasper, and we'll see what we can find.'

Sir Jasper passed over two cards to them. 'These cards, signed by me, will give you full access to anywhere in the museum. I've taken the liberty of doing them because, unfortunately, some of our staff can take their responsibilities a little too literally when it comes to some areas of the museum, and I don't want your investigation to be obstructed in any way.'

'Thank you, Sir Jasper,' said Daniel, taking the two cards and handing one to Abigail. 'Can I also ask if it's possible for us to have one of your lesser-used rooms as a base for our investigation? I'm thinking if information comes to us from outside, or if we wish to talk to people privately. I know that space is at a premium, so something small like a storeroom, or a broom closet, would be sufficient. So long as we could get a desk and a couple of chairs into it.'

'Of course.' Sir Jasper nodded. 'I'll talk to David Ashford, the museum's general manager. He'll arrange it for you. Give me an hour.'

'Thank you,' said Daniel. 'In the meantime, we'll start our investigation. The sooner we begin, hopefully the sooner we'll find out who was behind the killing.'

CHAPTER TWO

'So where do you plan to start?' asked Abigail.

'I thought I'd check the toilet where Pickering was killed. While I'm doing that, could you check the exhibition?'

'What am I looking for?'

'I don't know. Someone killed Lance Pickering. His book features in the exhibition. I'm hoping some kind of connection might show itself.'

While Abigail headed for the exhibition, Daniel went downstairs to the basement area, illuminated by gas mantles, where the conveniences were. The gentlemen's convenience was separated from that for the ladies by a door marked 'Private. Staff only'. He pushed open the door of the gents'. An attendant in an usher's uniform was sitting on a chair just inside the door, and he rose to his feet as Daniel entered with a 'Good morning, sir.'

'Good morning,' returned Daniel. He produced the card from Sir Jasper and handed it to the man.

The man nodded. 'Ah yes, we had word that you would be coming, sir. How can I be of service?'

'I believe there was no one in attendance here on the day the tragic event happened,' said Daniel.

'No, sir,' confirmed the man. 'It was only as a result of that, that it was decided to keep an attendant on duty here, to reassure patrons of their safety. There is also now a female attendant in the ladies' convenience.'

'And the door in between the two, the one marked "Private. Staff only"?'

'That is a storeroom, sir, for brooms and cleaning apparatus.'

Daniel stood and took in the room. White tiles on the floor and halfway up the walls to the level of the four handbasins. A hand towel on a brass rail by each handbasin. Three urinals, and three cubicles, the doors of which were closed.

'Are the cubicles in use at the moment?' asked Daniel.

'No, sir.'

'Then would you show me in which cubicle the body was found?'

The man nodded and led Daniel to the end cubicle, where he pushed open the door to show the water closet with its wooden seat and the cistern above it. Daniel reflected how rare this sight was even in a city like London. Most houses still had earth privies outside.

'Was the body clothed when found, or in a state of undress?' asked Daniel.

'Fully clothed, sir.'

'And on the seat, or on the floor?'

'On the floor. The door was locked, but when the attendant saw blood trickling out from beneath the door he went to the storeroom and got a hammer in order to break the door down.'

'Was that really necessary?' asked Daniel. He gestured at the space above the door. 'There is plenty of room above the door for someone to have climbed over from the next cubicle and unbolted the door from the inside.'

'The attendant who discovered the body was a former soldier, sir. He has a disability which would have made climbing over the top difficult.'

'What sort of disability?' asked Daniel.

'He only has one arm.'

Daniel nodded. 'I understand. In the circumstances, he did the right thing.' In truth, Daniel didn't feel this at all. The attendant should have got someone more agile to climb over the partition and unbolt the door, rather than destroying possible evidence by smashing the door open. But politics dictated it was better to let word spread among the staff at the museum that this Daniel Wilson, the private enquiry agent, was supportive of them. That he was on their side. People talked more freely if they felt at ease and safe with an investigator.

'Who was the attendant who discovered the body?' asked Daniel.

'Howard Wills,' said the attendant.

'Is he available?'

'I'm afraid he's off today. But he'll be in tomorrow.'

'What about the usher who escorted Professor Pickering down here? Where will I find him?'

'That was Gerald Dunton. He's on his break at the moment.'

'I see. Very well, I'll make a point of seeking them out. If you see either of them before I do, will you tell them I'd like to talk to them. Sir Jasper is arranging accommodation for me, an office, and I'll leave a note at main reception where that will be.'

'Certainly, sir.'

'And your name?'

'Rob Stevens, sir.'

'Thank you, Mr Stevens, you've been very helpful.'

Abigail was impressed by the way the exhibition had been put together and presented, with the more popular versions of the Arthurian legend – paintings by the Pre-Raphaelites, along with those by James Archer, depicting the death of Arthur, the Lady of the Lake, Lancelot and Guinevere, along with illustrated pages from Tennyson's *Idylls of the King* – and then introducing (in glass cases to protect them) pages from the manuscripts of the early sixth-century historian Gildas, Bede from the seventh century and a page from the Nennius's *Historia Brittonum*, compiled in the ninth century. From this, the key phrase was translated, displayed for all to see: 'The twelfth battle was on Mount Badon, in which there fell in one day 960 men from one charge by Arthur' – the first mention of Arthur as a king by name in any historical document.

There then followed pages from the works of William of Malmesbury and Geoffrey of Monmouth, and finally from Malory's *Le Morte d'Arthur*, alongside illustrations specially produced for the exhibition. And finally a whole section devoted to Ambrosius Aurelianus, the fourth century Romano-British cavalry leader who led the British resistance against the Saxon invaders, and was said to be the model for the legendary King Arthur. And neatly, and conveniently, stacked on a table close to this section were copies of *Ambrosius Aurelianus and King Arthur: The True Story* by Professor Lance Pickering. Abigail was just slightly cynical, wondering how much sales had increased by as a result of Pickering's brutal murder, when Daniel appeared beside her.

'The mystery of the murder in the locked cubicle is solved,' he told her. 'There's a large gap above each of the cubicle doors. The killer stabbed Pickering, put his body into a cubicle, bolted the door from the inside then climbed out of the cubicle over the top of the door.'

'So, no mystery,' she said.

'Except for who did it.'

'Mr Wilson!'

The cheery call made them both turn. A small man in his forties was approaching them, a beaming smile on his face.

'I heard they were calling you in! Like old times, eh!' Abigail noticed that Daniel didn't respond, didn't offer to shake the man's hand, just regarded the man calmly.

'Ned Carson, in case you've forgotten me.' The man beamed. 'The *People's Voice*. I was around during the Ripper investigation.'

'And, as I recall, you accused myself and Inspector Abberline of engaging in a cover-up to protect people you referred to as "the guilty parties".'

'Well, there was evidence, Mr Wilson!' said Carson, still smiling.

'There was no evidence of any cover-up,' retorted Daniel flatly.

'Well, that could be debatable,' said Carson, unfazed by Daniel's hostility. 'Still, all water under the bridge. This is a different day.' He doffed his hat towards Abigail. 'Sorry, miss, I guess I'm interrupting. Ned Carson at your service. Are you working with Mr Wilson?'

'This lady is an employee of the museum,' said Daniel quickly.

'Oh? In what capacity?'

'I am a historian,' said Abigail.

'Ah, then you're in the right place,' said Carson, and he gave a chuckle. Then he turned back to Daniel. 'So, are the rumours true? You've been brought in to look into the grisly murder here? Does that suggest the museum isn't satisfied with Scotland Yard?'

'I have no information on that. My own personal view is that Scotland Yard is – and always has been – the right organisation to investigate crime. Now, if you'll excuse me.' And Daniel moved off.

'So you don't think Superintendent Armstrong's a useless idiot!' Carson called after him, before giving another chuckle and heading for the museum exit.

Abigail hurried after Daniel and found him in the Etruscan Room. He looked annoyed.

'I'm an employee of the museum?' she queried.

'Technically, you are,' said Daniel. 'As am I.'

'But you didn't tell him that. Nor did you introduce me by name.'

'From my experience, the less you tell Mr Ned Carson the better.'

'I assume he's a newspaper reporter.'

Daniel gave a derisory laugh. 'I think that's stretching the description,' he said sourly. 'He writes for a gossip rag called the *People's Voice*. It prefers innuendo and rumour to hard facts. And smearing people.'

'You and Inspector Abberline, I gather, from your conversation with him.'

Daniel scowled. 'During the Ripper investigation there were all sorts of rumours circulating about who the killer was. They included members of the royal family. Abberline and I investigated those claims, but found nothing to back them up. Carson, in the pages of the *People's Voice*, suggested that we'd been bought off. The *People's Voice* has its own agenda, which is to attack and undermine the Establishment, in particular the government of the day, the royal family, the police and the armed forces. "The Arms of Brutal Repression", Carson calls them.'

'Why? He must have a reason. Or a political stance?'

'If he has, I don't know what it is,' said Daniel. 'I suspect it's some form of anarchy, the destruction of social order. But I'm not sure what he wants in its place.'

'His parting shot was to call Superintendent Armstrong an idiot,' said Abigail.

'Yes, well, there he's right,' admitted Daniel. 'But he's certainly not going to get me to endorse that opinion. Publicly, I will always support the Yard, however much privately I think that some of the top officials don't deserve to be in charge of a whelk stall, let alone the Metropolitan police force. But there are many good officers in the organisation I have a lot of time for.'

'Like this Inspector Feather you mentioned.'

'Exactly. John Feather is a superb policeman, and if the top brass had half a brain between them he'd have been promoted to superintendent long ago.'

'So why hasn't he been? What's stopped him?'

'I think the blockage lies with Armstrong. He needs the intelligence and detective skills of John Feather to get results, so he keeps him where he can use him, which is at inspector level. If John got promoted to chief inspector, which he deserves, he might be moved to a different department. So, Armstrong does his best to make sure *he* gets any credit, and John Feather is no threat to his position.'

'It sounds like the nastiest of politics,' said Abigail.

'It is,' said Daniel. 'And unfortunately, we could well get caught up in it. Which is why I'm off to Scotland Yard. Will you be alright here for a while?'

'Certainly. The way the exhibition's been done is most interesting. Sir Jasper should be very pleased. I assume you feel my presence will hamper you.'

'Not necessarily. I'm going to call on Inspector Feather at Scotland Yard and renew our old acquaintanceship. But there's a chance I might run into Superintendent Armstrong, and that could prove . . . difficult.'

'I assume he doesn't like you.'

'The feeling, as you may have guessed, is mutual. The thing is, he might have me thrown out of the building, and I don't want that humiliation to happen to you as well.'

'You must have done something very big to upset the superintendent.'

'Let's just say we never got on.'

'Very well, off you go.'

'Will you still be here when I've finished at the Yard?'

'Indeed, I will. There's a lot to take in.'

'Anything leap out at you?'

'Yes,' said Abigail. 'The exhibition has been very well done.'

CHAPTER THREE

Daniel stood across the road from Scotland Yard, surveying the imposing red and white bricked building and reflecting on the years he'd called it his working home. Then, he'd been an insider, a crucial part of Fred Abberline's elite squad of detectives. Now he was most definitely an outsider, and although he still had good friends amongst many of his former colleagues, there were certain people who had no desire to see him in the building again. And, unfortunately, some of them were quite powerful. Like his nemesis, Superintendent Armstrong. As he approached the building he wondered if Armstrong would be there, and what his reaction would be if they met. *What's the worst he can do*, thought Daniel, *order me to leave the building?* Yes, it would be an inconvenience, but not the end of the world. Still, he decided not to send a message up to John Feather telling him he was in the building and would like to see him, just in case it got intercepted. Instead, Daniel headed for the rear entrance and took the rather dingy concrete staircase up to the second floor, rather than the grand marble one of which the architect had been so proud.

Daniel walked along the familiar corridor, passing offices that housed old colleagues, before he came to John Feather's.

Here's hoping he's not got Armstrong with him, he thought.

He rapped at the door, and at the call 'Come in!', he opened it and stepped in.

Inspector Feather's face broke into a broad grin of welcome as he saw who it was. 'Daniel! Good to see you!'

The two men shook hands and Feather said, 'You didn't send a note up to say you were in the building. I'd have sent a messenger to bring you up.'

'I was reluctant to let too many people know I was here,' Daniel admitted. 'Certain people wouldn't be happy about it and might have had me thrown out.'

'Superintendent Armstrong.' Feather grinned.

'So, I took a chance you'd still be in the same office.'

'Indeed, I am,' said Feather.

Like Daniel, Feather was in his mid-thirties, but shorter. He'd also always looked younger than his years, and in his early days as part of Abberline's squad the others had taken to affectionately referring to him as The Kid. This had led Feather to grow and develop a rather luxuriant moustache, eclipsing most of his face, and he still proudly sported this same moustache, which, to Daniel's eyes, seemed to have grown even larger.

Feather gestured for Daniel to sit in a chair, then asked, 'So, is your visit for a favour, or are you planning to return to the fold?'

'Neither,' said Daniel. 'I've come to let you know that the British Museum has hired me to look into the murder there.'

'Good,' said Feather emphatically.

'You don't mind?'

'On the contrary, this case could do with your particular eye on it.' He grimaced. 'But I doubt if Superintendent Armstrong will see it the same way.'

'Sir Jasper Stone at the museum said Armstrong was taking charge of the case,' said Daniel. 'Why?'

'It's a high-profile case and he's looking for the top job when the commissioner retires,' said Feather.

'Armstrong as commissioner?' repeated Daniel, aghast.

'I know. Unthinkable, isn't it. But he's an example that you don't have to be a good copper to rise through the ranks; being a clever politician counts for more. You see the amount of coverage he gets in the papers? And he spends a lot of time at Parliament, mixing with the right people.'

'So a result here pushes him further up the ladder. But isn't he taking a chance with a high-profile case like this? If it isn't solved, it'll be a big mark against him.'

Feather shook his head. 'If it isn't solved, it won't be his fault, you can be sure of that. It'll be someone further down the chain.'

'Someone like you?'

Feather gave a rueful grin. 'Someone very much like me. Which is why he kept making sure my name was mentioned when he was talking to the press about the case. If we don't get our killer, it's down to yours truly. If we do, hail the hero, Superintendent Armstrong. So, what do you make of it so far, Daniel?'

'The killer got out of the cubicle over the top.'

'Yes, I worked that one out.' Feather grinned. 'So, someone who's agile. Not too big or fat.'

'And someone with a very cool nerve,' said Daniel. 'It was well planned. The "Out of Order" notice on the door. Have you spoken to the usher who showed Pickering to the gents' convenience?'

Feather nodded. 'He says he just escorted the professor downstairs and showed him into the convenience. He said he didn't notice anyone in there when they went in. The usher left and went back upstairs, and left the professor to it.'

'So, the chances are the killer waited for the usher to go back upstairs, and then went in to kill Pickering.'

'The usher said he didn't notice anyone following them, or hanging around downstairs. But that doesn't mean someone wasn't.'

'There's a ladies' just along from the gents', with a cleaning store in between the two,' said Daniel. 'Someone could have been hiding in one of them.'

'But why would they?' asked Feather. 'That assumes they knew that Pickering would be going to the gents' as his first port of call.'

'Yes.' Daniel nodded thoughtfully. 'It's more likely the killer followed them down.'

'But the usher said he didn't notice anyone.'

'It's one to think about,' said Daniel.

'Along with the fact that Pickering was stabbed not once but seven times, and there was no suggestion of robbery.'

'Seven times?' echoed Daniel.

'So, someone, despite having a cool head when planning the murder, was very angry indeed,' said Feather.

Daniel mused, 'Anger. Hate. Love. Jealousy. Seven stab wounds means a lot of passion was involved.'

'Unless it was the work of a lunatic, which is Superintendent Armstrong's favourite theory.'

'Always a possibility,' admitted Daniel. He hesitated, then said, trying to be casual, 'By the way, John, the other reason I came was to let you know I'm working with a partner on this case.'

'Oh? I thought you preferred to work on your own. The Lone Wolf.'

'Yes, well, this is someone who's got knowledge that I haven't. She's an archaeologist and historian. Got a degree in history from Cambridge. Been on archaeological digs all over the world. Egypt. Palestine.' He noticed Feather surveying him with an amused smile on his face.

'A woman?' asked Feather.

'Well, obviously,' said Daniel. 'That's why I said "she". I worked with her at the Fitzwilliam Museum in Cambridge. Circumstances brought us together because she was working there – and her insights into the history side of the case were invaluable. Same as here. The murder seems to be connected to this exhibition that's on: "The Age of King Arthur".'

'Perhaps,' said Feather. 'Perhaps not. We're looking into Pickering in case there might be some other reason anyone would want him dead.'

'And?' asked Daniel.

Feather looked as if he was about to say something, then stopped and gave a small smile. 'I'd prefer you to form your own opinion,' he said. He wrote something on a piece of paper and passed it to Daniel. 'This is the address of the late Professor Pickering, in case you want to call and talk to his widow.'

'You think there might be something there?'

'Let's see what you think,' said Feather. 'I don't want to

prejudice anything. But I'm guessing you'd be talking to her anyway.' He looked at Daniel with a quizzical smile. 'So, there's nothing between you and this female archaeologist . . .'

'Abigail Fenton,' said Daniel. 'Miss. And why should there be?'

'Daniel, you taught me everything there was to know about people, and how to read them. Little things like how people react when asked a question they don't really want to answer: shuffling their feet, twisting an ear, pursing their lips, putting on a bit of a front . . .'

'If you're thinking I'm doing any of those things . . .'

'I know you. I worked with you for years, and I can tell there's something about this woman that's special.'

Daniel hesitated, then he nodded. 'Yes, there is,' he admitted. 'But as far as this case is concerned, it's a professional relationship. When you meet her you'll see how sharp she is. She's intelligent, strong, resourceful . . .'

'And good-looking?'

'Yes, well, there's that, too,' said Daniel.

'Are you and she going to get married?'

'That's another issue,' said Daniel awkwardly. 'I just wanted you to know about her in case you come across her at the museum. We've arranged to have an office at our disposal during the investigation, so you can always get in touch with us there.' He put the piece of paper with the address in his pocket. 'And thanks for the tip about Mrs Pickering.'

'I didn't give you any tip,' said Feather.

'You say that after you've given me a talk about interpreting people's body movements,' chuckled Daniel.

He left Feather's office and headed towards the stairs that would take him back down to main reception. As he walked along the corridor, a door opened and Superintendent Armstrong stepped out. He stopped and scowled when he saw Daniel.

'What are you doing here?' he demanded.

The superintendent was a tall, broad-shouldered man with a protruding belly that showed a love of good food and wine. It was said that in his younger days he'd played rugby at a high level, and Daniel could well believe it. Even in his forties he had the imposing bulk that looked like it could still hold its own in a scrum.

'I came out of courtesy to report my involvement in the murder at the British Museum,' said Daniel.

'What involvement?'

'Sir Jasper Stone has asked me to do a separate investigation.'

'Why?'

'Because Professor Pickering was killed on their premises and they are concerned about their reputation.'

'I'm already protecting their reputation!' thundered Armstrong.

'Nevertheless, Sir Jasper has invited me and my partner to work on the case independently.'

'What partner?' growled Armstrong suspiciously.

'A historian and archaeologist called Abigail Fenton. She has a degree in history from Girton College in Cambridge, and is highly respected for her archaeological surveys in Britain and across the world.'

'How on earth did she link up with you?' demanded Armstrong.

'We completed a case together successfully at the Fitzwilliam Museum in Cambridge, where she was curating an exhibition of Egyptian artefacts. She has a great knowledge and understanding of history, and as this case seems to involve history . . .'

'It doesn't!' snapped Armstrong. 'It's some lunatic; that's obvious.'

'Surely, it's too early to draw that conclusion—' began Daniel, but he was cut off by the superintendent.

'Oh no you don't!' Armstrong snapped, waving a fleshy finger at him. 'You're not in Cambridge now. This is my manor. My case.' His eyes narrowed and he demanded, 'Who have you seen here?'

'I've just been to see Inspector Feather to advise him of my involvement. I was on my way to see you to inform you of the same,' said Daniel.

'There's no need,' growled Armstrong. 'You're not needed. We're doing this case. You have no part of it. And I won't have you strolling around here like you're part of this building. You're not. Don't come here again or I'll have you thrown out.'

CHAPTER FOUR

After Daniel left, John Feather was joined in his office by his detective sergeant, Jeremiah Cribbens. Cribbens proceeded to fill up his pipe with the evil-smelling black shag he seemed to love and lit it, then puffed away at it in between recounting his latest accomplishment on the Pickering murder. Or lack of accomplishment, as soon became clear.

'I had another word with the man who took the professor down to the convenience to see if anything had jogged his memory about that event, but sadly he said, no, that was all he could remember. He didn't see anyone hanging around. Then I went to have another word with the man who found the professor's body, but he wasn't in work today.'

'Oh? Why?' asked Feather, his interest aroused. People who went missing so soon after a murder were always worth looking into.

'It's his day off,' said Cribbens.

'Pre-arranged?' questioned Feather.

'Yes, sir. I had a word with the museum's Mr Ashford, who arranges the work schedules, and he told me today is Mr Wills' regular day off.'

'Good thinking.' Feather nodded appreciatively.

'Then I went in search of the person who cleans the conveniences to see if he knew any more about this "Out of Order" notice that someone stuck on the door . . .'

Feather was saved from being told, as he guessed, that this person was also either not in, or had nothing more to offer, because the door of his office crashed open and Superintendent Armstrong glared in at the two men.

Sergeant Cribbens leapt to his feet with alacrity and stood stiffly to attention, while Feather rose at a more leisurely pace.

'Is there a problem, Superintendent?' he asked.

'There is, and his name is Wilson!' growled Armstrong. 'I understand he was here in this office not many minutes ago.'

'That's correct,' said Feather. 'He popped in to inform us as a matter of courtesy that he'd been engaged by the British Museum to look into the murder of Professor Pickering, and he wanted to assure us that he would be doing nothing to interfere with our investigations.'

'Damn right he won't!' snorted Armstrong. 'I've just seen Wilson and told him he's banned from this building. Banned! Did you hear that, Inspector?'

'I did, sir,' said Feather calmly. 'He's banned.'

'Exactly! Do you know why, Inspector?'

Yes, I can certainly guess, thought Feather wryly. Aloud, he said, 'Because you don't like him, sir.'

'I don't like what he stands for.' Noticing Cribbens still standing stiffly to attention, he said curtly, 'At ease, Sergeant. You may sit.'

Gratefully, Cribbens sat down and picked up his pipe.

'Wilson is a maverick,' continued Armstrong. 'I disapprove of policemen who learn everything they can at the force's expense, and then go off their own private way, coining money hand over fist at our expense!'

'I don't think that Daniel – Mr Wilson – does that, sir. He only takes on an investigation when a private client hires him.'

'And what does that say about us?' demanded Armstrong. 'They don't have faith in us!'

'With respect, sir, I believe the British Museum has a great deal of faith in us. But Mr Wilson has a special relationship with Sir Jasper Stone after he solved that theft of that Saxon jewel.'

'Which we could have solved if we'd had more time!' shouted Armstrong angrily. 'Well, I've told him and now I'm telling you as you two seem to be such buddies, he's not to come in here. I won't have him using our expertise to prise fabulous sums of money out of gullible people. If you ask me, what he does is as good as criminal.'

'He's not the only one who's gone private, sir,' Feather pointed out. 'Inspector Abberline joined the Pinkertons and has done very well with them, I understand.'

'Better than he did here,' said Armstrong with a sneer. 'I've no time for Abberline either. Traitors to the force, the pair of them. Abberline and Wilson.' He glowered at Feather. 'I hope you're not entertaining any ideas of going private, Inspector.'

'No, sir. Absolutely not. I am very satisfied with my career here at Scotland Yard, and as long as I give satisfaction, I hope that career will be a long one.'

'It could well be, so long as you keep away from Wilson. He's a contaminant.' He strode back to the door, then turned. 'Remember, Inspector. Wilson is barred from this building. And don't you forget it.'

'It is indelibly inscribed on my memory, sir,' said Feather.

Armstrong gave Feather a quizzical look, searching for some sign of sarcasm in the inspector's face. Then he gave a last scowl and left, slamming the door behind him.

'Cor!' exhaled Cribbens. 'The super don't like Daniel Wilson, does he, sir!'

'Well spotted.' Feather grinned. 'We'll make a detective of you yet. Is there anything more to report?'

'Er, no, sir,' said Cribbens. 'I was just wondering what our next move is?'

'This business of the number of stab wounds bothers me,' said Feather.

'Someone didn't like the professor, sir,' said Cribbens.

'Exactly, but who?'

'When we saw Mrs Pickering she said her husband didn't have an enemy in the world,' said Cribbens.

'I've noticed that's usually the reaction of the nearest and dearest when something like this happens,' said Feather drily. 'We need to talk to someone else who knew the professor.'

'Who?'

'His publisher might be able to help,' said Feather. 'So, your next move, Sergeant, is to find out who published this book of his, and get their address.'

'Consider it done, sir,' said Cribbens.

After Cribbens had departed on his errand, Feather reflected on Armstrong's anger at former Scotland Yard detectives who became private investigators. Feather had meant what he'd said to the superintendent; he had no intention of going down that path himself. Not with a family of four children to support, as well as his wife's widowed mother, who also lived with them. And the truth was, there were other superintendents he might be working under who were far worse than Armstrong. Armstrong was many things Feather disliked: vain, bigoted, arrogant and not a quarter as intelligent as he believed himself to be. But he wasn't crooked or corrupt. And as long as it stayed that way, and as long as John Feather needed the regular salary he got from Scotland Yard, he was fine with the way things were.

It was different for Daniel. He was single. He didn't have to worry about making sure there was enough money coming in regularly to feed a large family. He could afford to take the chance on whether or not he'd earn anything that month.

Then Feather smiled. But that might change. Daniel had fallen for someone. A female archaeologist with a degree from Girton. Feather chuckled to himself as he recalled the embarrassed look on Daniel's face when he'd told him about her.

I'm looking forward to meeting her, he thought. *She must be someone special if she's able to make Daniel Wilson stammer and blush.*

CHAPTER FIVE

Abigail was still studying the exhibition when Daniel returned.

'Good?' he asked.

'Excellent,' she said. 'You really should spend time looking at it.'

'I have done,' he said.

'A cursory glance only.' She sniffed. 'How did you get on at Scotland Yard? Did this Superintendent Armstrong throw you out?'

'He did,' said Daniel. 'But fortunately not until after I'd met with John Feather, who's given us a tip.'

'Oh?'

'*Cherchez la femme*. He suggests we talk to the professor's widow.'

'Why?'

'He didn't say.'

'Surely it would be a matter of course to talk to his widow, find out if he had any enemies, that sort of thing.'

'Absolutely, but there was something in the way he said it.'

'He suspects her?'

'Mr Wilson! Miss Fenton!'

They turned and saw a tall, thin man in his middle forties approaching them, immaculately dressed in a dark three-piece suit, shoes shined to a gleam.

'I'm David Ashford. Sir Jasper asked me to find a space you can use as your base while you are here. I've arranged a room halfway up one of the spiral staircases just off the main reception. It's quite bijou, but I hope it will suffice. There's room in there for a small table and a couple of chairs, but unfortunately little else. If you'll follow me, I'll show you the way.'

'I'm sure the room will be fine,' said Daniel.

'Thank you for accommodating us at such short notice,' added Abigail, as Ashford led the way up the spiral staircase.

'The thanks is ours,' said Ashford. 'I fear this tragic incident could adversely affect the visitor numbers to the exhibition on King Arthur. Sir Jasper has spent so long preparing it and it was intended to be the highlight of the season.'

'It deserves to be,' said Abigail. 'I've taken the opportunity to spend time looking at it. The displays are superb, and the assembled information remarkably wide, taking in so many different aspects of the Arthur story.'

'Thank you.' Ashford smiled. 'It's always gratifying to receive praise from someone as knowledgeable as you, Miss Fenton. I know of your work, of course, in the area of ancient Egypt. Perhaps while you are here you'd care to take a look at our Egyptian rooms?'

'I would love to,' said Abigail.

He stopped at a landing and indicated a door. 'This is your room.'

He pushed the door open and they followed him in. He'd described it as bijou, but Daniel thought 'tiny and cramped' might be a better description.

'Again, I must apologise for the smallness of the accommodation . . .'

'This will be fine, Mr Ashford,' said Abigail. 'There will only be the two of us in it, and much of the time we will be around the museum and elsewhere, following leads. We very much appreciate your arranging this at such short notice.'

Ashford gave a smile and a small bow, and left.

'Flatterer,' muttered Daniel.

'That's something I learnt from you,' said Abigail. 'A kindly smile gets more results than a sharp command.'

'Yes, you were certainly more brusque when we first met.'

'I was not brusque,' bridled Abigail. 'I was efficient. I was also at a disadvantage because I was a woman in what was essentially a man's profession, and I had to appear to be stronger than a man if I was to be considered as an equal.'

'But now, because of me, you have softened?' Daniel smiled.

'I saw the results you achieved when you interviewed people, especially the disadvantaged and those of lower social status. They appreciated the respect you showed them and were more helpful to you than they could have been to others. It was a salutary lesson.'

'It doesn't always work,' said Daniel. He looked around the room. 'Still, you're right to compliment Mr Ashford. The room may be tiny, but at least he found us something, and in a short space of time, and without fuss. When I was at Scotland Yard, if a new senior officer was appointed and needed an office, it usually took months, and then only after endless red tape had to be untangled. Anyway, now I suggest we go to see Mrs Pickering, and see what light she may throw on what happened.'

The late Professor Pickering and his wife lived in a large and luxurious-looking house in Park Square East, one side of a private square overlooking Regent's Park. The gardens that formed the centre of the square were very well kept and ornately planted with all manner of blooms.

'It must cost a pretty penny to keep the gardens looking like this,' observed Daniel. 'I hadn't realised writing books on history could be so lucrative.'

'Appearances can be deceptive,' pointed out Abigail. 'We don't know that the professor owned the house. It could have belonged to his wife's family or be rented.'

'Even if it's rented, it would be expensive.'

'Some people live for show to impress others, regardless of expense,' said Abigail. 'You'd be surprised at how many aristocrats are living in debt.'

'No, I wouldn't,' said Daniel. 'I've met many of them in my time.'

They mounted the steps of white stone to the front door and rang the bell. The door was opened by a plump woman in her sixties, who looked at them enquiringly.

'May I help you?' she asked.

Daniel and Abigail handed the woman their cards.

'My name is Daniel Wilson, and this is my colleague, Abigail Fenton. We would appreciate it if we could talk to Mrs Pickering.'

'For what reason?' demanded the woman.

'We are here at the request of Sir Jasper Stone of the British Museum,' said Daniel.

It was no proper answer, but enough for the woman to nod.

'If you'll wait here, I'll see if Mrs Pickering is available,' she said and closed the door.

'Very protective,' commented Daniel.

'The sign of a good housekeeper,' said Abigail.

The door opened again, and the woman gestured for them to enter. 'Mrs Pickering is in the drawing room. If you'll follow me.'

The house was as opulent and luxurious inside as it was outside, the walls adorned with paintings, along with statues that Daniel recognised as Roman and Greek. Most likely copies, he guessed, but even then, he reflected that it showed there was money here.

Mrs Pickering was sitting in a chair by the bay window, looking out. A young man, well-dressed, with long hair that curled over his collar, was standing by the window next to her. As Daniel and Abigail were escorted in by the housekeeper, Mrs Pickering rose and looked at them enquiringly.

'Good afternoon, Mrs Pickering. My name is Daniel Wilson, and this is my colleague, Abigail Fenton. We're very sorry to intrude at this difficult time, but we are private enquiry agents hired by the British Museum to look into the death of your late husband.'

'I thought the police were already doing that,' she said suspiciously.

'They are, and we are working closely with Inspector Feather,' replied Daniel. 'But the museum has its own concerns that the professor's death may have had something to do with his work on the exhibition they are currently presenting. We understand that the attack on him happened when he'd gone there to deliver a talk connected to it.'

'Yes,' she said.

The young man suddenly moved from the window into the room.

'I can see this is a difficult time,' he said. 'I'll take my leave for the moment.'

'I'm sorry if we are interrupting anything,' said Daniel. 'We will be very happy to come back later.'

'No, no, Mr Tudder was just leaving.' She turned to the young man and said, 'I'll show you to the door, Mr Tudder.'

'No, I'll be fine,' said Tudder. 'Once again, Mrs Pickering, my condolences.'

He bowed his head and held out his hand to her. She shook it, giving him a wan and grateful smile; then he left.

With Tudder gone, she gestured for them to sit. 'I'm still not sure what else I can tell you that I haven't already told the police,' she said.

'I promise we won't keep you long,' said Daniel. 'Did your husband say anything to you before he went to the museum to suggest that he was apprehensive about anything?'

'To be honest, I didn't see my husband on that morning. I had another engagement that day, and I left for it while my husband was in his study preparing for the talk he was to give.'

'Was this other engagement local?' asked Daniel.

She gave him a glare. 'I don't see that is relevant,' she said curtly.

'No,' agreed Daniel, 'but it may be. Say someone was watching the house, for example, in preparation for the attack on your husband.'

'But why would they do that?' she demanded. 'I understand it was just some lunatic, that he was just a victim chosen at random. At least, that's what Superintendent Armstrong informed me.'

'That may be right, Mrs Pickering, but we and the police are also looking into the possibility that your husband was deliberately chosen. We now have evidence to suggest that his death was quite carefully planned.'

Mrs Pickering's face had gone white, and now she said angrily, 'That is a ridiculous thing to say! Who would want to murder my husband?'

'That is why we're asking questions,' said Daniel.

She fell silent for a moment, then asked, 'You say you have been hired by the British Museum?'

'Yes, ma'am. By Sir Jasper Stone. By all means you can contact him to verify that.'

She shook her head. 'There is no need,' she said. She looked at Daniel and Abigail, her expression fearful. 'You say that my husband was deliberately targeted. Do you think that I might also be at risk from this . . . this person?'

'I would hope that's unlikely, ma'am,' said Daniel. 'As I say, at this moment we're just trying to put together the professor's movements on the day of the tragedy. You say you had another engagement on that day. Did you notice anyone loitering outside when you left the house?'

'No. But then, I wasn't paying that much attention.'

'If you'll pardon me, Mrs Pickering, where was your other engagement?' asked Abigail.

Mrs Pickering fixed her with a cold glare. 'It was a private matter and nothing to do with this.'

'With respect, Mrs Pickering, at this moment everything may be to do with what happened,' said Daniel.

'I can assure you that is not the case here,' she said curtly. She stood up. 'I've told you all that is relevant. I did not see my husband before he left for the British Museum. The first I heard of what had occurred was when I returned home and received a visit from Superintendent Armstrong to inform me of the dreadful news. I now wish to be left alone.'

Daniel saw that Abigail was about to say something more, most likely to press her for detail of this other engagement, so he rose quickly and said, 'Absolutely, Mrs Pickering. And we apologise for taking up your time.'

After they left the house and walked towards Albany Street, Abigail said, 'We should have insisted on getting details of this other engagement from her. She's obviously hiding something.'

'Yes, she is,' agreed Daniel, 'but pressing her would have had no effect except to get us thrown out of the house. We are not the police. And, even if we were, she could still have us thrown out of the house. The wealthy and those with titles live by different rules.'

'No one is above the law,' said Abigail.

'Tell that to a policeman trying to arrest an MP, or a lord or lady, or magistrate,' said Daniel ruefully. 'What did you make of Mr Tudder?'

'The young man? She's having an affair with him. Did you see the way she stroked his arm when they shook hands goodbye?'

'Yes, the same thought struck me.' Daniel nodded. 'And the fact she didn't see the professor that morning suggests they don't share sleeping accommodation.'

'She may not even have been in the house that morning,' said Abigail.

'No, indeed. Did you notice the religious images and items on the walls and shelves? A small picture of the Bleeding Heart. A rosary. Catholics.'

'So, if Mrs Pickering and Mr Tudder wished to make their union official . . .'

'They couldn't, not while the professor was alive. There's no divorce for Catholics.'

'I can't see either of them wielding a knife that way.'

'Nor can I,' said Daniel. 'But there are plenty who will, for a price.'

CHAPTER SIX

The offices of Whetstone and Watts publishers, were in Fitzroy Mews, a small cobblestone cul-de-sac not far from the busy junction of Euston Road and Tottenham Court Road, and very near to the outer circle of Regent's Park.

'Just a few moments' walk from the Pickerings' house,' observed Feather. 'Very convenient.'

He rang the bell beside the highly polished black door, and the door was opened by a smartly dressed woman of middle-age.

'Detective Inspector Feather from Scotland Yard. This is Sergeant Cribbens,' Feather introduced them. 'And you are?'

'Miss Roseberry,' said the woman. 'Is this about what happened to poor Professor Pickering?'

'It is, indeed. We wonder if it would be possible to speak to the person who worked with him most closely on his book on King Arthur?'

'That would be Mr Whetstone,' said Miss Roseberry.

'Mr Whetstone?'

'Mr Mansfield Whetstone. He's the senior partner. The book of King Arthur was as much his pet project as it was the professor's. They were both inspired by the subject.'

'Would it be possible to talk to Mr Whetstone?'

'He's in his office. I'll go and see if he's free. If you'll just step inside and wait in there.'

She guided them to a small and comfortably furnished waiting room whose walls were adorned with paintings and caricatures of distinguished-looking people, mostly men, before heading up a flight of stairs.

'Is this a sort of art gallery?' asked Cribbens, looking at the pictures.

'I would suspect they are the firm's authors,' said Feather.

Cribbens frowned as he examined the pictures. 'I can't see everyone being impressed by them,' he observed. 'Some of these cartoons make the subject look . . . well . . . idiotic.'

'Never underestimate the vanity of authors,' said Feather. 'For some, being mocked in a caricature is the height of flattery.'

There were the sounds of heavy footsteps crashing down the stairs, then Mansfield Whetstone appeared. He was a big man in every respect: tall, broad-shouldered, and with a large stomach that suggested a man of healthy appetites. With his full beard, he reminded Feather of actors he'd encountered, particularly those who played the larger-than-life Shakespearean roles such as Lear or Falstaff. His booming voice when he spoke added to this image.

'Scotland Yard, I presume! I have been expecting your visit ever since this tragedy happened. You have come to ask me about poor Professor Pickering.'

'We have, sir. I'm Inspector Feather and this is Sergeant Cribbens.'

'Welcome to the offices of Whetstone and Watts, specialist quality publishers,' said Whetstone. He gave a long and theatrical sigh, then a tortured, 'Lance Pickering! One of the greatest historians of our generation! The world is a lesser place for his tragic departure, and in such a cruel way! Who could have done such a thing, Inspector?'

'That's what we're trying to find out, sir. You must have got to know him during the preparation of his book.'

'We were like brothers! Kindred spirits!'

'In which case, we're hoping you might be able to cast some light on whether he had any enemies.'

'Enemies? Lance? Never! The man was universally loved. And respected, not just by his peers in the sphere of historical research, but by everyone who knew him. Have you met his wife, Laura, Inspector?'

'I have, sir.'

'Never was there a more loving couple! That will tell you the kind of man Lance was. A devout husband with a loving wife who doted on him. A marriage made in heaven!'

'What about in his profession? Were there any rumours of professional jealousy? From other historians, or other authors?'

'None!' thundered Whetstone. 'Lance was revered! In the halls of academe, in the corridors of archaeological establishments, the name Lance Pickering shone like a beacon of integrity and benevolence! The man had no enemies at all!'

* * *

'What did you think of that, sir?' asked Cribbens as he and Inspector Feather walked out of Fitzroy Mews.

'That I've never heard such tosh in all my life,' said Feather. 'You've met Mrs Pickering, Cribbens. Did she strike you as someone stricken by grief at the loss of a marriage made in heaven?'

'I must admit, she didn't, sir,' said Cribbens. 'But then, some people are very successful at hiding their feelings. Maybe she's one of them.'

'You may well be right,' said Feather. 'The question is, what feelings is she hiding?'

That evening Daniel served the supper he'd made for them: a roasted chicken, roasted potatoes, carrots and cabbage.

'You must let me cook a meal for you,' said Abigail as Daniel laid the plates heaped with food on the table in the kitchen.

'A kitchen range takes some getting used to,' said Daniel. 'And, as a single man, I cooked for myself for many years, while you always had a cook.'

'I can learn,' said Abigail.

'I'm sure you can,' said Daniel.

'I shall start with something simple,' said Abigail. 'Sausages.'

'Sausages need to be cooked right through, it's not enough that the outside skin is brown.'

'I have seen sausages cooked before,' responded Abigail primly.

'Very well,' said Daniel. 'I suggest sausages and bacon with eggs for tomorrow. With bread on the side.'

'Why not potatoes?'

'You can try potatoes, if you wish, but if you boil them too much they can turn to mush.'

'If that happens I shall make them into mashed potato. Or I could roast them, as you've just done.'

'The oven part of the range is the one that takes most getting used to,' cautioned Daniel. 'It's experience of using it that tells you when something is cooked right the way through.'

'But how does anyone get experience without using it?' asked Abigail.

'Yes, that's true.' Daniel nodded.

'It seems to me you are very protective of your kitchen range,' Abigail observed.

'You're probably right,' admitted Daniel. 'It took me a long while to get used to it, and I was very proud of the first meal I cooked successfully on it. It was about getting the right amount of coal in the grate, not too hot, not too cool. Knowing which shelf in the oven was the hottest.'

Abigail smiled. 'I promise I shall only do it under your watchful eye until you are confident in me.' As she ate, she asked, 'Why did you not employ a cook?'

Daniel laughed. 'When I was a working police officer, there wasn't the money to pay for one. Nor could I guarantee what time I'd return home for meals.'

'And when you became a private agent?'

'Again, I was never sure what time I'd be home for meals, or if at all. And also, there didn't seem any need, having looked after myself all these years.' Then, rather awkwardly, he added, 'I suppose it's a class thing, as well. This is Camden Town. You must have noticed it's one of the poorer districts. People here are employed as cooks in better houses; they don't employ them. That's for the middle classes and upwards.'

She smiled and said, 'Is that a dig at me for being middle-class?'

'No, no dig. Just an observation.' He smiled as he said, 'I'm just so grateful that you've settled in here as you have. And turned a house – and a rather cold and austere one – into a home.'

'I'm grateful that you've allowed me to. Many men would resent a woman coming in and changing things. Bringing in paintings and ornaments to decorate. Cushions for the chairs.'

'Much more comfortable,' said Daniel. 'I should have done it before.'

'But you didn't. I did.'

'You've made it our house.'

She shook her head. 'No, it's your house. I've just brought some of me into it.'

'You've brought everything I could ever want.'

'Oh really, Daniel, you're getting sentimental!'

'I suppose I am. But then, I haven't felt this way about anyone before.'

'I'm surprised you never married. Most men are married by the time they're thirty.'

'I could say the same about you,' countered Daniel.

'Perhaps we never met the right person before,' said Abigail. 'But it is strange, isn't it, how two people from very different walks of life should find themselves in this situation.'

'I will always be grateful to the Fitzwilliam for bringing us together so we could discover that,' he told her.

'And you don't mind that I still go off on digs?' asked Abigail.

'It's what you do,' said Daniel. 'What you are. Why would I want to change you?'

'Most men want their wives to fit into their pattern.'

'Ah-ha! You said wives!'

'We are husband and wife in all but name. Don't you feel that?'

'You know I do. I missed you terribly while you were up at Hadrian's Wall.'

'You could have always come with me,' she said.

'And done what? Watched you dig?'

'You could have dug with me.'

He shook his head. 'It's not what I do. I'm a detective. That's what I do.'

'There are mysteries to be solved in archaeology,' she said.

'But no culprits to be brought to book. You may find evidence of an ancient murder from two thousand years ago, but there won't be any arrests made.'

'This case may prove you wrong,' she said. 'If the exhibition is at the heart of the murder of Professor Pickering, then we might have to dig back into ancient history to find out why.'

'If,' said Daniel doubtfully. 'At the moment I feel we should concentrate on the living.'

'You mean Mrs Pickering and her lover?'

'Her *assumed* lover,' Daniel stressed. 'I think it's time to pool our resources with Scotland Yard and see what they have.'

'I thought you were *persona non grata* at Scotland Yard.'

'I am. So, I suggest we invite John Feather to meet us at the museum tomorrow. It'll be good for you two to meet. I think you'll like him.'

CHAPTER SEVEN

As Superintendent Armstrong entered through the main doors of Scotland Yard the next morning, he was surprised to see one of the Yard's messengers get off his stool beside the main reception desk and scurry towards him.

'Superintendent!' said the messenger, a small wiry man. 'The commissioner says he wants to see you as soon as you arrive.'

Armstrong was bewildered. He looked at the clock to confirm that he wasn't late. No, it was half past eight. He'd rarely known the commissioner to arrive at the Yard before nine-thirty, except for an emergency. This was obviously such an emergency.

He didn't stop to go to his own office, but hurried up the wide staircase to the first floor, and along the wide passageway to the commissioner's office. As he mounted the stairs various thoughts ran through his mind, none of them good. What disaster had brought the commissioner in at this hour? And was he being summoned because he was involved – and therefore in trouble – or because he was needed to solve a difficult situation?

The commissioner's secretary looked up as he entered the outer office.

'Ah, Superintendent,' she said. 'The commissioner's expecting you. Please, go straight in.'

The commissioner looked up from his desk as Armstrong entered. He wasn't smiling. There was no welcome in his look; instead he glared at Armstrong in an accusing manner.

What have I done wrong? thought the superintendent.

The commissioner gestured for Armstrong to take the seat across from him on the other side of his wide desk.

'My cousin, Sir Cheriot Windrush, is on the board of the trustees at the British Museum,' he intoned.

'Ah, yes, sir. The murder of Professor Pickering. Rest assured that my men are working on it at this very moment.'

'I am not assured, Superintendent,' snapped the commissioner. 'Sir Cheriot informs me that the museum has brought in a private enquiry agent to investigate the murder.'

'Yes, sir,' said Armstrong. 'I believe that to be the case.'

'Will you explain to me why the museum feels the need to engage the services of a private detective on such an important matter as this?' the commissioner demanded.

'I believe this particular agent has an existing relationship with the museum, sir. He helped resolve a situation regarding a stolen Saxon jewel.'

'Helped?' snapped the commissioner.

Armstrong hesitated, then admitted, 'I understand he solved it, sir. He brought the identity of the culprit to the attention of the police, and we subsequently charged the thief with the crime.'

'*He* solved it. Not *you*.'

'I was not involved with that particular case, sir.'

'That's not the point!' snapped the commissioner angrily. 'The fact is that the museum, by engaging this person, has expressed its lack of confidence in the police to solve this crime. And a very high-profile crime, I may add, the murder of a leading academic and author in such an institution as the British Museum.'

'With respect, sir, we haven't had sufficient time yet to investigate,' protested Armstrong. 'The murder only happened a few days ago. We are still gathering evidence.'

'But not fast enough to satisfy the museum!' barked the commissioner. 'I don't like this, Armstrong. There have been too many cases recently where the reputation of the police force in the eyes of the public has been undermined. This is just one such example, and it's happening on a case you are in charge of. I want this situation dealt with, Superintendent. *You* will solve this heinous crime. You and your men. Not some private detective. I will not stand by and let the reputation of this force be tarnished. Solve this crime, Superintendent, and solve it quickly! And that is an order!'

First thing next morning Daniel sought out Howard Wills, and found him on duty in the rooms that housed the Saxon collection. Wills looked every inch a former sergeant major, tall, rigid, straight-backed, although in civilian life his muscle had mostly turned to fat. With the left sleeve of his uniform pinned up to show his missing arm, and his excess weight, Daniel understood why it would have been difficult for Wills to climb over the toilet cubicle partition.

Daniel introduced himself and showed Wills the card Sir Jasper had given him.

'Terrible tragedy, sir,' said Wills. 'It was lucky it was me who found him, being used to sudden violent death. One of the other attendants without that experience might have gone to pieces.'

'Indeed,' said Daniel. 'I understand you were in the army.'

'Northamptonshires, 58th Regiment,' confirmed Wills. He indicated his empty sleeve. 'Lost my arm at Majuba Hill. 1881.'

The Battle of Majuba Hill, reflected Daniel. The final battle of the Boer War, the crushing defeat of the British which led to the Boers' victory and the reinstatement of the Republic of South Africa.

'It must have been a terrible experience,' said Daniel sympathetically.

'No war is a good experience when you lose, sir,' said Wills.

'True,' agreed Daniel. 'Tell me about finding the body.'

'He was definitely dead, sir. There was a lot of blood. There was blood on the back of his coat as well as on his shirtfront, so I could tell he'd been stabbed more than once. And there was a wound in his throat, just below his chin.'

'It sounds like a savage attack,' said Daniel.

'That was my thought, sir. I heard later that the doctor who examined the body found seven stab wounds. Two in the back, four in his front, and that one to the neck.'

'And you didn't see anyone when you came down?'

'No, sir. Mr Ashford sent me to find the professor because the audience was waiting. I came down the stairs and went into the conveniences. There was no one else in, just the one cubicle door closed. It was when I saw the blood trickling out from under the door I knew at once something was wrong. I banged on the door but there was no answer. I went into the next cubicle and climbed on the toilet seat and looked over, but all I could see was an arm lying on the toilet seat.' He indicated his empty sleeve. 'Because of this I couldn't climb over the partition, so I went to the storeroom and got a hammer and bashed the lock open. And there he was. Lying on the floor between the wall and the toilet bowl.'

'What about the sign on the door?' asked Daniel. 'The one that said "Out of Order".'

'Yes, sir. That puzzled me,' said Wills. 'It wasn't there when I showed the professor down, that I'm sure of. When I saw it, I thought it meant there was a cleaner inside, but when I entered there was no one at all, just that closed cubicle door.'

'So, you saw no one?'

'No one at all.'

Daniel thanked Wills and then started back towards their small office to share Wills' account with Abigail. But instead, he made for the exhibition, remembering their conversation the previous evening when she'd urged him to study the displays.

'You told me that the exhibition may contain the clues we're looking for, but I can only look at it from a historical perspective,' she'd told him. 'You are the trained detective.'

'I shall be groping in the dark,' he'd protested. 'Much of this is strange to me. Yes, I know the stories about Arthur and Guinevere, and Lancelot and the Lady of the Lake . . .'

'The fictional Arthur,' said Abigail. 'Pickering's book is about the historical Arthur.'

And so, Daniel directed his attention to the later parts of the exhibition, those focusing on the *real* Arthur, and found himself looking at pages from ancient texts displayed in glass cases. But the language of them wasn't even English. Latin, possibly, but not a Latin he'd seen before.

'Taking it all in?' said a voice.

Daniel turned and saw John Feather.

'John! You got my note?'

'I did,' said Feather.

'I thought meeting here would be better for us, as Superintendent Armstrong threatened to throw me out if he saw me in the Yard again,' said Daniel.

'Yes, he came to see me after he'd bumped into you and warned me about allowing you in the building. He still remembers.'

'It was a long time ago,' said Daniel. 'When he was just an ordinary detective sergeant, the same as me.'

'He was never the same as you, Daniel. I also heard that the commissioner was looking for him first thing this morning, and seemed to be on the warpath; so I took the opportunity to head out of the Yard before whatever wrath the commissioner is feeling gets passed on to me.' He indicated the display cases. 'What have you learnt?'

'That I can't understand what the writing says, so I don't know the half of what this is all about.' Daniel sighed. 'Come up and meet Miss Fenton.'

Daniel led the way towards a narrow winding staircase to one side of the main reception area. 'We've been allocated a room just up here. It's small, but it serves us.'

He mounted the stairs, Feather following, to a small landing, and then through the open doorway into the tiny room. Abigail got up from the small table she was sitting at and gave a smile of welcome.

'You must be Inspector Feather,' she said. 'Daniel said he'd asked you to call.'

'Please, call me John.'

'Abigail,' said Abigail, and they shook hands.

'Luckily, we've been able to squeeze a third chair in,' said Daniel. 'As I mentioned, Abigail is working with me on the case.'

'Yes, Daniel has been singing your praises loudly,' said Feather.

'To be taken with a very large pinch of salt,' said Abigail. 'When it comes to detective work, I am very much the novice.'

'As we all are,' said Feather. 'Always learning. Right, Daniel?'

'Very true,' said Daniel. 'Anyway, I thought it might be useful to catch up. We met Mrs Pickering yesterday afternoon. There was a young man at her house. A Mr Tudder.'

'The artist.' Feather grinned.

Daniel and Abigail exchanged puzzled looks.

'The artist?' repeated Abigail.

'That's the official story, according to the servants.' He winked. 'I used one of your old tricks, Daniel. Sending someone out to pick up gossip. Some of it may be just that, idle chatter, but often you find a nugget of gold. It seems that Mrs Pickering is having her portrait painted by this Joshua Tudder, who is said to be a rising young artist. In fact, their joint alibi for the time Professor Pickering was killed was that they were in his studio.' He hesitated, then said, 'However, according to the gossip, what they were doing there is open to speculation.'

'They are having an affair,' said Abigail. 'That was obvious from the way they were with one another.'

'Yes, that was my guess,' said Feather.

'Mrs Pickering was very reluctant to give us any information about her portrait being painted,' said Daniel.

'That is because she claimed it was being done as a secret gift for her husband,' said Feather. 'At least, that's what she told her servants, so they were sworn to keep her visits to Tudder's studio a secret from the professor.'

'Very convenient,' commented Daniel. 'And clever. I have no doubt that if you investigated, you would indeed find a portrait of Mrs Pickering in Tudder's studio. Unfinished, of course.'

'Exactly,' said Feather. 'What interests me more is who Tudder might have been in contact with.'

'An assassin.' Daniel nodded. 'You spotted the items that showed they were Catholics?'

'The Bleeding Heart. A rosary. So, the only way that Tudder and Mrs Pickering could be legally married, and Mrs Pickering to inherit his wealth and property, is if Pickering died. Which, conveniently, he did.'

'So, they're your main suspects at the moment?' asked Abigail.

Feather frowned. 'Only because we haven't got anyone else in the frame, not if it was a calculated killing.'

'Superintendent Armstrong told Mrs Pickering it was the work of a lunatic. A random killing,' said Daniel.

Feather shrugged. 'Yes, that's his opinion. Makes for an easier defence when he fails to turn up the killer. It wouldn't surprise me if some poor soul fished out of the Thames fits with the profile of the person Armstrong says he's looking for.'

'Case solved. Kudos for Superintendent Armstrong.' Daniel sighed.

'But that's outrageous!' burst out Abigail. 'That would be a fraud!'

'And who would question it?' asked Daniel. 'Especially if the person pulled out of the Thames has no family to defend him.'

'You'd be surprised how many people have reached the top of their particular profession through false credentials, Miss Fenton,' added Feather. 'And unfortunately, the police force is not exempt.'

'So, apart from Superintendent Armstrong's lunatic, and our suspicions about Mrs Pickering and Joshua Tudder, what other options are the Yard looking at, John?'

Feather sighed and gave a shrug. 'None, truth be told. We've taken a look into Pickering's life, but he seems to be exactly what he appears to be: a respectable professor of history who writes books and lectures. There seems no reason why anyone would want to kill him. Which leaves us with the other option: that it was the museum itself that was the target.'

Daniel walked Feather back downstairs, both men promising to keep in touch, and then Daniel returned to the exhibition. He still wasn't sure how it could help him come to any conclusions about why Pickering had been killed, but Abigail seemed to be of that opinion, and he'd learnt that she had one of the sharpest minds he'd ever encountered. He was studying the exhibits, when a cheerful voice beside him said, 'Daniel. I heard you were here.'

Daniel turned and grinned in delight at seeing the portly figure of Joe Dalton. 'Joe!' he said. 'This is a pleasure! Long time, no see.'

Dalton was a reporter for the *Daily Telegraph* and his speciality was crime. They'd first met seven years before, when Daniel had been part of Abberline's team investigating the Jack the Ripper murders.

'A little bird told me you'd been brought in by the museum to look into the professor murder,' said Dalton.

'There must be a lot of talking birds around,' grunted Daniel. 'I was caught by Ned Carson the other day. Remember him?'

Dalton laughed. 'The *People's Voice*. How could I forget him? Still claiming to be a reporter?'

'Who buys the *People's Voice*?' complained Daniel. 'It's just a rag!'

'Lots of people like that sort of stuff.' Dalton shrugged. 'They prefer to read dirt about people rather than hard news.'

'Most of the time the stuff they write isn't even true!' burst out Daniel. 'It's just hints and innuendoes. Smears.'

'And not enough so they can be sued for libel. So, what about this case. Any leads?'

'Early days, Joe. You'd be better advised to have a word with John Feather.'

'I already have,' said Dalton. 'The trouble is he has to be careful what he says because he's got Armstrong watching over his shoulder the whole time.' He gestured at the exhibition. 'So, crime of passion? Or is the answer here somewhere?'

'I wish I knew,' admitted Daniel. 'What have you picked up yourself?'

'Nothing.' Dalton sighed. 'I've tried digging into Pickering's life looking for a motive, but no one's saying anything off about him, just that he was a pillar of society.'

'And you have doubts about that?'

'I've no idea,' said Dalton. 'I never met the man. But it strikes me that for someone to get stabbed to death, he must have upset someone. That is, if he was the target.'

'Is there any reason to think he wasn't?'

'Well, we've both known of people being killed because of mistaken identity.'

'True, but those are usually people who look anonymous, or have a resemblance to someone else. Looking at the picture of the professor on the book display, he looks fairly individual.'

'I don't know,' said Dalton thoughtfully. 'To me, he looks like a lot of the toffs you see around London. So, are you back in the metropolis for a while? I keep hearing about you going off to distant parts. There was that case in Cambridge. The reanimated murderous mummy.'

Daniel laughed. 'A reporter's invention.' He chuckled. 'Yes, I'm certainly back while this case is on.' He gestured towards the stairs. 'In fact, come on up to our office and meet my investigating partner.'

'A partner?' said Dalton, surprised. 'I thought you worked on your own, ever since you left the force.'

'Yes, but now and then two heads can be better than one, especially with her mind. She's clever. I also think you'll like her.'

'Her?' Dalton smiled. 'Now this *is* intriguing.'

CHAPTER EIGHT

Abigail was writing something when Daniel appeared, but she stopped as soon as she saw Daniel had someone with him.

'Abigail Fenton, meet Joe Dalton,' Daniel introduced them to one another. 'Joe's a reporter for the *Daily Telegraph*, and highly reputable. Miss Fenton is a history graduate from Girton College, Cambridge, a celebrated archaeologist who has conducted major digs at most of the major sites of the pyramids in Egypt, and has just returned from a series of explorations along Hadrian's Wall.'

They shook hands as Dalton asked, 'Pardon me for asking, Miss Fenton, but with all those qualifications, what on earth are you doing here with Daniel?'

'Call me Abigail, please. If Daniel counts you as a friend and someone to be trusted, then so shall I. The answer is, Daniel has asked me to help him solve the murder of Professor Pickering.'

'So, you're a detective as well,' said Dalton admiringly.

'A trainee detective,' she corrected him.

'Joe and I first met when Inspector Abberline and I were on the Ripper case. Joe was one of the few who was after facts rather than sensational garbage.'

'And there was a lot of garbage around at that time,' said Dalton. 'Black magic. Witchcraft. Ritual killings.'

'The royal family,' added Daniel. 'A mad surgeon.'

'But he was never caught, was he,' said Abigail.

'Sadly, no,' said Daniel.

'But Daniel and Fred Abberline got close,' said Joe. 'It was only the powers-that-be that stopped them making an arrest.'

Abigail looked quizzically at Daniel. 'You never told me,' she said.

'It was a long time ago,' said Daniel.

'It's only eight years,' she said.

'True. But the person we had our eye on is dead now. So, better to concentrate on the here and now. What were you working on?'

Abigail showed him a short list she'd written. 'I was thinking about what John Feather said: that perhaps the museum itself was the target,' said Abigail. 'So, I was making a list of possible reasons. There's a lot of resentment in some foreign countries about artefacts that have been taken from them to be displayed somewhere far away. Like the Elgin Marbles, for example, which were taken from the Parthenon and brought to Britain. The Greeks are still very angry they're here in the British Museum instead of being on display in their native Greece.'

'It's an interesting thought, but in my experience, most crimes are committed against people rather than institutions,' said Daniel.

'That's not strictly true,' said Dalton. 'Look at the recent attacks there have been on government buildings by Irish home rule terrorists.'

'That's different, that's politics,' countered Daniel. 'They claim they're fighting for Irish independence.'

'But they're still crimes,' said Dalton.

'Exactly.' Abigail nodded. 'Mr Dalton and I are as one on this.'

Dalton grinned at Daniel. 'You're right, Daniel. Clever indeed.'

'Only because she's agreeing with you,' grumbled Daniel. 'But why would anyone want to attack the British Museum?'

'Museums are always being attacked,' said Abigail. 'When I was in France . . .'

'Yes, but that's in France!' argued Daniel. 'They have revolutions, we don't.'

'The Civil War,' said Abigail crisply. 'Oliver Cromwell.'

'King Charles I losing his head, just as the French aristocrats did,' added Dalton.

'Yes, alright,' said Daniel uncomfortably. 'My point is that *most* crimes are committed against people, rather than . . .'

He was interrupted by the sound of angry raised voices and crashing sounds from somewhere below, including the sound of glass breaking.

'Trouble!' he said.

He rushed out of the room and down the spiral staircase, Abigail and Dalton close behind him.

In the exhibition hall two young men were struggling with four uniformed stewards who were having the greatest difficulty in keeping hold of them. Daniel shot a glance at the exhibition and saw that one of the cases was smashed, glass scattered around the floor. One of the young men was wielding a walking stick, which Daniel guessed had caused the damage to the case, and he was now using it to try and ward off the stewards. The young man raised the walking stick and brought it down hard, trying to hit another of the glass cases, but missed.

Daniel moved forward and kicked the young man at the back of his knee. The young man uttered a yelp of pain and fell to the ground, the two stewards collapsing on top of him.

Daniel turned to the other attacker and saw him struggling to break free from the two stewards holding him, lashing out with his elbows and his feet. Abigail stepped forward, a look of fury on her face, and punched the young man so hard in the stomach that her fist disappeared into his clothing. He sagged, gasping for air, and as he sank to his knees, Abigail grabbed him by his hair and yanked him face down to the floor, shouting angrily, 'How dare you!' With that, she plonked herself down on the fallen man and ordered the stewards, 'Tie his hands and feet while I sit on him.'

The young man began to struggle and jerk, trying to throw Abigail off, but Abigail simply grabbed him by the hair again and banged his face on the stone floor.

'I abhor violence!' she snapped. 'But if you struggle any more I shall do worse to you.'

The young man that Daniel had kicked in the knee was also under control, the stewards tying his hands behind his back with a length of cord.

'And his ankles,' ordered Daniel. 'He'll kick, otherwise.'

'What's going on?' Sir Jasper had arrived, a look of shock on his face.

'For some reason, these two decided to attack the exhibition,' said Daniel. 'They smashed the glass of one of display cases, but everything else seems to be alright. Luckily, we caught them before they could do too much damage.'

Sir Jasper stared at the two young men lying on the floor. 'What on earth . . . ?' he said, still in a state of shock. Then his voice broke as he appealed, 'Why?'

'We're here, sir!' said a voice.

Daniel saw that two uniformed constables had arrived, brought by a steward who'd run out into the street for help. One of the constables reached down, grabbed one of the young men by the collar of his jacket and hauled him up to a sitting position. Then he frowned and asked, 'You sure this is them? They look like toffs.'

Yes, Daniel thought, they didn't resemble the kind of youths he expected the constable was used to arresting for vandalism. Both young men were dressed in neat and expensive-looking clothes: long jackets with velvet collars, tailored trousers, patent leather shoes.

'This is certainly them,' said Daniel. 'Caught red-handed.'

The constable shook his head. 'Toffs doing this sort of thing. I don't know what the world's coming to. The judge ought to throw the book at 'em.' He hauled the young man completely to his feet. 'You leave it to us, sir. We'll call a wagon and have them in a cell before they know what's hit them.'

'Wait!' said Sir Jasper suddenly. He took hold of Daniel's arm and steered him to one side, out of earshot of the constables. 'Is there a way to avoid this, Mr Wilson? A court appearance could reflect badly on the museum, especially following on from the murder. This is a very important exhibition for us, and the idea that people may stay away because they're frightened of what might happen . . .'

Daniel nodded. 'I understand, Sir Jasper. Your preference is for the matter to be treated with discretion.'

Abigail joined them, her face registering outrage. 'Did I hear you right, Sir Jasper? These two vandals have committed the worst outrage I've ever experienced in any museum, or any other place of education, and you are preparing to ignore it?'

'Not ignore it, no,' said Sir Jasper. 'But the bad publicity . . .'

'They deserve to be flogged!' said Abigail angrily. 'Ten years' hard labour each!'

Daniel bit his lip to stop himself from smiling at this enraged outburst of Abigail's.

'There could be a way, Sir Jasper,' he said. 'They look like they can afford to pay for the damage.'

'Never!' shouted one of the young men.

Daniel strode to him and hissed, 'I would strongly advise you to keep your mouth shut. You heard what my colleague has said: she would like you flogged and sent to jail with hard labour. The constables will agree with her. If you go to prison, you will die, I can assure you of that. The flogging will weaken you, then the other prisoners – which include some very, very vicious men – will take advantage of you in every way possible. As will the warders. In the end you will beg for death to release you. Or you can let me try and negotiate some safe way out of this.'

The shorter of the two young men opened his mouth to protest, but the other shot him a warning look and nodded.

Abigail glared at Daniel. 'You're not seriously going along with this! These so-called men are criminals! That page from Nennius is rare beyond belief. If it had been damaged . . .'

'This is the second such attack,' Daniel whispered to her. 'We need to find out if it might be connected to the one where

Professor Pickering was stabbed. Is there a link? This is our chance to question them, in our way. Once they have been taken away by the police and put into the system, that chance will be lost.'

She looked at him suspiciously. 'I suspect you are trying to gull me, Daniel Wilson,' she said accusingly.

'Not at all,' he said, still keeping his voice low. 'If, after we have talked to them, you still want them punished, to include flogging and imprisonment, then so be it. I shall support you in trying to persuade Sir Jasper of that. But, right now, they are more valuable to us here, with just you and I asking the questions.'

She turned and studied the two young men, who now looked white-faced and nervous. Then she nodded. 'There is merit in what you say. But they must be taught a lesson.'

'They will be,' Daniel promised her. He went back to Sir Jasper and told him, 'I'll see what I can arrange, Sir Jasper.'

'Thank you, Mr Wilson,' said Sir Jasper. 'If it can be achieved, the museum will be very grateful.'

Dalton, who had been standing at one side observing everything, approached Daniel as Sir Jasper walked off. 'I'm guessing you don't want anything about this in the paper?' he said in a tone of amusement.

Daniel nodded. 'I owe you one, Joe,' he said.

'You owe me a big explanation to my editor if he finds out about this,' commented Dalton. 'If he asks I'll say it was part of a deal with the museum to get an exclusive if you catch the murderer. How does that sound?'

'Like blackmail,' said Daniel ruefully.

Dalton grinned. 'Let me know how it goes,' he said. 'I'll be in touch.'

As Dalton left, Daniel walked to where the constables were waiting, their eyes on the two young men.

'Can we take 'em now?' asked one of the constables.

'There is a problem,' said Daniel, his voice barely above a whisper. 'The British Museum won't press charges. Which means, as employees of the museum, neither I nor my colleague, nor the stewards who overpowered the young men, will be able to give evidence against them.'

'Why not?' demanded the constable.

'Because, as you rightly observed, they are toffs,' said Daniel quietly. 'You can be sure their families will have high-powered lawyers at their disposal. Barristers who will do their best to destroy the reputations of the only persons giving evidence against them. You and your fellow constable. A clever barrister will ask if you saw the actual vandalism happening, and under oath you will be forced to admit that you didn't. All you saw was a struggle going on, and the two young men being trussed up. There might even be doubt cast by a good barrister as to whether the two young men were actually the victims, assaulted while conducting a peaceful protest, and the glass case got broken during the assault on them.'

'No one's going to believe that!' snorted the constable.

'No?' said Daniel. 'Look at them. Imagine them in the dock, with a clever and very expensive barrister asking the questions, in front of a judge or magistrate who's possibly on social terms with these men's families. And because we will be unable to speak up, it will be a case of your word against theirs. And you will have to admit you saw nothing, because it all happened before you arrived.'

The constable looked at the young men and scowled. 'I hate it when this happens!' he growled. 'If they'd been two working class young men from the streets they'd be in jail over this. But this pair . . .'

Words failed him, and he glared angrily at the two young men.

'I agree with you,' said Daniel sympathetically. 'It's an unfair world. But I promise you, they will not go unscathed.'

'No?'

'No,' said Daniel. 'I doubt if their families will take kindly to their activities when we tell them what happened. I'm sure there will be repercussions for them, especially when the families find they have to make good the damage.' He gave them a smile. 'People with money hate parting with it.'

'True,' said the constable. 'Very well, then, sir. We'll leave them with you. And I hope their families thrash 'em.'

CHAPTER NINE

The young man sitting in the chair in the small office seemed to have recovered his bravado. He had been the one who'd wielded the walking stick and smashed the glass case. Now, released from the ropes that had bound him, he sat, arms folded, staring defiantly at Daniel and Abigail. Daniel guessed his age at about nineteen.

His fellow conspirator was languishing, locked in a laundry room, his wrists and ankles still bound, waiting to be questioned once Daniel and Abigail had finished with this young man.

'First, your name,' said Daniel.

'Sir Galahad.'

'Your real name,' said Daniel wearily.

'That is the only name I answer to,' said the young man.

'Very well,' said Daniel. 'If that is your answer, I shall have you locked away in Bedlam and your photograph published in the newspapers in order to find out if anyone recognises you.' He leant forward and said warningly, 'Your family, for example.'

The young man went white and swallowed hard. 'You can't do that,' he said hoarsely.

'To someone called Sir Galahad, I can do whatever I want,' said Daniel. 'A citizen with a proper name and address, however, has rights. The choice is yours.'

The young man hesitated, then announced, 'My name is Alan Markham. I am a member of the Order of the Children of Avalon.'

This brought a slight groan from Abigail. Daniel looked enquiringly at her, but she shook her head.

'Why did you attack the exhibition?'

'We had a message.'

'Who from?'

'Emrys.'

When Abigail saw Daniel give a puzzled frown, she said quietly, 'Merlin.'

Markham shot her a quick glance then rapped out a few words in what Daniel took to be a foreign language. To his surprise, Abigail responded in words that sounded similar. Markham looked taken aback, then asked, 'You are a bard?'

Instead of answering his question, Abigail asked, 'How did you receive the message?' When he hesitated, she prompted, 'A seance?'

Markham nodded.

'And Emrys – Merlin – told you to attack the exhibition.'

'He told us it denigrates the true Arthur. The spirit of Avalon is being turned into a sideshow. The miracles are explained as if they were just . . . nothing.'

'Very well,' said Daniel. He pushed a piece of paper and a pencil across the table to Markham. 'You will write down the name of your companion, and also a list of the members of your order. With addresses, where you can.'

'I will do no such thing!' said Markham defiantly, folding his arms.

Daniel shrugged. 'Have it your own way. I'll have you taken to prison on a charge of causing criminal damage, with a recommendation you are refused bail. I'm guessing you'll receive a year's hard labour, and may the experience be a salutary one.' He turned to Abigail and said, 'Would you ask the security men to come and join us and take Mr Markham away. Newgate would be as good as any police station to take him.'

As Abigail got up to leave, Markham shouted, 'Wait!' He snatched up the pencil and began to write. When he finished, he pushed the paper across to Daniel, who ran his eye down the list, then nodded.

'Thank you, Mr Markham.'

'What's going to happen to me?' asked Markham, and for the first time he showed his fear beneath his bravado.

'That will be up to the museum authorities,' said Daniel. 'But, as you have been cooperative, they might consider leniency of some sort. We shall see.'

'No prison?' said Markham hopefully.

'As I said, the final decision rests with the museum authorities.

We'll now talk to your fellow conspirator' – he looked at the list Markham had provided – 'Edward Chapman, and then we'll discuss your situation with Sir Jasper Stone.'

This time, Abigail left the small room, reappearing with two security men who took Markham away.

'You seem fairly sure that Sir Jasper won't press charges,' said Abigail.

'You heard what he said. He has no desire for bad publicity. We'll see what we can get from the other miscreant, and then suggest to Sir Jasper he brings their families in and gets them to pay compensation for the damage as a way of avoiding the case being taken to court. They'll pay up, I'm sure.' He looked at her, curious. 'By the way, what was that language you and he spoke? Some kind of magical tongue?'

Abigail laughed. 'Welsh.'

'You speak Welsh?'

'I had to study it for part of my degree, along with Gaelic. Both are the original languages of these islands, and when researching early British history those are the languages you're most likely to come across.'

'You groaned when he mentioned the order he belonged to.'

She nodded. 'The Children of Avalon.'

'You've heard of them?'

'No, I but can guess what they are, which is nothing to do with real Arthurian history. Do you know Sir Thomas Malory's *Le Morte d'Arthur*?'

'No,' replied Daniel. 'Should I?'

'If you'd taken a proper look at the exhibition, you would. It's a work of fiction written in the fifteenth century on which Tennyson's *Idylls of the King* is largely based. It contains all the elements of what became the later Arthurian legends: Guinevere, Camelot, Sir Lancelot, Excalibur, courtly love, all those things the Pre-Raphaelites were so obsessed by. There's a whole section on Malory, as well as Tennyson, in the exhibition. I keep telling you, you ought to at least take a look at it.'

'I will,' promised Daniel. 'So this order . . . ?'

'They've taken on board Malory's Arthur as the reality, rather than the earlier works of people like Gildas, Bede, Nennius and William of Malmesbury, which are more fact-based – as far as we can call them "facts" when they're recorded that far back and they could be supposition or propaganda.'

'Propaganda?'

'Gildas was a particularly angry man with a lot to say about the decline of the British people, so he skewed some of what he reports for his own agenda.'

'So things like Merlin . . .'

'Malory again, although you find mention of him in Geoffrey of Monmouth. But many historians view Geoffrey's work as more fiction than historical fact. As I said, you need to take a look at the exhibition.'

They were interrupted by the arrival of the other young man, pushed into the room by the security men. The ropes that previously tied him had been removed.

'Thank you,' said Daniel. 'We'll bring him back to you after we've talked to him.'

The men left, and Daniel gestured at the empty chair. 'Sit,' he ordered.

The young man sat and assumed a stuff posture, arms folded in defiance, just as Markham's had been. Daniel judged him to be even younger than Markham, possibly seventeen.

'First,' said Daniel, 'your name.'

'My name is Gawain,' snapped the young man.

'No, it isn't,' said Daniel. 'It's Edward Chapman and you live at 43 Peabody Street. In a moment I shall be sending a police officer to your home to bring your parents here.'

'No!' burst out Chapman, aghast. 'Please, don't bring them here!'

'Why? They have a right to know what their son has been up to. Committing criminal damage. You'll probably go to prison for two years.'

Chapman stared at them, his mouth open, shocked and ashen.

'P-prison?' He gulped.

'Well what did you expect?' demanded Daniel. 'You came here to commit a crime of violence. At the same place where a man was recently savagely stabbed to death. In view of that, I think two years would be generous. Four years is more likely. I'm only bringing your parents here so they can say goodbye to you before you are taken to prison while you await trial.'

'No!' howled the young man, and he dropped his head into his hands and began to sob.

After that, words tumbled out of him: the seance, the decision by the Children of Avalon to protest at the way their revered King Arthur had been denigrated, and finally – under Daniel's stern gaze – Chapman wrote out his list of the members of the Children of Avalon.

'Why did you ask them both for the list?' asked Abigail after the security men had taken Chapman away.

'To compare,' said Daniel. 'It's quite likely each will decide to leave certain people's names off it.' He put the two sheets of paper side by side. There were eleven names on one sheet and fifteen on the other.

'Hardly a mass movement,' commented Daniel. Then he smiled. 'Well, well,' he said.

'What?' asked Abigail.

Daniel pointed to a name at the bottom of the longer list. 'Joshua Tudder,' he read.

CHAPTER TEN

At home that evening, Daniel sat in his favourite wooden armchair in the kitchen and watched as Abigail moved a saucepan about on the hob of the range. Cabbage bubbled away inside the saucepan. In the range's oven she had two roasting trays, one bearing a chicken, the other potatoes.

'Are you sure you're confident about this?' asked Daniel.

'Yes, I am confident,' retorted Abigail, irritated. 'You're the one who isn't.'

'If you're not sure, there's a very good pie and mash shop in Royal College Street.'

'I am not having pie and mash.'

'It's very good,' said Daniel. 'The white parsley sauce is really tasty.'

'I have worked hard preparing this meal,' Abigail told him. 'I watched what you did the other day, which is why I'm confident I can do the same dish, roasting a chicken and potatoes. If it turns out to be inedible, then and only then will I consider pie and mash.'

'I thought you were going to start with something easier, like sausages,' said Daniel. 'To roast a chicken at your first attempt is quite brave.'

'When you say "brave", what you mean is foolish. But I have seen chickens cooked before, and not just by you. When I was in the desert out in Egypt . . .'

'They don't have kitchen ranges in the desert,' said Daniel.

'They have their equivalent, an ash pit in which the chicken is placed.'

'The chicken needs to be cooked right the way through,' said Daniel.

'As you've already said about five times. Really, Daniel, you are being a complete fusspot over this. I would have thought, rather than finding fault and undermining me, you would have been encouraging me, giving me confidence.'

'I am,' said Daniel. 'I want you to achieve this, that's why I'm giving you my advice, based on my experience of using this particular range.'

'Did you have anyone watch you when you cooked your first meal on this thing?' asked Abigail.

'No,' said Daniel.

'There you are, then. You did it without supervision and it was alright.'

'Actually, it wasn't,' admitted Daniel. 'I burnt the potatoes, boiled the cabbage to a mush, and the meat was raw inside.'

Abigail opened the oven door, took out the basting tray with the chicken on it and pushed a thin knife into it, which she took out and examined. She then did the same with the roast potatoes.

'Five more minutes,' she announced, putting both trays back into the oven, and sat down at the table.

'I have to say I was very impressed with the way you dealt with those vandals today at the museum,' said Daniel. 'Where did you learn to step in like that?'

'Egypt,' said Abigail. 'I was on a dig and had got separated from my fellow archaeologists – it was a very large site – and a local Egyptian decided to try and take advantage of the fact that I was alone.'

'And?'

'I beat him with a shovel that was lying nearby.'

'Badly?'

'Enough for him to need medical treatment,' said Abigail. 'And for word to spread about what had happened. No one ever attempted to molest me again.'

'I can imagine.' Daniel grinned.

'I have a question,' she said. 'This reporter, Dalton.'

'Joe,' said Daniel.

'How can you be so sure he won't put anything in the paper about the attack at the museum? He's a newspaper reporter, it's his job to write about things like that.'

'Because I asked him not to,' said Daniel. 'I've known Joe for a good few years. He's honest, but he also takes the long view. So long as he keeps my trust, he knows I'll always keep him informed when something really big happens. And often before anyone gets to know about it.'

'Unlike that other reporter. Carson,' said Abigail.

'I wouldn't trust Ned Carson as far as I can throw him,' said Daniel. 'There is a man who'd promise you anything in order to get a story, and go back on his word at the first opportunity. Joe Dalton is a news reporter; Ned Carson is a parasite.'

'Getting back to the lists of names those two idiots gave us, what are we going to do about Joshua Tudder?'

'I thought I'd go and visit him with John Feather.'

'Without me?'

'Yes.'

'Why?'

'Because if the conversation turns to the affair we all think he's having with Mrs Pickering, he might be reluctant to talk about it with a woman present.'

'Whereas, with all men, he's likely to boast?'

'No, I don't think he'd boast. I know we didn't see him for long, but he didn't come across as the type who'd boast about his sexual conquests.'

'Appearances can be deceptive,' observed Abigail. 'And we didn't see him for long. But, yes, I take your point. He might be more frank without a woman there. But do you think there's anything in it? Him being part of this ridiculous Children of Avalon?'

'I know it seems unlikely, but say the situation is as we suspect, that Professor Pickering was an obstacle to Tudder and Mrs Pickering being able to be together. We've seen how gullible those two idiots were today, Markham and Chapman. Perhaps Tudder whispered in the ear of one of the others about having King Arthur's revenge on Pickering. He could even have arranged a fake seance for the purpose. It's easy enough for someone to make sure the planchette moves to the right letters on a Ouija board to spell out what's wanted. Fake mediums do it all the time.'

'What do you want me to do, while you and Inspector Feather are interrogating Mr Tudder?'

Daniel shrugged. 'Just be at the museum, in case anyone arrives who might have some information. Talk to the staff, see if any of them can remember something about the day that Pickering was attacked that they'd forgotten. That often happens.'

'I'm happy for that,' said Abigail. 'And also for the opportunity to look properly at the museum's Egyptian rooms. With everything that's been going on I haven't had much chance to do that.' She looked at the clock on the mantelpiece. 'Five minutes. Time for the test on the proof of the pudding being in the eating.'

That night, as they lay in bed contentedly wrapped in one another's arms, Daniel whispered, 'I do love you so, Abigail Fenton.'

'And I do love you, Daniel Wilson,' returned Abigail. 'You don't feel this is sinful, living as we do? Bella has barely been in touch with me since I told her about us.'

'No, not at all,' said Daniel. 'If this is sin, then I'm all for it.'

'Be careful who you say that to,' cautioned Abigail. 'You could offend a lot of people.'

'I'm hardly going to be saying that outside these walls,' Daniel assured her. 'But, within these walls, I have everything I need with you.'

'You might need a more modern oven.'

He smiled. 'The meal was perfect.'

'I didn't get the potatoes right.'

'I like them like that, very crispy.'

'Partly burnt.'

'Not at all. And that chicken was perfection. You are a marvel, Abigail.'

'And you are a liar, Daniel, but I love you for it.'

CHAPTER ELEVEN

Tudder's studio was at the very top of a tall, narrow building, squeezed in between other similar tall and narrow buildings. Daniel and Feather climbed the steep and winding staircase to the top. They reached the door to Tudder's studio and were met with a smell of oil paints and turpentine mixed with linseed oil. Feather knocked on the door and Tudder opened it to them. He wore a smock, daubed with paint.

'Inspector Feather,' he said, 'Mr Wilson. What can I do for you?'

'We've got a few questions we'd be grateful if you could help us with, sir,' said Feather. 'Can we come in?'

The smell of oil paint, linseed and turpentine was even stronger inside than out. The slanted windows in the ceiling remained firmly shut, reducing any chance of fresh air getting in. Squeezed tubes of oil paint in all colours lay on every surface, on benches, on the table, on the two easels that adorned the studio. A dozen untouched canvases on wooden stretchers were stacked against the walls, waiting to be used. On one of the easels sat a canvas in the process of becoming a painting.

The face was of Mrs Pickering, but the pose and the setting were very similar to some of the paintings and images Daniel had seen at the exhibition. Mrs Pickering was depicted wearing long flowing robes, sitting regally on a large rock in a pastoral setting, a leafy glade that opened up into a verdant green valley behind her, with mountains and forests beyond. A small gold crown adorned her head, and sticking out of the rock was the lavishly decorated hilt of a sword.

'Guinevere and Excalibur?' said Daniel.

'Yes,' said Tudder. 'It was to be a present for Lance in honour of his book, representing the Arthurian legends. I shall still finish it and it will hang in his memory.'

'But I understand that Professor Pickering's book concentrated on the realistic model for Arthur, Ambrosius Aurelianus, at the expense of the more romantic version of Malory that you have depicted,' murmured Daniel.

Tudder shot Daniel a look of surprise. 'You are a scholar?' he asked.

'No,' said Daniel. 'But the difference between the two views was brought to our attention as the result of an attack on the exhibition at the museum by a group calling itself the Children of Avalon.'

Daniel saw that flicker of recognition in Tudder's face at the mention of the name.

'As a result of that attack, we are now considering this group as possible culprits for the killing of Professor Pickering,' said Feather.

'No, that's impossible!' Tudder exclaimed.

'Not from what the two young men from the Children of Avalon told us,' said Daniel. 'They were very vehement in their condemnation of the professor, and his book.'

'They also physically attacked the exhibition and the stewards at the museum,' added Feather. 'That certainly indicates they are capable of violence.' He paused, then added, 'They named you as one of the members of the Children of Avalon. Would you care to explain your connection to them?'

Suddenly, Tudder appeared shrunken, defeated. He sat down on a chair.

'It was an error of judgement on my part,' he said dully. 'An artist friend of mine mentioned them to me because he knew I was interested in the romantic aspects of the Arthurian legends.' He gestured at the paintings and sketches around the studio. 'Much of my work has been inspired by James Archer.'

Feather frowned. 'The name is unfamiliar to me, sir.'

'*The Death of King Arthur*,' said Daniel. 'The painting is on display as part of the exhibition at the museum.'

'Yes.' Tudder nodded. 'You have a good eye, Mr Wilson. And a good memory.'

'This artist friend who mentioned the Children of Avalon to you, his name?' asked Feather.

'William Epsom. As I said, he knows that I am very keen on the work of James Archer, and he suggested it might be interesting to learn what these people were doing, in case our interests coincided.'

'And did they?'

'No. I only went to a couple of their meetings.'

'But you allowed your name to be added to their list of members.'

'It was one of their things, trying to get as many names as possible to make it appear they were a large organisation.'

'Were you at the seance?' asked Daniel. 'The one where the spirit of Emrys was conjured up?'

Tudder groaned and nodded. 'To be honest, that was the last straw for me. I draw the line at mediums.'

'When was this seance?' asked Feather.

'The week before Lance was killed.'

'Yet you didn't mention it to Mr Pickering, or Mrs Pickering, as a warning for him to be careful.'

'I didn't believe in it. It was a hoax.'

Feather moved a chair near to Tudder and sat down on it, then said in a quiet but very firm tone of voice, 'Mr Tudder, an acquaintance of yours has been killed in the most savage manner. What we are looking for is a reason, and so far the only one we've come across is this Order of the Children of Avalon, and we find you are connected with them. I'm sure you can understand why we'll be looking into you in greater depth over your relationship with Mr Pickering – and Mrs Pickering.'

Tudder fell silent, but Daniel could see that he was in an emotional turmoil. Daniel and Feather waited, and finally Tudder said, in a low whisper, 'It was nothing to do with the Children of Avalon.'

'What was it to do with?' asked Feather.

There was a longer pause, and finally Tudder let out an anguished moan and said, 'There was a child.'

Daniel and Feather exchanged looks, then Feather said, 'Mrs Pickering's?'

Tudder shook his head. 'Lance's.'

'And how does that relate to his murder?'

'There were threats,' said Tudder hesitantly.

'You'd better explain,' said Feather.

Tudder nodded. 'It seems that eighteen years ago, Lance was staying with some friends of his during a weekend. He – er – was attracted by their maid and it seems he had a brief relationship with her.'

'With her consent?' asked Feather.

'I'm not sure,' admitted Tudder.

'Was he married at this time to Mrs Pickering?' asked Daniel.

'Yes.'

'And did Mrs Pickering know of this . . . incident?'

'No,' said Tudder. 'Not until earlier this year. A girl turned up at the house demanding to see Lance. Lance was away at the time, doing some research on his latest historical project. The girl was in an agitated state, and Laura – Mrs Pickering – took pity on her and invited her in. The girl told her she'd just discovered she was Lance's child by the maid.'

'So, this girl was seventeen.'

Tudder nodded. 'Laura didn't want to listen to it, wanted the girl to leave, but the girl was insistent on telling her story. According to her, when her mother found herself pregnant after what had happened between her and Lance, she was dismissed by the household. She told them that Lance Pickering was responsible, and the master of the house contacted Lance, who denied it and threatened to have the police on her if she repeated the allegation. So, the maid was sacked.'

'What was the maid's name?' asked Daniel.

'Maude Bowler. She called the child Elsie. Her relatives suggested she give the baby up for adoption, but Maude refused. She dedicated her life to raising Elsie, but she never told her who her father was.'

'I expect she was still terrified about Pickering's threat to have her charged by the police,' grunted Daniel.

'Earlier this year, Maude died. And it was then that Elsie's aunts, Maude's sisters, broke their silence and told Elsie the truth about her parentage. How Lance had got Maude pregnant, then abandoned her. And how she'd been sacked and had a hard life of struggle ever after, but she'd always taken care of her daughter.'

'And the girl, Elsie, came looking for . . . what? Money?'

'A confession,' said Tudder. 'She wanted Lance to admit what he'd done all those years ago, and how he'd got Maude sacked, and had abandoned her and his baby daughter. She wanted him to publicly acknowledge her as his daughter.'

'I assume Mrs Pickering told her husband about this visit?'

'She did.' Tudder nodded. 'He, of course, denied it. He was angry. He demanded to know where he could find the girl, said he would have her arrested for slander. The girl had actually left an address where she could be contacted with Laura, but Laura didn't pass that on to him. She told him the girl had left no address.'

'That was very brave of her,' said Daniel.

'It was,' said Tudder. 'Lance could be very . . . overbearing. Intimidating.'

'A bully?'

'Sadly, yes. He was used to getting his own way. Anyway, Laura wrote to the girl telling her what Lance had said, warning her that he had threatened to charge her with slander. She advised Elsie to drop her accusations, but she did say that she would do her best to try and talk to Pickering and see if she could change his mind.'

'I doubt if there was any real chance of that,' said Daniel.

'None at all,' said Tudder. 'Laura just added that to try and make the girl feel not too let down.'

'Do you happen to know Elsie's address?'

Tudder shook his head.

'You understand that we'll need to ask Mrs Pickering for it,' said Feather. 'It's important that we talk to Elsie Bowler.'

'You think she might have been the one who stabbed Lance?' asked Tudder.

'Don't you?' asked Feather. 'Seventeen years of anger building up over what happened to her mother, and once again this man denying he was responsible, and feeling she has no way to get him to admit what he did.'

Tudder nodded. 'I'd like to talk to Mrs Pickering first, tell her I've told you, so she is prepared.'

'Of course,' said Feather.

'Would it be better if you were present when we talk to Mrs Pickering?' suggested Daniel.

Tudder hesitated. 'I'm not sure,' he said. 'She told me while she was in a state of distress. I'm not sure how she will feel about the fact that I've told you. She might feel I've betrayed her.'

'Can I suggest that when you talk to her about this, you ask her if she would like you to be with her,' said Daniel. 'Also, to take some of the stress out of the situation for her, I also suggest that my colleague, Miss Fenton, is present. Having another woman there might make it feel less oppressive for her.'

CHAPTER TWELVE

Abigail stood looking on the Rosetta Stone with the same sense of awe and wonder she'd always felt ever since the first time she'd laid eyes on it. Three separate sections carved on a stone of black granodiorite, the middle and upper texts in ancient Egyptian hieroglyphic and Demotic script, the lower section in ancient Greek; possibly the most famous of all the ancient artefacts to come from Egypt. Originally unearthed by a French soldier during Napoleon's campaign in Egypt in 1799, it had been taken by the British following their defeat of the French in 1801, and it had been permanently on display at the British Museum since 1802. For Abigail, and for many Egyptologists, the importance of the stone was that it was the key to deciphering Egyptian hieroglyphics, due to the incredible work by the Briton Thomas Young and the Frenchman Jean-François Champollion. Thanks to them there was now a far greater understanding of the meaning of the hieroglyphics being brought to the museum.

'Good afternoon, Miss Fenton.' Abigail turned and saw an elderly man in a steward's uniform smiling at her. 'Mr Ashford said he hoped you might get the chance to take a look round our Egyptian section.'

'I'm delighted to take the opportunity.'

'He said you've been at most of the famous digs in Egypt.'

Abigail nodded. 'Quite a few of them.'

'I'd love to go there,' said the steward. 'To see the pyramids for myself. To be there where the builders hauled those huge stones, thousands of years ago.'

'Yes, it is impressive,' said Abigail. 'The first time I was there, I was awe-struck by their magnificence, their splendour.'

'But not so much the second time?'

'Actually, I was just as awe-struck the second time. And the third. It's not something, as an Egyptologist, you ever tire of.' She looked admiringly again at the Rosetta Stone. 'I'm glad Mr Ashford suggested I look. I will make a point of thanking him.'

'He's a wonderful man,' said the steward. 'And to think, we might have lost him.'

'Lost him?' asked Abigail.

'Because of that Professor Pickering,' said the steward. 'I know you're not supposed to speak ill of the dead, but there was a nasty piece of work if ever there was one.'

'In what way?'

'The way he treated people he considered his inferiors, which – according to the professor – was almost everyone. Certainly, all the staff here. Except for Sir Jasper, of course. He buttered him up. But the way he was with the stewards and the other staff was terrible. That's what caused the row.'

'Between him and Mr Ashford?' said Abigail, guessing.

'That's right.' The steward nodded. 'Mr Ashford came across the professor giving one of the stewards a real telling-off, claiming he hadn't shown him enough respect. He told the steward he was going to get him sacked, and it was at that point when Mr Ashford arrived. Well, Mr Ashford told the Professor good and proper that he wasn't in charge of the staff, he – Mr Ashford – was. And if he had a complaint he was to bring it to him, not take it out on the staff. And he told him that at the museum the staff were to be accorded equal respect – those were his exact words – and he expected the professor to apologise to the steward.

'Well, talk about setting off a tornado! The professor started ranting at poor Mr Ashford – I think it was because Mr Ashford had said all this in front of the steward – and said he'd get Mr Ashford sacked, and he'd make sure he never worked at this or any other museum again.'

'It was an empty threat, surely,' said Abigail. 'Sir Jasper wouldn't have sided with Pickering against Mr Ashford.'

'It wouldn't have been down to Sir Jasper, miss. Pickering reckoned he had the ear of important members on the board of the museum. Luckily, he got killed before he could do anything about it. Lucky for us, that is, not for the professor.'

'When was this confrontation?'

'On the Saturday, two days before Professor Pickering was killed.'

'As you say, that was very fortunate for Mr Ashford,' said

Abigail. 'Do you happen to know who the steward was that Professor Pickering was abusing, the one who witnessed the exchange between the professor and Mr Ashford?'

'Henry Smith. Lovely old man. Been here years.'

Daniel returned to their small office at the museum to find a note from Abigail: *I have news. I'll see you at home.*

Concerned, Daniel headed for Camden Town, and found Abigail studying Professor Pickering's book.

'Your note said you had news,' he said. 'Good or bad?'

'I'm not sure,' she said. 'We have a new suspect, and as it's Mr Ashford I couldn't leave a note to that effect, and it's not something we could talk about there in case we were overheard.'

'Ashford?' said Daniel, bewildered.

Abigail told him about the altercation between Ashford and Pickering, and Pickering's threat to get the board at the museum to have him dismissed.

'That was on the Saturday. Pickering couldn't have done anything about it on the Sunday, and he was killed on Monday morning before he could make good on his threat.'

Daniel shook his head. 'I don't see it,' he said. 'Ashford doesn't come across as a killer.'

'You've said yourself, the successful killers – those who get away with it – don't. That job at the museum means everything to him, you don't think he'd kill to keep it?'

Daniel sat down, deep in thought. 'It's plausible,' he said. 'And he's fit and agile enough to climb over the partition of the toilet cubicle. And he knows the way the museum operates.'

'And he's very efficient in the way he goes about things,' added Abigail. 'What shall we do? Talk to him?'

'We have to,' said Daniel. 'But first, we're due to meet Mrs Pickering at her house in the morning.'

'You and Inspector Feather?'

'And you. This is going to be a delicate matter, and your presence could be crucial on whether we get some satisfactory answers from her or not.'

'About what?' asked Abigail.

'About her late husband fathering a child, on the maid of some friends, and then denying it.'

He told her what Tudder had told them about Elsie Bowler turning up at the house. 'She was obviously angry.'

'And you think it might have been this Elsie Bowler who stabbed Pickering?'

'I don't know, but we might have a better idea when we talk to Mrs Pickering tomorrow. And then, afterwards, we'll seek out David Ashford and talk to him.' He sighed. 'We started out with no suspects, and now we're accumulating them at a rate of knots.'

CHAPTER THIRTEEN

'Thank you for talking to us, Mrs Pickering,' said Daniel, 'We are aware this is a difficult time for you, made worse by the revelation about Elsie Bowler.'

They were back in the drawing room of the Pickering house by Regent's Park, but the atmosphere was different from the rather tense one of their previous visit. Daniel guessed that was thanks to Tudder having spoken to Mrs Pickering beforehand. Nevertheless, he had decided that friendly civility was the right tone to adopt if they were to get the information they needed.

Mrs Pickering sat in the same chair as she had before, Tudder once more standing in the bay window, looking on, while Daniel,

Abigail and John Feather sat in a semicircle of chairs drawn up to face Mrs Pickering.

'I've asked my colleague, Miss Fenton, to be here in case you would prefer to engage with her, rather than myself or Inspector Feather,' said Daniel.

'No, I am happy to answer your questions, Mr Wilson. Although I do appreciate your thoughtfulness in bringing Miss Fenton into this discussion.'

'First, as I'm sure you can appreciate, we need to talk to Elsie Bowler, even if just to eliminate her from our enquiries. We understand you have her address.'

'I have the address she gave me earlier this year,' said Mrs Pickering. She handed Daniel a piece of paper. 'Whether she is still there is another matter.'

'Thank you. I'm sure, if she isn't, this will give us enough information to be able to find out where she went to. Next, we understand the substance of the allegation made by Elsie against your late husband. Without wishing to appear prurient in any way, is it possible there might have been other such cases in your husband's past?'

Her face appeared to become pinched as she weighed up this question. Then she said, 'My husband was a selfish man when it came to his appetites. It is possible there may have been other such incidents. I assume you are looking for people who might have felt enough anger at him over them to have carried out the attack on him?'

'It is possible.' Daniel nodded. 'It would help us if you are able to let us have the names of people he might have upset in this way.'

She gave a bitter laugh. 'Upset? My husband raped women. Usually servants, but I know of two occasions when his victims were women of the house. One a daughter, one a wife.'

'But no charges were ever laid against him?'

'And risk the shame such exposure would bring?' she said angrily. 'Yes, I will give you the names of the families. I know of them because I know my husband was barred from their houses ever after. But I would ask you to be discreet. Not to protect my late husband's reputation, but for the sake of the women and their families.'

'I promise you we will be the soul of discretion,' Daniel assured her solemnly.

As the front door closed behind Daniel, Abigail and Feather, all three were aware of the intense feelings there had been in that house: the anger of Mrs Pickering, the protectiveness of Joshua Tudder.

'What a hideous man Pickering was!' burst out Abigail. 'How could she have remained married to him for all those years?'

'Catholics don't divorce,' said Feather.

'But she could have left him! Lived her life without him as an odious presence.'

'And how would she have survived financially?' asked Daniel. 'You yourself said about the difficulty a married woman has with owning property, or her own finances.'

Feather indicated the cab waiting for him at the kerbside. 'I'm heading back to the Yard,' he said. 'Can I offer you a lift?'

Daniel was just about to accept, when Abigail cut in with, 'That's very kind of you, John, but I was going to suggest that Daniel and I catch an omnibus. For me, it's the ideal way to get to know London, sitting on the open top deck and seeing the hustle and bustle of the city, the different areas. A cab is more comfortable and quicker, but . . .'

'I understand.' Feather smiled. 'When I was young that was the way I learnt my way about London. That, and on foot.' He doffed his hat to them and made his way to the waiting cab.

'So, an omnibus it is,' said Daniel. 'There's a good service from Parkway which will take us.'

They strolled through the park to Parkway, where they boarded a horse-drawn omnibus. They were lucky enough to find two seats at the front of the upper deck, giving Abigail the view she desired as the bus rattled slowly along over the cobbles.

'This is wonderful,' she said.

'Providing it isn't raining,' said Daniel. 'And being at the front does rather put us in the line of fire whenever the horse breaks wind or decides to evacuate its bowels. Which, I've noticed, horses tend to do with great frequency.'

Abigail laughed. 'You have no romance in your soul, Daniel Wilson!' she chided him.

He took her hand in his and squeezed it gently.

'On the contrary, I can imagine nothing more romantic than seeing the London I love from the top deck of a bus in company with the woman I love.'

The bus rolled on, making frequent stops on its journey along Parkway, then southward along Camden High Street. As the bus neared Plender Street, Daniel suggested, 'We could get off and take some leisure. After all, our house is just a few paces away.'

'We have a job to do,' she said firmly. 'I already feel that this bus journey is a luxury we should not be taking. We should be back at the museum, reporting the information about Elsie Bowler to Sir Jasper.'

'And we will,' said Daniel. 'At a slow pace, perhaps, but the horse pulling the bus is a dray, a Shire, not a racer. Slower, but more reliable.'

The bus continued its journey south, and as it drew up at the junction of Eversholt Street and Euston Road, the conductor called out, 'St Pancras New Church!'

Abigail looked at the huge edifice, built in the Roman style, the whole of the front faced with a row of tall Doric columns supporting a decorated frieze, the same as at the British Museum, and asked, 'What happened to St Pancras Old Church?'

'Ah, that still exists,' said Daniel. 'It's not far away from here. It's in St Pancras Gardens, quite near St Pancras Railway Station.'

'Why did they build a new church if there was already an old one?'

'Because the old church is tiny. It's also said to be the oldest Christian place of worship in Britain.'

She looked at him and frowned. 'Surely not older than Canterbury, or Westminster?'

'Yes, indeed,' said Daniel. 'Someone dated it as being built around the year 500. Someone else claimed it was built even earlier, about 300, but if it was much of that has gone. 500 seems about right.'

'I have to see this!' she said excitedly. 'Has anyone carried out any archaeological surveys there?'

'Hallowed ground.' Daniel smiled. 'I don't think you'd get official approval for digging it up. There was enough controversy when they had to move some of the graves from the old cemetery to bring the railway lines into St Pancras.'

As they journeyed, Daniel pointed out that the one street they rode down bore various names: Woburn Square, Tavistock Square, Bedford Square, Russell Square.

'So called because this area is owned by the Russell family, who also bear the titles of the Duke of Bedford and the Marquis of Tavistock, not to mention others.'

'If you ever decide to abandon being a detective you'd make a very good tour guide,' said Abigail.

When the bus pulled up at Great Russell Street they alighted and headed for the museum.

'I feel for a short while we were on holiday,' said Abigail, then sighed. 'But now back to the matter in hand.'

They walked up the steps and into the main entrance, and saw the figure of David Ashford at the reception desk. He looked in an agitated state.

'Something's happened,' murmured Daniel.

As they headed towards Ashford, he turned and saw them, then rushed towards them, relief writ large on his features. 'Thank heavens you're here!' he exclaimed. 'I was trying to find out where you were.'

'We were at Professor Pickering's house, talking to his widow,' said Daniel. 'What's happened?'

'Sir Jasper's received a threatening letter. It claims to be from the person who killed Professor Pickering, and is demanding money or more people will die.'

CHAPTER FOURTEEN

Daniel and Abigail sat opposite Sir Jasper and took the note he handed to them. David Ashford had tried to sit, but his agitation over the letter made stillness impossible for him, and he stood, every now and then pacing the room.

The letter was unsigned, just a few lines on a sheet of writing paper.

Professor Pickering was the first. More will die unless you pay £1,000. Leave the money in a parcel tonight at midnight under the bench nearest to the Clarence Gate entrance to Regent's Park. Do not tell the police or someone will die.

'When did it arrive?' asked Daniel.

'Late this morning. It was handed in at reception, marked for my attention.'

Daniel examined the letter and the envelope that had contained it, then passed them both to Abigail.

'An educated hand,' she said.

'What shall we do?' asked Sir Jasper.

'Tell the police,' said Daniel. 'It may be a hoax, or it may be someone using the murders to make some money, or it may actually be connected to the murders. Whichever it is, you have to tell the police. Which means Superintendent Armstrong, as he's in charge of the case.'

Sir Jasper sighed, then nodded. He reached for a sheet of notepaper and wrote a few words, then handed it to Ashford.

'Arrange for a messenger to get this to Superintendent Armstrong as a matter of urgency.'

Superintendent Armstrong looked taken aback when he and John Feather entered Sir Jasper's office and found Daniel and Abigail already there. He scowled at Daniel.

'So, you're here, Wilson.'

'I am indeed,' said Daniel. 'Allow me to introduce my partner, Miss Abigail Fenton.'

Armstrong looked at Abigail and gave a sniff of disapproval, then grunted, 'A woman.'

'I see you have good powers of observation, Superintendent,' said Abigail. 'It is a pleasure to make your acquaintance. Mr Wilson has told me so much about you.'

Armstrong glared at them, then said in frosty tones, 'I can see no reason why they should be involved in this, Sir Jasper.'

'It was Mr Wilson who insisted I contacted you when I received the letter, despite the threat contained in it,' countered Sir Jasper.

'And we have been engaged by the museum to look after their interests in this matter,' said Daniel.

'That was about the murder,' said Armstrong curtly. 'This is different.'

'Not according to the letter,' Daniel pointed out. 'The threat is that if the money is not paid, there will be further murders.'

'Let's see this letter,' grunted Armstrong.

He and Feather took the seats that Sir Jasper waved them to, and Sir Jasper handed the superintendent the letter. Armstrong studied it carefully. 'The handwriting looks like that of an educated person,' he said. 'It could be a hoax. Someone trying to make money out of this tragic situation. That's happened before.' He handed the letter back to Sir Jasper. 'I suggest a stake-out. The parcel is left as specified, and a trap set.'

Sir Jasper looked doubtful. 'It won't be easy to raise that amount of money in such a short space of time,' he said.

'No money,' said Armstrong firmly. 'Newspaper in the parcel. If it's a hoax, no one will turn up. If they do, we'll catch them. There's no sense in putting a thousand pounds at risk.' He turned to Feather. 'I'll leave you to organise this, Inspector. You've been involved in this sort of thing before.'

'Yes, sir,' said Feather. 'As has Mr Wilson.'

Armstrong scowled. 'You're not suggesting a civilian be involved in this?'

Before Feather could answer, Sir Jasper said, 'Mr Wilson and Miss Fenton are the museum's representatives in this case.'

Armstrong glowered and said, 'With respect, Sir Jasper, Mr Wilson may have experience of this sort of thing, but Miss Fenton – as a woman . . .'

'I am perfectly capable of taking care of myself,' said Abigail crisply. 'When I was attacked in Egypt I defended myself so robustly the would-be assassin needed hospital treatment.'

The superintendent looked at them, obviously silently seething. Finally, he said, 'It's your decision, Sir Jasper. My instinct is to be against it.'

'I respect that, Superintendent, but the museum has been impressed by Miss Fenton so far, and we would like her to be part of this stake-out, as I believe you term it.'

'Very well, Sir Jasper. I leave that in your hands.' He stood up. 'Inspector Feather will make arrangements for the action. We'll return to the Yard now and he'll be in touch later to make the final arrangements.'

With that, Armstrong swept out, his face still grim. Feather rose from his chair and grinned at Daniel and Abigail.

'Let's meet at the Yard at ten o'clock,' he said.

'I'm banned,' Daniel pointed out.

'From inside the building,' said Feather. 'We'll meet by the stables where the vans are kept.'

'Feather!' came the barked command from the superintendent.

Feather smiled farewell and left.

CHAPTER FIFTEEN

Daniel and Abigail arrived at the stables in the cobbled courtyard to the rear of Scotland Yard to find John Feather had assembled five constables. Introductions were made, then Feather outlined the plan.

'I did a reconnaissance of the bench this afternoon,' he said. 'There's a small copse not far from it, and a few ornamental bushes and shrubs also within easy distance. Constables Adams and Nixon will secrete themselves behind the trees of the small copse. Daniel and Miss Fenton, with your agreement, you'll hide yourselves in the larger ornamental shrub. There's room for two people to hide there without being seen, providing you tuck yourselves in to the main stem of the bush. Constables McCartney and Yewtree will take position behind a hedge in Cornwall Terrace virtually opposite Clarence Gate. Constable Bean' – Feather indicated the last uniformed officer – 'will be the van driver and he'll park the horse and van about fifty yards away from the gate. He'll be inside the van, ready to come into action if needed.'

'Say the horse wanders off?' asked Abigail.

'No fear of that, miss,' said Bean. 'I'll put old Dobbin's nosebag on him and he'll be happy munching his way through some oats. And the handbrake will be on, just in case.'

'We should arrive at Clarence Gate at about quarter to eleven, and once there we'll take up positions and wait. I've already made up the parcel with the paper inside, which I'll put under the bench at a quarter to midnight. I'll then walk off in the direction of Albany Street, just in case anyone's watching. I'll double back using York Terrace and Allsop Place and climb back in the van so I can keep watch from there. If anyone does arrive to collect the parcel, Adams and Nixon will be closest to the bench. Mr Wilson and Miss Fenton will be the next nearest. Whistles will be at the ready at all times. The signal to go into action will be someone either opening the parcel or going off with it. We take no action if someone just turns up and looks at it, then goes off again leaving it unopened. Frankly, gentlemen and lady, this could be a long night with nothing happening. For all we know, it's a hoax. But we can't take the chance it might be real. And, if it is, remember we're dealing with a murderer behind all this. It could be that the person who comes to pick up the parcel is merely a messenger, but just in case it is our murderer, and we already know how ruthless he is, the superintendent has allowed me to draw a firearm from the store.' He tapped his jacket pocket. 'So, if you hear me shout "Down!", drop like a stone. But I'll only use it if I have to. Any questions?'

There were silent shakes of heads all round.

'Right, let's get in the van and get going.'

As they walked to the van, where the horse Dobbin was already in the shafts, Daniel said, 'So Armstrong isn't coming himself.'

'The super decided to leave the surveillance to me and the officers,' said Feather.

'So, if it goes wrong, he can't be blamed,' said Daniel. 'But if it goes right and we catch someone, he gets the credit.'

'One of the benefits of being a superintendent.' Feather shrugged.

They climbed aboard the interior of the van, while Constable Bean climbed onto the driver's seat.

'Nervous?' whispered Daniel to Abigail.

'No,' she said briskly.

The van rolled on its way, the occupants keeping silence. When it reached Clarence Gate on the outer circle of Regent's Park, they all climbed down and Bean took Dobbin and the van to his appointed parking space.

'I'll show you where your hiding places are,' said Feather.

They were heading towards the gate to the park when they became aware of another uniformed constable heading towards them.

'Did you alert the beat copper?' Daniel whispered to Feather.

'Short notice,' Feather whispered back. He called the party to a halt and let the new arrival catch up with them.

'Excuse me, sir,' said the constable. 'I saw the police van arrive and saw you all get out . . .'

'Inspector Feather from Scotland Yard,' Feather introduced himself.

The constable saluted, then said, 'PC Johnson, sir. This is my beat, so if there's anything happening and I can do anything . . .'

'Thank you, Constable. We may need your assistance. All I can say at the moment is this is a stake-out and we've got the cover we need. But if you wouldn't mind staying inside the van along the road, out of sight; if anything untoward happens we'd be grateful for your help. The driver of the van is PC Bean. Tell him I sent you.'

'Certainly, sir,' said Johnson. 'I'll keep my ears peeled for a shout.'

As Johnson headed towards the van, Feather led the group into the park. They stood for a moment, adjusting their eyes to the darkness, then Feather gestured towards a very large ornamental shrub. 'That's yours, Daniel and Miss Fenton,' he said. 'You going to be alright with that?'

Daniel shot a quizzical look at Abigail, who said a confident 'Yes' and headed towards it. Daniel followed, and the pair pushed their way between the branches of the shrub until they were hidden from outside view.

'Can you see the bench?' asked Daniel.

'Yes,' said Abigail.

'Good,' said Daniel. 'So can I.'

There was a pause, then Abigail said quietly, 'You know when you asked me if I was nervous?'

'Yes.'

'Well, I was. I still am. But I didn't want to admit it in front of the others.'

'If it's any consolation, I'm nervous, too,' said Daniel. 'And so are the others.'

'Even Inspector Feather?'

113

'Especially John. This is his responsibility. If it goes wrong, it'll be on his head. Also, he's got a loaded firearm. No one likes carrying one of them in case they have to use it. Take my word, Abigail, I've done a lot of stake-outs in my time, and they are awful experiences. You get nervous because you don't know what's going to happen, and all you can think of is the worst possible outcome: death or being badly wounded.' After a thoughtful pause, he added, 'In fact, thinking about it, I'm not sure it's a good idea you being here.'

'Why?' whispered back Abigail. 'Am I not a part of this team?'

'Yes, but it could be dangerous.'

'You don't think I can deal with danger?' she demanded indignantly. 'You forget . . .'

'Yes, I know, you beat a potential molester with a shovel. But we don't have any shovels to hand. And these people may be armed.'

'Inspector Feather has a pistol,' pointed out Abigail.

'Yes, he has,' agreed Daniel.

'And there are also some very sturdily built constables in hiding as added protection.'

'Yes, but it is cold at night,' said Daniel.

'You don't think I have spent nights out?' countered Abigail. 'When I was in Egypt . . .'

'Egypt is not the middle of London,' said Daniel. 'It is the desert, in the Middle East.'

'And if you don't think the desert gets extremely cold at night, then you have been very badly misinformed. Contrary to the public's view of deserts in the Middle East as hot and parched places, that may be true during hours of daylight, but once night falls the temperature often drops to below freezing. A colleague of mine froze to death overnight while in the Atlas Mountains . . .'

'Mountains,' stressed Daniel. 'Very cold.'

'This was in Morocco. And he was on the lower slopes of the mountains.'

'Yes, alright,' said Daniel. 'I take your point. So, I assume you have dressed for the occasion . . .'

'I have two pairs of drawers on, plus woollen stockings . . .'

'You're just saying that to excite me,' muttered Daniel with a smile.

'I suggest we stop this conversation before it gets out of hand,' said Abigail. 'We need to concentrate our attention on the bench.'

Time passed. Nothing happened. No one entered the park through Clarence Gate, or exited through it. No one was around.

At what they guessed to be a quarter before midnight they saw the shadowy figure of John Feather appear, walk to the bench, push a bulky parcel beneath it, then turn and walk out of the park.

'If the letter is genuine, hopefully we shouldn't have long to wait,' murmured Daniel.

But wait they did. Patiently, they sat, their eyes firmly focused on the park bench. No humans were to be seen, but they were aware of lots of activity by small mammals, scurrying across the short grass as they went from copse to bush to shrub in search of nocturnal mouthfuls.

Suddenly, after what seemed like an age, they were aware of a man entering through the park gate and slowly walking towards the bench. He hesitated, then sat down upon it, and then lay full length on it.

'A tramp,' whispered Abigail.

'Look at his arm,' Daniel whispered back.

One of the man's arms was dangling down, his hand gently

stroking the ground. Then his hand moved beneath the bench and came into contact with the parcel.

Slowly, the man uncoiled himself and sat up, dragging the parcel out from beneath the bench. He lifted it up and put it on his lap.

'Any moment now,' whispered Daniel, alert.

The man tore at the paper of the parcel, reached inside and took out a handful of folded pieces of newspaper.

Immediately, the shrill sound of a police whistle tore through the silence of the night. The man leapt to his feet, then as he saw the shapes of two constables hurrying towards him from the small copse of trees, he threw the parcel down on the ground and broke into a run, straight towards the ornamental shrub where Daniel and Abigail were in hiding. Daniel began to scramble to his feet amongst the shrub's branches, ready to launch himself at the man, but he was too late; Abigail had already rolled out into the open from beneath the plant and she stuck out a leg just as the man reached them.

Smack! The man tripped over her outstretched leg and tumbled face first to the ground, where Daniel hurled himself at him. As Daniel took a firm grip on the man, the two constables arrived, with John Feather and the other constables close behind.

'Got you!' cried Constable Adams triumphantly.

CHAPTER SIXTEEN

They hauled the terrified and handcuffed man out of the park and over to the waiting police van, their prisoner loudly protesting his innocence of whatever it was he was supposed to have done.

'I ain't done nothing!' he howled in anguish.

It was left to the beat constable, PC Johnson, to confirm who he was.

'His name's Martin Pye, sir, and he's a vagrant,' Johnson informed Inspector Feather. 'He sleeps in the park.'

'Always on the same bench?' asked Feather.

'Not always,' said Johnson. 'Sometimes one of the others,

sometimes under a tree if it's raining.' He hesitated, before adding, 'He doesn't do any harm. There've been no complaints about him, or I'd move him on.'

It turned out that Pye was illiterate, so there was no chance it could have been him who'd written the extortion letter.

'But he could be working for whoever did,' said Feather.

But Pye was firm in his protestations of innocence when questioned.

'No one asked me to pick the parcel up. I only opened it in case there might be something useful in it. Food. Clothes. You'd be surprised what people leave behind.'

'What are we going to do with him, sir?' asked Constable Nixon. 'Let him go?'

Feather shook his head. 'We'll take him back to the Yard. He can sleep in a cell for the night. At least that way he'll be in the warm. And he'll be there if Superintendent Armstrong decides to question him tomorrow morning.'

'I ain't done nothing!' repeated Pye desperately.

'In that case, you won't have anything to worry about.'

'Will I get a cup of tea?' asked Pye hopefully.

'Yes,' said Feather. 'I'll arrange that.'

As Pye was loaded into the back of the van, Feather turned to Daniel and Abigail. 'Hop in. We'll drop you off at Plender Street on the way.'

'A false alarm,' commented Daniel.

'At least I didn't have to use the gun,' said Feather, doing his best to put a positive spin on it.

Next morning, after just a few hours' sleep, Daniel and Abigail arrived at the museum to be met by a worried-looking David Ashford.

'It's terrible, Mr Wilson, Miss Fenton,' he said. 'The exhibition's been attacked again!'

Daniel and Abigail hurried with Ashford to the exhibition area. The display of books had been pushed to the floor, the volumes lying scattered, and on the wall just behind them someone had used red paint to scrawl 'Who killed Ambrosius?' in large letters. Cleaners were .already at work with buckets of soapy water and scrubbing brushes, trying to remove the words, but the paint had dried sufficiently to make it an impossible task.

'We're going to have to hang a curtain or something over the paint until we can start to chip it off. It's going to be the devil of a job,' said Ashford unhappily.

'Does Sir Jasper know?' asked Daniel.

'No,' said Ashford. 'He hasn't come in yet. I sent a messenger to his house with a note telling him about it. But I've assured him the damage will be sorted out so the exhibition can open. We might be a few minutes late, but we're not going to let these people – whoever they are – close us down.'

'Have the police been informed?'

Ashford nodded. 'We told the local beat constable who was in Great Russell Street. He came in and examined the damage, then sent a message to Superintendent Armstrong at Scotland Yard. We're expecting him.'

'We'll take a look at the situation while we wait for Scotland Yard, Mr Ashford,' said Daniel.

'I'd appreciate it if you could be quick about it,' said Ashford. 'I want to get that paint covered up so we can open.'

'Can I suggest a series of screens, rather than a hanging curtain?' proposed Abigail. 'The police will want to inspect the writing, and that way they can do it while hidden from the public.'

'Yes, good idea, Miss Fenton,' said Ashford. Then, in an anxious whisper, he asked, 'May I ask what happened last night?'

'Nothing,' said Daniel. 'We had a long, cold night, but no one turned up.'

'So, a hoax then?'

'Possibly,' said Daniel.

'I'll arrange the screens,' said Ashford.

He moved off, at the same time giving orders to the cleaners and stewards to check the books for damaged copies and restore the displays.

'That was good thinking about the screens,' said Daniel.

'We used them often in displays at museums,' said Abigail. 'They can conceal cleaning equipment, storage boxes, all the unsightly things you don't want the public to see.'

They walked to the wall and examined the red painted writing. Daniel tested the paint with his finger and sniffed at it.

'Red lead,' he announced. 'The stuff people use for painting their doorsteps. It's dry, so this was done some hours ago, in the early hours of the morning.' He looked quizzically at Abigail. 'Another attempt at disruption by the Children of Avalon, do you think?'

'No,' said Abigail. 'The Children of Avalon are only interested in promoting the later medieval Malory version of Arthur: knights in armour, courtly love, quests for the Grail, that sort of thing. If you remember the two young idiots we talked to disdained the earlier references, anything to do with the reality of Ambrosius is anathema to them.'

'So, who would want to do this? And why?' Then he stiffened as a realisation hit him. 'And how?'

He hurried to where Ashford was still supervising the checking of the books.

'Mr Ashford, was there any sign of a break-in during the night?'

'No, Mr Wilson. I sent the stewards to check every window, every door, for any sign of forced entry. And I spoke to the two nightwatchmen who were on duty. They reported nothing.'

'Didn't they notice the damage while they were on their rounds?'

'They don't do rounds, as such. They guard the two main entrances. The museum is so vast that it can be difficult to find your way around it in the dark, even with an oil lamp to help. It was decided that if there was trouble it would come from someone trying to break in through one of the entrances, so that's where they're stationed. There's also a nightwatchman who patrols the outside of the building.'

'And he saw nothing?'

'Nothing.'

'And there were no signs of disturbance either inside or out?'

'None.' He gestured at the writing on the wall. 'Have you finished? I'd like to get the screens up.'

'Yes, of course,' said Daniel. 'Thank you, Mr Ashford, and may I congratulate you on the way you've handled this with great speed and efficiency.'

'Just doing my job, sir,' said Ashford.

Daniel and Abigail moved to the undamaged part of the exhibition to allow the cleaners and ushers to set about their work under Ashford's direction.

'Well?' asked Abigail.

'No sign of forced entry. Which leads us to only one conclusion.'

'The spirit of Emrys working his magic,' said Abigail.

When Daniel shot her an inquisitive look she said swiftly, 'That was a joke.'

'Sorry,' he said. 'With no sign of forced entry . . .'

'The person who did it must have already been in the museum,' finished Abigail.

'Yes,' said Daniel. 'Hiding. And they made their escape when the doors were opened, just slipped out.'

'They were taking a chance,' said Abigail. 'They weren't to know the nightwatchmen didn't patrol inside the museum.'

'Unless they did,' said Daniel.

'You're thinking the culprit is someone who knows how the system works at the museum?'

'It makes sense,' continued Daniel. 'They'd know the best place to hide when the stewards do their last round to make sure everyone has left the building. They'd know the nightwatchmen wouldn't be patrolling.'

'Someone who works here?'

'Or who *worked* here,' said Daniel. 'Someone with a grudge against the museum.'

'Someone who was dismissed?' asked Abigail.

'It's worth looking into. When Sir Jasper arrives, we'll ask him if he knows of any disgruntled ex-employees.' He frowned, thoughtful. 'But why write "Who killed Ambrosius"? Why fixate on that?'

'Ambrosius is the key,' said Abigail. 'He's the subject of Professor Pickering's book, and Pickering was killed here.' She gestured at where the staff were putting the display of Pickering's books back together. 'Look at the way the books were hurled around. Nothing else in the exhibition was touched except the books, and the graffiti on the wall.'

'Alright, I can see where this is going.' Daniel sighed. 'You've been telling me I should have examined the exhibition properly, and I will. And I will read the professor's book and see if there's anything in there that arouses such anger. But, right now, tell me the short version. Who was Ambrosius, and how does he relate to the person of King Arthur?'

'The main link is the Battle of Badon, which is believed to have taken place in about 500, between the Britons and the invading Saxons,' said Abigail. 'Some accounts talk of the Britons being led by Ambrosius Aurelianus, some by Arthur, which is why they are believed to be one and the same.

'There are five main sources for the tales of Ambrosius and his connection with King Arthur: Gildas, a monk who was writing in the sixth century; Bede, a seventh-century monk based in Jarrow; Nennius, a ninth-century Welsh monk; and two who wrote in the twelfth century: William of Malmesbury and Geoffrey of Monmouth. Of these, most scholars discount Geoffrey because his text is less about historical fact than myths and legends. It was Geoffrey who added Merlin to the Arthurian cycles – or Emrys, as he initially called him, then changed his name to Merlin.'

'King Arthur's magician,' said Daniel.

'Yes and no,' said Abigail. 'Geoffrey says that Merlin was Ambrosius's magician first when Ambrosius was King of the Britons, then when Ambrosius died, Merlin gave service to Uther Pendragon, and then to Uther's son, Arthur.'

'How did Ambrosius die?'

'According to Geoffrey, he was poisoned by his enemies. Interestingly, William of Malmesbury also calls Ambrosius the

King of the Britons, and names Arthur as Ambrosius's general, when they defeated the Saxons at the Battle of Badon. Nennius also describes Ambrosius as "King among all the Kings of the British nation".

'Gildas and Bede describe Ambrosius as the leader of the Britons, but not a king, though Gildas says he "wore the purple", which means he was of royal birth.'

'So, there's some agreement there.'

'Again, yes and no,' said Abigail. 'All these early historians copied one another; so Bede would have taken his information from Gildas, and Nennius from Bede, and so on.'

'So this graffiti saying "Who killed Ambrosius"?'

'I don't know,' admitted Abigail. 'The only real mention of his death is Geoffrey saying he was poisoned, but as I said, Geoffrey's account is considered suspect. More fiction than history.

'The things that link Ambrosius and Arthur – even the later Arthur of Geoffrey and Malory – are that Ambrosius was the fearless leader of a cavalry troop.'

'Knights on horseback,' said Daniel.

'Exactly. And the fact that Badon is generally assumed to be a hill outside Bath. The "D" in Badon is the linguistic giveaway; it was how the "TH" sound was written at that time.'

'So that puts Ambrosius and his mounted cavalry around Bath.'

'Which later became the area where Arthur was active, around Glastonbury and up to and across the Welsh border. Geoffrey of Monmouth locates Camelot at Caerleon just across the border in Wales, for example. As does Chrétien in his poem "Lancelot, the Knight of the Cart".'

'I need to read the book,' said Daniel.

'You do. And to examine the exhibition properly.'

They were interrupted by the sound of raised voices from the main entrance, and a bellowed, 'Who's in charge here?!'

'I think Superintendent Armstrong has just arrived,' said Daniel.

CHAPTER SEVENTEEN

Armstrong made his way up from the steps from the main reception and scowled when he saw Daniel and Abigail.

'You're still here,' he growled disapprovingly.

'We are indeed, Superintendent,' said Daniel. 'I assume you heard about last night. No one turned up.'

'A hoax,' grunted Armstrong. 'I suspected as much.' He turned to Ashford and demanded, 'Where's Sir Jasper?'

'He's . . .' began Ashford. Then, as a familiar movement at the entrance caught his attention, he said, 'He's just arrived.'

Sir Jasper hurried towards them, out of breath. 'Superintendent,' he said. 'Thank you for coming. I apologise for

126

the fact I wasn't here to greet you, but I've only just received the message about the attack.' He turned to Ashford and asked, 'Was there much damage?'

'Red paint used to write on the wall,' replied Ashford. 'I've had it concealed behind screens so that we could open the exhibition to the public, but also to allow room for the police to examine the evidence.'

'Well done, Ashford,' said Sir Jasper.

'Yes, good, clear thinking,' put in Armstrong.

'It was Miss Fenton who suggested using the screens,' said Ashford.

Sir Jasper turned to Abigail and smiled. 'Thank you, Miss Fenton.'

Armstrong scowled. 'What about the rest of the damage?' he demanded. 'The constable reported mayhem here.'

'The books from the display had been thrown about and were on the floor,' said Ashford. 'I've had the display put back together, again so we could open the exhibition to the public.'

'Good man, Ashford,' said Sir Jasper. He indicated the screens. 'Shall we examine the damage?'

'Miss Fenton and I have already examined the paintwork,' said Daniel. 'So, as there is limited space there, we'll let you gentlemen do that, and then we can discuss our findings.'

'You are not part of the official police investigation,' scowled Armstrong. 'I will not be discussing any conclusions I reach with you.'

'You don't think that's a bit narrow-minded?' asked Daniel. He looked at Sir Jasper. 'Surely, on a case like this, the more minds and thoughts we have on it the better.'

Sir Jasper nodded. 'I have to agree.'

Armstrong looked at Sir Jasper, then at Daniel, then back at Sir Jasper again, and both Daniel and Abigail could see he was doing his best to control an outburst of temper. What he wanted to do was order Daniel and Abigail out in the most brutal fashion. Instead, he swallowed hard and forced out, 'That's your prerogative, Sir Jasper. This is your museum.'

'Then we'll wait for you here while you examine the paint, and perhaps afterwards we could all repair to your office, Sir Jasper,' said Daniel.

'Very good,' said Sir Jasper.

He headed for the screens, and the superintendent threw a last scowl at Daniel before following the museum director.

'He really doesn't like you,' said Abigail.

'No, he doesn't,' agreed Daniel.

'Why?'

Daniel shrugged. 'It's a long and old story.'

'We have time,' said Abigail.

'Possibly, but this is not the place for it. They won't be behind those screens for very long, and I'd rather Armstrong didn't come back and hear me talking about it.'

As Daniel had predicted, the two men were behind the screens for just a few minutes before they reappeared and headed for the stairs that led up to Sir Jasper's office. Daniel and Abigail followed. Sir Jasper's first words once they had sat down was to ask about the previous night and the ransom.

'A non-event, so Inspector Feather tells me,' grunted Armstrong. 'I suspect it was a hoax. Someone making mischief.' Then he turned to look accusingly at Sir Jasper, and Daniel and Abigail. 'But on a serious note, I understand from the constable who brought me the message about this vandalism that this is the second such attack in just a few days. That before there was serious damage, a glass case being smashed.'

'That is correct, Superintendent.' Sir Jasper nodded.

'But the constable told me the museum decided not to press charges, and had decided not to involve the police further,' added Armstrong angrily.

'That is also correct,' said Sir Jasper. 'I asked Mr Wilson and Miss Fenton to deal with the situation to avoid publicity that could adversely affect the museum and the exhibition.'

'With respect, Sir Jasper,' grunted Armstrong in a tone of voice that showed he had very little respect, 'that was completely the wrong decision. The two attacks are obviously connected. If we'd been allowed to investigate the first one, instead of it being left to amateurs, we could have prevented this one.'

'Miss Fenton and I must disagree with you, Superintendent,' said Daniel calmly. 'The first attack was by some people calling themselves the Children of Avalon, who are devotees of the King Arthur of . . .' He looked at Abigail.

'Of Geoffrey of Monmouth and Sir Thomas Malory,' said Abigail.

'As opposed to this attack, which – as you will have seen – refers to Ambrosius.'

Again, he turned to Abigail, who added, 'Ambrosius Aurelianus was a Romano-Briton war leader of the fifth and sixth centuries, far removed from Malory's and Geoffrey's Arthur. The Children of Avalon, who launched their attack against the exhibition, were protesting at its linking their romantic Arthur with the historical Ambrosius. They deny such a connection. The two attacks are not connected.'

'Nonsense!' snapped Armstrong. 'How can you say that? The evidence is there!'

'The evidence is there to show that the reasons for the attacks were not the same,' stated Abigail firmly.

'But they attacked the same exhibition!' insisted Armstrong. 'It doesn't matter whether this is about Arthur or this . . . this . . .'

'Ambrosius,' said Daniel.

'Him.' Armstrong nodded. 'They're the same.'

'No, Superintendent, they're not,' said Abigail. 'There is a parallel here with religion. I have spent a lot of time in the Middle East and it is assumed that all Muslims follow the same religion. They do not. There are different branches, and the Shi'a and Sunni factions are resolutely opposed to one another and would never work together. As is the case with the Catholic and Protestant forms of the Christian religion. To a non-Christian they may appear the same, but to a Protestant or a Catholic who are fundamentally opposed to one another, again, they would never work together. It is the same with those Arthurian scholars who accord Ambrosius a place in his history, and those who subscribe to the romantic later visions, where Ambrosius has no place.'

Armstrong stared at her, looking in a state of bewilderment.

'Miss Fenton can explain it further to you, if you wish, Superintendent,' said Daniel. 'But if you read the texts at the exhibition, you'll see the value of her argument.'

Armstrong scowled, then spat out, 'I don't have time for this mumbo-jumbo and hocus-pocus. Two crimes have been committed here. Regardless of what this woman says, I would be failing in my duty, Sir Jasper, if I did not proceed with my own investigation, using proper policemen.'

'Of course.' Sir Jasper nodded.

Armstrong stood up. 'I will be sending Inspector Feather along to conduct his own investigation into both these attacks, as well as him continuing to investigate the murder of Professor Pickering. I wish you good day.'

With that, the superintendent left.

Sir Jasper turned to Abigail and said, 'I, too, accept your very plausible argument, Miss Fenton, but it is important we keep Scotland Yard on our side.'

'Of course, Sir Jasper. I understand,' said Abigail.

'Have you yourselves reached any conclusions about today's attack?' asked Sir Jasper.

'That there was no sign of any forced entry, nor any reports of intruders from the nightwatchmen or the patrol outside the building, suggest to us the person who did it may have been hiding inside the museum,' said Daniel.

'Inside?'

Daniel nodded. 'The fact that the paint had dried suggests it was done in the early hours of the morning, possibly between midnight and two. We think the person hid inside the museum, then left when the doors were opened. If we are right, that would suggest someone with an intimate knowledge of the layout of the museum, and the routines, such as the fact that the nightwatchmen stay at their posts by the entrances rather than make internal patrols.'

'You are suggesting an employee?' said Sir Jasper.

'Or possibly a former employee. Someone who might have a grudge against the museum. Or, if this was connected with the murder of Professor Pickering, which is suggested by the fact that the only real damage were the copies of his books being thrown about, someone who might have a grudge against the professor. But again, this attack indicates it was by someone with an intimate knowledge of the museum and how it works.'

Sir Jasper looked unhappy. 'It is awful to think that any of our employees, or former employees, would have such feelings. We've always thought of ourselves as one big happy family, from the curators to the cleaners, the stewards and the cloakroom attendants, everyone has always worked so well together. Everyone here loves what we are doing at the museum, and they are proud of what we do.'

'That may be, Sir Jasper, but there's always one person in any organisation who feels slighted for some reason, imagined or otherwise. Is it possible to let us have a list of people who've left the museum's employ recently, people who may feel they have a grudge against the museum? Was there anyone who left after an argument with Professor Pickering, for example?'

'I'll talk to Ashford about it,' said Sir Jasper thoughtfully. 'If there is any such person, he'll know, I'm sure.'

'Would you mind if we talked to Mr Ashford?' suggested Daniel. 'We understand that you're very busy, and we do have an idea of what we're looking for in this situation.'

'Not at all, I'm happy for you to do that,' said Sir Jasper.

CHAPTER EIGHTEEN

As Daniel and Abigail made their way to Ashford's office, Abigail said in a tone heavy with disapproval, 'You've got a nerve.'

'What do you mean?' asked Daniel.

'Telling Superintendent Armstrong to read the texts at the exhibition. You haven't even read them yourself! You only said that to annoy him.'

Daniel smiled. 'True,' he said. 'But I promise I will. In fact, once we've talked to Mr Ashford, I promise I will take a copy of Professor Pickering's book and read it thoroughly.'

'Will you raise the issue of the row with Professor Pickering with Ashford?'

'After we've got the information about possible disgruntled former employees. I'm thinking he'll be more relaxed then.'

'What did you think of the superintendent's reaction to last night? The failure to collect the money? Do you think it was a hoax?'

'I don't know,' said Daniel. 'It's possible, but then we see what happened during the night here, the attack with the red paint. Could that be connected? Making sure we were busy occupied watching a bench at Regent's Park while they carried out this attack?'

Once Daniel had explained what they were looking for, Ashford left his office and returned a few moments later bearing a large ledger.

'This is the payments record for the current year,' he said. 'It shows the employment record of everyone at the museum on a weekly basis: the hours they worked that week, rate of pay, and if they left for any reason.' He placed the ledger down on his desk. 'How far do you want to go back?' asked Ashford.

'We'll start from now and work back over the last three months,' said Daniel. 'We know that some people can harbour resentment for many years before it erupts into action, but for the moment I suggest we limit ourselves to a number of names that can be handled relatively easily.'

'Fortunately, staff turnover at the British Museum is mainly through people retiring. People tend to stay. It's actually rare that anyone is dismissed, mainly because we're quite careful about the type of person we take on.' He turned over the pages, leafing backwards, and said, 'In fact, within the last three months we've had to dismiss just two people. And in the two months before that, there were no dismissals, although some older staff retired.'

Daniel followed his finger down to the name Horace Bell,

which had 'D' against it dated the month before, and thereafter no record of his being at work.

'I assume "D" stands for dismissed?' asked Daniel.

Ashford nodded.

'The reason?' asked Abigail.

'Sadly, it was drink,' said Ashford. 'Horace gave no indication of being a heavy drinker when we first engaged him, but shortly after that his problem became apparent.'

'Turning up late for work smelling of drink?' suggested Daniel.

'And sometimes not turning up at all. Or, even worse for us, turning up drunk, which meant we had to send him home rather than have him breathing fumes over the visitors and falling over.'

'How did he take his dismissal?' asked Abigail.

'He cried,' said Ashford. 'It was very unpleasant, for him and for me. I could tell that he was deeply remorseful. He begged to be given a second chance, but I had to tell him that we'd already given him many second chances, and third ones.'

'He was drunk on his last day, I assume?' said Daniel.

'Sadly, yes. Which was what prompted his dismissal. It was not an action I wanted to take, but the secure and efficient running of the museum has priority over everything else.'

Daniel wrote down Horace Bell's address, then asked, 'The other person dismissed?'

Ashford scowled and leafed further back. 'Exactly two months ago,' he said. 'For once, my judgement of character eluded me. Or, perhaps, I was preoccupied with other matters. This was a young man called Algernon Pope. He was very personable, charming, and he had impeccable references. As I discovered when I checked on them, there was a good reason his references were so good: they were false. He had conjured them up himself. Unfortunately, it took some time for the answers to my letters checking his references to be answered, and by that time Mr Pope had been with us for almost three weeks.'

'So, you dismissed him because of the forged references?' asked Abigail.

'No, because we discovered that he was stealing items from the museum. Just small items, and most of them from the storerooms rather than the displays, otherwise we'd have picked up the situation sooner.'

'You challenged him about the stolen articles?'

'Of course, and he denied it flatly. He also denied forging the references, insisting it must have been a mistake by the people who'd checked the references. In fact, when I – along with another steward as witness – searched his bag in his presence and found small items taken from the storeroom, he denied initially it was his bag. Then, when it was pointed out that his name was inside it, he insisted that someone else must have put the items in his bag to "frame him", as he said.'

'Caught red-handed. Did you inform the police and have him charged?'

'No,' said Ashford. 'I discussed the matter with Sir Jasper, and we both felt that a trial would not reflect well on the museum's public image. People would feel uneasy if it got out that one of the stewards was a thief.'

'Understandably.' Daniel nodded. 'What about this one? John Kelly. His wages seem to have stopped for a couple of weeks, and then there are no entries to show he's been at work since, but he's being paid, although not as much as before.'

He pointed to the entry in the register for Abigail to see. Beside

Kelly's name some of the regular entries were just blanks, then the initials SB appeared; and after a few days money appeared in the wages paid column, but smaller sums than had been entered before.

'Ah,' said Ashford awkwardly. 'Yes. That's an unfortunate situation.'

'Unfortunate?'

'Mr Kelly has been at the museum for some years, a very reliable person. But about a month ago he didn't turn up for work, and there was no word from him, which was unusual. In the past, if he'd had a problem, he always sent a message explaining. So, after two days, I sent a messenger to his home to see if everything was alright with him. The messenger found his wife very distressed. It seems that he'd been arrested by Special Branch.'

'Special Branch?' queried Abigail, puzzled.

'I'll explain about them later,' Daniel told her.

'You are familiar with them, Mr Wilson?' asked Ashford.

'As a former detective at Scotland Yard, yes.' Daniel nodded. 'I assume they hadn't said why they'd arrested him. In my experience, Special Branch don't give out information.'

'No, you're right,' said Ashford. 'I passed this on to Sir Jasper, and it was he who took the matter up. At first, he got nowhere, Special Branch initially refusing to even admit their actual existence. So Sir Jasper got in touch with the Home Secretary. They are old friends. They were at school together.'

'That was very fortunate for Mr Kelly,' said Daniel.

'Yes, it was. They still refused to divulge what was going on, but Mr Kelly was released. Unfortunately, he was in need of hospital care, which Sir Jasper arranged.'

Abigail shot a look at Daniel, and saw the angry expression which darkened his face, but he said nothing.

'It turns out his arrest was a case of mistaken identity,' said Ashford. 'Because Mr Kelly has been a faithful servant of the museum for many years, Sir Jasper said that we could keep his job open for him until he was fit enough to return, and in the meantime, we would pay him a token wage. '

'That's very generous,' said Daniel. 'I can't think of many organisations that would do that.'

'The museum cares for everyone who works here. Sir Jasper sees it as one large family.'

'Yes, although we believe that Professor Pickering rather betrayed that idea,' said Daniel.

Ashford shot him a sharp, wary look.

'We heard about the row between you and the professor on Saturday. We applaud you for standing up for your staff the way you did. From other accounts we've heard, he was an objectionable man.'

'Yes, he was,' said Ashford quietly. He looked at them, his expression grim. 'But I didn't kill him.'

'We never suggested you did,' said Daniel.

Ashford's mouth tightened and he looked annoyed. 'Yes, you did, in an oblique way. And I understand why you should think it. But I'd already decided to challenge his threat to have me dismissed. If it was even a real threat, that is. Part of me felt it was just bluster, a braggart and bully feeling the need to try and reassert his authority.'

'Did you mention the incident to Sir Jasper?'

Ashford shook his head. 'No. I had intended to when we returned to work on Monday. Neither Sir Jasper nor I were at the museum on the Sunday. But then, the killing made it irrelevant.' He looked firmly and directly at Daniel and Abigail. 'I suppose you want to know where I was when Professor Pickering was stabbed.'

'It would help to eliminate you from the enquiries,' said Daniel.

Ashford gave a rueful chuckle. 'Such a bland phrase, don't you think. I was in my office. I went straight there when I arrived on the Monday morning. Unfortunately, no one came in, except one of the ushers to report that Professor Pickering had arrived. I told him to take charge of the professor and that I would be down to join them in due course.'

'You chose to avoid seeing the professor face-to-face after what had happened?' asked Abigail.

'Possibly,' admitted Ashford. 'In fact, I was busy compiling a report on the incident which I intended to give to Sir Jasper. It was my defence should Pickering decide to lodge a complaint against me with the board of trustees.'

'Do you have that document?' asked Daniel.

'No,' said Ashford. 'I destroyed it. After Pickering was killed it no longer seemed of any value.'

'And when did you leave your office?' asked Daniel.

'When one of the stewards came to me and told me of what had happened. I went with him to the gentlemen's convenience and saw Pickering dead.'

'Thank you, Mr Ashford,' said Daniel. 'I'm sorry to put you through this, but you understand, we had to ask.'

'Of course,' said Ashford. 'I would have thought the less of you if you hadn't. By the way, tomorrow we will be having a visit from Mansfield Whetstone, the senior partner of Whetstone and Watts, the publishers of Professor Pickering's book. I assume he's coming to check on how many copies of the book have been sold and to see if more should be delivered.'

'Isn't it unusual for a senior partner to involve himself at that level?' asked Abigail. 'I would have thought that a sales representative of the firm would have sufficed.'

'Yes, but these are not what could be termed "usual circumstances",' said Ashford. 'The murder of an author can greatly increase sales. I mention this to you in case you'd like to talk to Mr Whetstone. I'm sure he can tell you much more about the professor than I.'

'Thank you, Mr Ashford.' Daniel nodded. 'Yes, we will most certainly make a point of seeking out Mr Whetstone. Has he indicated what time he will be here?'

'He says about ten o'clock.'

'Then we'll let you do your business with him first and talk to him afterwards.'

CHAPTER NINETEEN

After Ashford had gone and they were alone, Abigail said quietly, 'He's still a suspect, isn't he?'

Daniel nodded. 'He has no alibi. He could have very easily slipped down to the convenience, killed Pickering, then returned to his office and waited for the steward to come and summon him.'

'Surely his clothing would have been splashed with blood,' said Abigail.

'A long raincoat and a change of shoes would have dealt with that,' said Daniel. 'Mr Ashford is a very efficient planner, and he'd have had all Sunday to prepare.'

'So, what do we do to find out if he is the guilty person?'

'We talk to the other members of staff who were around the area at the time Pickering was killed, see if they happened to spot Mr Ashford outside of his office at any time before the body was discovered. At the same time, we'll make time to talk to the people whose names popped up: Horace Bell, Algernon Pope and John Kelly.'

'John Kelly,' said Abigail. 'You said you'd tell me about Special Branch. Who are they? Part of the police, I assume.'

'But separate,' said Daniel. 'Special Branch was set up as a separate branch of the Metropolitan police just over ten years ago. Its full title is the Special Irish Branch because it was set up to combat the Irish Republican Brotherhood, and that's still its primary function.'

'Yes, I've read about the Irish Republican Brotherhood,' said Abigail. 'They've carried out assassinations and explosions to further the cause of home rule for Ireland.'

'The Special Branch way is to pay informers to keep up with what's going on. So, this suggests that some informer told them that this John Kelly was involved with the Brotherhood in some way.'

'And they just arrested him, with no word to anyone?'

'Special Branch have powers far in excess of those of the ordinary police force. Because their role is to keep the nation safe from terrorist attacks, they've been given carte blanche as to how they do that. They're a law unto themselves.'

'Who should we talk to first of the three?'

'My instinct tells me John Kelly.'

'But surely he's the least likely to launch an attack on the museum. By all accounts, it was Sir Jasper who got him released from custody, and they're paying him while he recovers.'

'Yes, but I'm curious to find out what was behind Special

Branch being involved, and where the Irish Brotherhood fits in.'

'Mistaken identity, Ashford said.'

'I'd still like to find out for myself,' said Daniel. 'I also think we need to bring John Feather into this. And not just about Kelly, but also talking to Whetstone tomorrow when he comes to the museum.' He gave an unhappy groan. 'This being barred from Scotland Yard is so annoying, it makes seeing John so difficult. I can send him notes asking him to meet us, but who's to say he's there to get them?'

'I'm not barred,' said Abigail.

Daniel gave a sour laugh. 'I get the impression Superintendent Armstrong views you as even less welcome there as me.'

'That may be, but he can't stop me entering the building and sending a message to Inspector Feather asking if he will come and meet me in reception. And then he and I will join you somewhere nearby outside.'

Daniel nodded. 'I think that's the only way round the problem. But first, we'll go and talk to John Kelly and get his version of events.'

John Kelly lived in a tiny cramped house on the fringes of Seven Dials, on the edge of Covent Garden. Seven Dials itself was notorious as one of London's worst rookeries, a warren of alleyways and rat-runs with houses on opposite sides of these alleys so close together that their fronts almost touched. It was said that a criminal on the run could enter Seven Dials at Covent Garden and make his escape in Leicester Square without once setting foot on the ground, using windows to go from house to house and then over roofs.

The reason for Kelly's house feeling so cramped was his large family: nine children with ages ranging from twenty to a baby in a cot. Mrs Kelly cleared the children out of the living room so that Daniel and Abigail could talk to him without infant shrieks and interruptions.

John Kelly was a short, round man in his fifties. At this moment his face still bore the bruises from his incarceration in the cells of Special Branch, and his left arm was encased in plaster below the elbow. Abigail's face tightened in distaste when she saw what had happened to Kelly, but decided to leave the talking to Daniel. This was his area of expertise.

'Mr Kelly, my name is Daniel Wilson, and this is Miss Abigail Fenton. We've been hired by Sir Jasper Stone to look into the recent tragic event at the British Museum, the death of Professor Lance Pickering.'

Kelly nodded, his look suspicious. 'I know who you are, Mr Wilson,' he said warily. 'I saw your name in the papers over the Ripper case. You were Inspector Abberline's sergeant.'

'I was, but I've left the police force. I'm now working as a private enquiry agent.' Carefully, he added, 'And, to let you know, from my experience when I was at Scotland Yard, I have no time and even less respect for the actions of Special Branch, the people who did this to you.'

'You say that, but you were a part of Scotland Yard.'

'I was at Scotland Yard in Fred Abberline's team, but I was never party to anything that Special Branch did, nor some of the other dubious activities. And nor was Fred Abberline.'

'Was that why you both left and set up private?' asked Kelly.

'Let's just say, it was time for me to move on,' said Daniel. He smiled. 'And, if it's any help, I'm currently banned from even going into Scotland Yard.'

'You must be doing something right,' grunted Kelly.

'We'd like to ask you what happened to you with Special Branch.'

Kelly scowled and gestured at his plaster-encased arm. 'You can see what happened.'

'Yes, but why did they pick you up?'

'They said they'd been given good information that a John Kelly of my address was part of an attack the Brotherhood was planning on the British Museum.'

'Why the British Museum?'

'They said the Brotherhood saw it as a figurehead of the Empire, so it was a good target.'

'I assume you told them you knew nothing about this.'

'Of course I did! Over and over again! The museum's been good to me. I've loved working there all these years, and with Sir Jasper Stone and Mr Ashford there are no finer people to work for. In fact, if it wasn't for Sir Jasper, I doubt if I'd have made it out alive.'

'When did they find out for sure they were wrong?'

'It seemed they went back to their informer to ask him about me, and he told them they'd got the wrong John Kelly.'

'But they'd got the right address,' said Daniel. 'Is there another John Kelly who lives here?'

'No,' said Kelly quickly. Too quickly, registered Daniel.

'But there was,' said Daniel quietly. 'I'm guessing you have a son, also called John.'

'He's nothing to do with this!' burst out Kelly.

'I think he is,' said Daniel. 'When Special Branch told this informer about you, and your age, he must have told them he meant a younger John Kelly at this address. Your son, John Kelly Junior.'

'John's a good boy!' Kelly told them.

'But lately he's got into bad company,' said Daniel. 'Where is he?'

Kelly fell silent, then he groaned and said, 'I don't know. He

145

was gone when I came out of hospital. My wife, Eileen, told me he packed a bag and left the same day I was lifted by Special Branch.'

'And you've no idea where he's gone?'

Kelly shook his head. 'And I don't want to know. I don't want them bastards beating it out of me so they can lay their hands on him.'

CHAPTER TWENTY

John Feather sat at his desk in his office going through his notes with a gloomy feeling. Nothing leapt out, everything so far had been a dead end. The supposed ransom pick-up had been a disaster. Why? Had the blackmailer spotted the stake-out and retreated? That was possible, but Feather still had his doubts as to how real it had been in the first place.

Joshua Tudder and Mrs Pickering had looked promising, but now he doubted them as potential suspects. Then there was this recent spate of vandalism at the museum, in particular this daubing of graffiti using red lead paint. With no signs of forced entry, that suggested it had been done by someone with inside knowledge of the museum, someone who either knew how to get in and out without raising any alarms, or who knew the museum well enough to spend the night there, and was then able to slip out easily the next morning. That certainly seemed the most promising. But who? And why? And was it the same person who'd stabbed Professor Pickering?

There was a knock at the door, then a messenger entered with a note for him.

'There's a lady downstairs who asks if she can see you, sir,' he said.

Feather opened the note and smiled as he read: *I'm downstairs in the main reception. Do you have a moment to see us? Yrs, Abigail Fenton.*

Us. Of course, Daniel was hiding somewhere outside.

'Is there an answer for her, sir?' asked the messenger.

'No thank you. I'll see the lady myself. Thank you, Leonard.'

Feather took his coat from the coat-stand and headed out of his office and down the stairs to the main reception hall. Abigail was stood waiting and she came towards him as he reached the bottom of the stairs.

'I hope I haven't got you in any trouble?' she asked.

'None at all,' he reassured her. 'The superintendent's at the Houses of Parliament, seeing important people. Where's Daniel?'

'In a coffee shop almost opposite,' said Abigail.

'Freddy's.' Feather nodded. 'We used to do as much business in Freddy's as we did in the Yard: swapping notes, meeting up with informers. The top brass thought it was a low place – they still do – so they never bothered us.' He gestured at the main door. 'Shall we go?'

Abigail and Feather left the Yard, and strolled along the Victoria Embankment a short distance, turning into a narrow lane where the smell of freshly roasted coffee wafted into their nostrils.

Daniel was sitting inside Freddy's, three cups of steaming coffee on the table in front of him.

'I took the chance that you'd be in the office,' said Daniel, shaking Feather's hand, and they all sat.

'My turn to look after the shop,' said Feather. 'The super's at the Houses of Parliament, cultivating the powerful.'

'The ones who can land him the role of commissioner?' enquired Daniel.

'You've got it,' said Feather. 'So, what's happened?'

'It's struck us that there's an inside element to this case.'

'Someone inside the museum?'

'Or someone who may harbour feelings of revenge against them. For example, someone who may have been sacked, in their opinion, unfairly.'

'It's a bit extreme, to take revenge by killing someone,' said Feather.

'We agree. But nevertheless, we took a look at people who've left under a cloud, and there were only two who we're looking into. But another person popped up. A man called John Kelly, who's been working at the museum for years. Very respected. Nothing against him. But it seems that Special Branch took him in after they got word that the museum was going to be attacked by members of the Irish Republican Brotherhood, and that John Kelly was one of the attackers.'

'Special Branch.' Feather shuddered. 'I don't like the sound of that.'

'No, and they didn't give him a nice time,' said Daniel. 'Until they realised that the John Kelly they had wasn't the one they were after. That was his son, also called John Kelly. So, they let Kelly Senior go.'

'How sure were Special Branch that the son, John Kelly Junior, was going to launch an attack on the British Museum?' asked Feather. 'And what sort of attack? Murder? Assassination?'

'The only people who'd be able to answer that are Special Branch,' said Daniel. 'It seems one of their informers passed on information about this attack to them, and the name he gave them was John Kelly of such and such an address. We've been to see John Kelly, the father, and that's where we got this from.'

'I assume he won't say where his son is?'

'He says the boy ran off after he was picked up and he's not heard from him since. The question is, did the Republican Brotherhood abandon their proposed attack once the elder John Kelly was picked up, or did they go ahead with it? And if so, did it involve the stabbing of Professor Pickering?'

'You think that's likely?'

'I don't know,' admitted Daniel. 'If it had been the Brotherhood, I'm sure they would have taken the credit for it as part of their push for home rule. Unless the attack went wrong and Pickering was killed in mistake for someone else.'

'Like who?'

'Sir Jasper Stone. On one level, the two men look quite similar. They're about the same height, about the same age.'

'So, you think it may have been them who did the attack, but when they discovered the wrong man had been killed – not the head of a place they described as being a keystone of the British Empire, but an author – they just kept quiet about it?'

'I know it sounds far-fetched,' said Daniel. 'But I think it's a possibility we need to look at.'

'And how do you suggest we do that?'

'This informer of Special Branch's. Maybe he knows if Sir Jasper was the real target.'

Feather looked doubtful. 'I can't see Special Branch revealing anything to me. They don't reveal anything to anyone.'

'They're more likely to talk to you than to me. You're an inspector at Scotland Yard. One of their own. I'm not even allowed in the building.'

'I'm never one of their own,' snorted Feather. He gave a sigh. 'Alright, I'll have a word and see what I can find, *if* they talk to me.'

'Tell them we think John Kelly Junior might be the person who killed Pickering, and why.'

'The mistaken identity?'

'It might nudge them into saying *something*. There's another thing. A man called Mansfield Whetstone is coming to the British Museum tomorrow morning at ten.'

'Pickering's publisher,' said Feather. 'I met him. Loud, boastful, and definitely a man not to be trusted, particularly whatever he tells you about Lance Pickering. He told me that Pickering was a paragon of virtue who had the respect and admiration of anyone who ever met him.'

'Huh!' snorted Abigail indignantly.

'That's a pity,' said Daniel. 'We were thinking he might be able to tell us more about Pickering.'

'He might have changed his tune in light of the latest information about Elsie Bowler,' said Feather. 'So, yes, I'll join you. Especially because at the moment I feel we're just clutching at straws. Though this Kelly business might lead somewhere. There have been a few incidents lately with these home rule fanatics getting more dangerous. The big fear is there might be another attempt to assassinate the Queen. In one way, it's fortunate she's largely kept herself away from the public since Prince Albert died.'

'The last attempt was some time ago, wasn't it?' said Abigail.

'Six years ago. 1882,' said Feather. 'Roderick Maclean tried to shoot her at Windsor Station soon after she arrived from London, but the boys from Eton College who'd been waiting to cheer her when she arrived overpowered him. Ten years before that, Arthur O'Connor tried to shoot her in 1872. Then there was a whole rash of attempts in the 1840s, most of them claiming to be in revenge for the Irish Famine – or the Great Hunger, as they called it.' He sighed. 'As if we haven't got enough to keep us busy without assassins roaming the country.'

CHAPTER TWENTY-ONE

The address they had for Algernon Pope was a terraced house in Coram Fields. Daniel knocked at the door, which was opened by a middle-aged woman wearing a flower-pattern apron.

'Good day,' he said. 'We're sorry to trouble you, but is this right the address for Algernon Pope?'

The woman looked at him, curious, and then burst into laughter. 'It was,' she said. 'But his latest address is Newgate.' And she laughed again.

'Do I assume you mean Newgate Prison?' asked Daniel.

'You assume right,' said the woman. 'If you're here to serve a summons on him, you'll have to get in the queue behind me. He owed me rent for two months.' She sighed. 'I guess he saw me as a soft touch. Kept spinning these stories about how his wealthy family was due to send him money, just as soon as his mother could get it out of his dad, who was a regular old tight-fist, according to Algie.'

'Why was he sent to Newgate?' asked Daniel.

'Stealing a wallet,' said the woman. 'He claimed it fell out of the gentleman's pocket and he was chasing after him to return it to him, but when they found he'd done the same thing just the week before and been let off with a caution . . . well. That was it for Algie.'

'How long ago was this?' asked Daniel.

The woman thought. 'It was a month ago he went in,' she said.

'And he's been there all that time?'

'Unless he's managed to talk his way out,' said the woman. She gave a chuckle. 'I wouldn't put nothing past Algie. He may have done me for two months' rent, but he was always amusing. And he did help out when he could. He used to bring things home for me. "Here you are, Mrs P," he'd say. "A little something for you until my dear ma persuades my tight-fisted old pater to cough up with the readies."'

'What sort of things?' asked Abigail.

'Trinkets,' said the woman. 'Little things. Old-looking. Nothing valuable though.'

'How do you know?' asked Abigail.

'Cos I used to take 'em to the pop shop at the corner, Mr Moses. He's always been fair. He said they were old, but not valuable. Nice-looking things, though. A couple of brooches. An ornate-looking hat pin.'

After they left the house, Abigail strode off with great determination along the street.

'Where are we going?' asked Daniel.

'To this pop shop at the corner,' said Abigail. 'I'm interested to see how many historic items from the British Museum's collection are on display there.'

'Even if they are, we won't be able to get them back,' said Daniel.

'Yes, we will. We'll call a constable and have them impounded.'

'Your proof?' asked Daniel. 'This Mr Moses will insist he bought them in good faith, and there'll be no proof that they are actually from the British Museum.'

'The curator will be able to identify them,' insisted Abigail.

'But who's to say they are the same ones that came from the British Museum?' queried Daniel. 'Someone else could have got similar items from another source. And once you've identified something as potentially stolen, that item will soon disappear from the display, before it can be examined properly.'

'You're saying we should just turn a blind eye to this crime?' asked Abigail.

'No,' said Daniel. 'Algernon Pope is currently in prison. Not for this offence, admittedly, but he was sacked for stealing from the museum. His landlady has had some recompense for the two months' rent he didn't pay her. Mr Moses is keeping the wheels of his local small business turning. If we were looking into thefts from the museum, then I agree we should follow this up. But we are looking into a murder, and that I feel is where we should be putting our energy. So, the first thing we do is go to Newgate and make sure that on the day of the murder, Algernon Pope was still locked up.'

'I don't approve.' Abigail sniffed. 'But I suppose what you're saying does make sense. Even though it still seems to me that a serious crime will go unpunished.'

'The museum know that Pope stole things from them. Ashford told us so. They don't expect to get them back. But, I'm happy, once the main case – the murder – is solved, to pass this information on to them and let them deal with it, if they choose to. Would that make you happy?'

Abigail nodded. 'Happier.'

John Feather strode along the basement corridor that connected the main building of Scotland Yard with an annexe where Special Branch had their offices. The setting was very apt, he thought: underground and out of sight, just the way that Special Branch operated. Unlike in the main building, none of the doors had identification on them to show who was behind a particular one, or even which department. Fortunately, Feather was on his way to see an old friend of his, Walter Grafton, who'd transferred from the detective division to Special Branch the year before. They still occasionally saw one another at police events, and Walter had given Feather the door number of his office in the annexe 'in case anything ever turns up which you think might be of interest to us'.

It had been a while since he'd last seen Grafton, and he wondered if the invitation still stood, or whether Grafton had evolved into the same kind of person as other Special Branch personnel Feather had met: suspicious, wary, close-mouthed, trusting no one. It was time to find out.

He knocked at the office door and waited until he heard Grafton call, 'Enter!'

Grafton looked up in surprise when he saw who his visitor was. 'John! We don't often see you in this corridor.'

Feather gave him a rueful grin. 'Hallowed ground, Walter. Not for the feet of we ordinary coppers.'

Grafton snorted. 'Come off it, John. Either you're here for information – which you know I can't give you – or you're here to pass on something. Which is it?'

'A bit of both,' said Feather. 'You know Superintendent Armstrong and I are investigating the murder at the British Museum.'

Grafton nodded, his eyes wary.

'A name's come into the frame that appears to cross over into your area. John Kelly Junior. Son of an attendant at the museum who I believe you pulled in for questioning.'

'Not me,' said Grafton quickly.

'No, but your lot. Anyway, we're looking for him, and I'm about to initiate a manhunt for him. I thought, before I did, I'd check with you that we're not treading on your toes.'

'In what way?'

'Well, according to whispers we've picked up, this John Kelly is rumoured to be part of an Irish Brotherhood group, and the stabbing of Professor Pickering might be part of an attack they carried out that went wrong. We think they had another target in mind. One of the top dogs in the museum itself. So, you see, we don't want to go blundering in if you're already involved. We don't want to mess things up.'

'Very considerate of you,' grunted Grafton. He lapsed in thoughtful silence for a moment, then said, 'This Kelly business isn't one of mine, but I can have a word with the person whose it is. I'll get back to you.'

'That would be good,' said Feather.

'You say you're about to initiate the manhunt,' said Grafton. 'Has it got Armstrong's backing?'

'Not yet,' said Feather. 'I was just about to take it to him when

I thought I'd check with you first. But he'll be wanting to know what's going on about it.'

Grafton nodded. 'Give me half an hour,' he said.

'Thanks,' said Feather. 'Will you come to me, or shall I come back here?'

'You come here,' said Grafton. 'I don't trust anyone outside this corridor.'

'Not even me?' said Feather with a smile.

'Especially you,' said Grafton. 'In my book, you spent too long working with Abberline and Wilson. Renegades both.'

And Feather noticed he wasn't smiling.

CHAPTER TWENTY-TWO

Daniel and Abigail walked away from the grim granite building at the corner where Newgate Street met the Old Bailey, Newgate Prison.

'What an awful place!' said Abigail.

'It used to be a lot worse,' said Daniel. 'And at least we know that Algernon Pope has the perfect alibi for the murder.'

'I suppose the length of time he stays in there will depend on how harsh the judge views him.'

'No,' said Daniel. 'Newgate's now only used for prisoners who are to be executed, or those awaiting trial at the Central Criminal Court. Once Pope is found guilty he'll be sent elsewhere.'

'Don't you mean *if* he's found guilty?' asked Abigail.

Daniel chuckled. 'That's true. You never know; from past form, Mr Pope seems perfectly capable of evading justice.'

'It's still a horrible place,' said Abigail. 'I'm quite glad we didn't go in any further than the front gate.'

'There's not that much more to see,' said Daniel. 'There's the central courtyard, where the prisoners are exercised. Under the eyes of the guards, of course. There's a chapel, where prisoners of both sexes attend services. The men sit on benches in the lower area while the women are in the gallery. The gloomiest part is the passageway between the Old Bailey and the prison, because it's also the prison graveyard. Prisoners who've been executed are buried beneath the flagstones that mark the pathway of the passage.'

'I suppose you've had to visit it often during your career.'

'Yes,' said Daniel. 'Sometimes for information when a prisoner has something to trade for a reduced sentence. Sometimes just to confront someone you've been chasing for a long while.' He headed towards a waiting omnibus. 'Well, with Algernon Pope accounted for,' said Daniel, 'our next stop will be Horace Bell. And I must warn you, this may not be pleasant. People who are sacked for drunkenness are invariably foul-mouthed, filthy and liable to be violent when challenged. Are you sure you want to seek him out?'

'You'll be with me,' said Abigail. 'And I can take care of myself.'

John Feather sat in Grafton's office and waited. He could tell that Grafton was deliberating just how much to tell him. Yes, his old friend had definitely taken on the persona of Special Branch.

'I've had a word,' said Grafton. 'It might be useful, this manhunt for Kelly. There's a possibility he's fled over the water, back to Ireland. But he might still be here. And if he is

160

and we can lay our hands on him, that would be good.'

'So, was Pickering the target for the killing, Walter, or was it someone else?' asked Feather.

Grafton shook his head. 'I'm not at liberty to say,' he said. 'But if your boys bring him in, it will be appreciated.'

Instead of the shuffling, dribbling, filthy drunken wreck Daniel had anticipated, Horace Bell was a man who positively glowed with good spirits of the spiritual rather than the alcoholic kind. And his small house, rather than being a hovel filled with empty bottles and reeking of cheap gin, was clean and neatly cared for.

'We're sorry to trouble you, Mr Bell, but we've been asked by the British Museum to investigate the recent difficult events there.'

'The murder,' said Bell. 'I saw it in the paper.'

'And other incidents,' said Daniel. 'Some vandalism.'

Bell smiled. 'And I'm guessing you've come to ask me whether the vandalism might have been me because of them sacking me.'

Daniel and Abigail exchanged surprised looks.

'Well . . .' began Daniel.

'Nothing could be further from the truth!' said Bell cheerily. 'Getting the boot from the museum was the best thing that ever happened to me. It brought me to my senses! You see, the museum had always been good to me, Mr Ashford in particular. But how did I repay his kindness and concern? By getting blind drunk, time and time again! I was a mess, sir and madam! Truth to tell, I took the museum for granted because they were so caring. What I needed, sir and madam, was not worried looks and concern, I needed the iron rod to bring me to the right path! Yes, sir and madam, being told I was dismissed, and seeing the hurt look on Mr Ashford's face and realising the pain I'd brought on that good man, I couldn't live with myself. Not the way I was. So, I stopped drinking, sir and madam. Not even a small beer passes my lips these days. I have done with it! The demon drink is my downfall no longer!

'I now have regular employment at a greengrocer's. Not as nice as when I was at the museum, a lot of it is outdoors, unloading crates of vegetables from the wagons when they deliver. But it is honest work! And it keeps me healthy and away from taverns. Yes, sir, getting the sack saved my life. And, if you see Mr Ashford, I'd be appreciative if you'd tell him so. That what he was forced to do – by my selfish and unsocial behaviour – saved my life.'

'Well, I think we can also cross Horace Bell off our list of possible suspects,' said Daniel, as they headed home.

'A veritable conversion,' said Abigail. 'And Algernon Pope also out, that means we are left with Mr Ashford . . .'

'Very unlikely, in my opinion,' said Daniel doubtfully.

'I agree,' said Abigail. 'From the way that Bell spoke of him, and our own experiences with the man, I would hate it if he turned out to be the murderer.'

'Then there are Tudder and Mrs Pickering working together with an unknown assassin,' continued Daniel. 'But, again, very doubtful, especially now we know about Elsie Bowler.'

'Elsie Bowler is a possibility,' said Abigail.

'Indeed, if we can find her. As is John Kelly Junior.' He frowned thoughtfully. 'I'm not sure of our next move.'

'I am,' said Abigail. 'You need to read Professor Pickering's book.'

'Why?' asked Daniel.

'Because you promised you would.'

'But you've already told me everything I need to know about Ambrosius,' protested Daniel.

'Second-hand information,' countered Abigail. 'You're always saying how important it is to go back to the source. Well, I suggest you start the book this evening, and then continue reading it when we get to the museum tomorrow morning while we're waiting for Mr Whetstone to arrive.'

CHAPTER TWENTY-THREE

Abigail stood at the kitchen range, poking the potatoes bubbling away in the saucepan on the hob with a thin knife.

'How are you getting on?' she asked Daniel, who sat in his armchair turning over the pages of Professor Pickering's book with a perplexed expression on his face.

He gave a sigh. 'I cannot see anything in here that would a reason for murder,' he said. 'It's interesting, linking this Ambrosius with King Arthur, but so what?'

'The Children of Avalon were upset by it,' pointed out Abigail.

'Yes, but enough for a couple of idiots to smash a glass case.

That's a far cry from killing someone.' He shook his head. 'There's nothing here.'

'You've only read about a quarter of the book.'

'And it feels like a lifetime.' He looked at the clock. 'Those are two lost hours I'll never get back.' He shut the book and put it aside. 'Frankly, from what I've read and everything we've learnt so far, I'm of the opinion that John Kelly Junior and the Irish Republican Brotherhood are starting to look the most likely.'

'Why?'

'I'm coming back to what you, Joe Dalton and John Feather have already suggested: maybe it's the institution itself that's being attacked. The British Museum is seen as one of the bastions of the Empire. And the Irish Republican Brotherhood hate the British Empire.'

'Why?'

'Haven't you been following the arguments for and against home rule in the newspapers?' asked Daniel. 'It's been going on for long enough.'

'To be honest, although I was aware of the campaign, other things were my priority.'

'Digging in Egypt.'

'Not just Egypt. Palestine. Rome. Greece.'

'It's often struck me that, after those places, being in England must seem very boring.'

'How can you say that?' demanded Abigail. 'I'd hardly describe being part of a team investigating violent murders as boring!'

'Yes, but it's not very exotic, is it. Not after the Middle East and places like that.'

'You were going to tell me about this home rule issue,' she said firmly, turning her attention back to the potatoes.

'What do you know about it already?' asked Daniel.

'What everyone else does. That Ireland wants independence from Britain. The thing is, the level of violence that seems to be happening in the name of this independence seems to indicate something much stronger. Angrier.'

'Indeed,' said Daniel. 'The Act of Union which made Ireland part of Britain only came into effect at the start of the century, in 1801. But British occupation of Ireland has caused anger in Ireland for hundreds of years. You could trace it back to Henry VIII and the break from the Catholic church.'

'Religion again!' Abigail sighed.

'I'm afraid so. The population of Ireland remained mainly Catholic after Henry's break with Rome, with no sign of changing to the new Protestant faith. So, after Henry's death, his daughter Elizabeth and then King James I took large areas of Ireland away from the Irish and gave it to English Protestant gentry to rule over the Catholics.'

'Surely there must have been uprisings against them?'

'There were, but they were suppressed by the army. And then even more so under Oliver Cromwell, who was fiercely anti-Catholic. It was calculated that at the siege of Drogheda, Cromwell's forces massacred about 4,000 people. Not all soldiers.'

Abigail smiled. 'I thought I was supposed to be the one with a history degree, but here I am being given a course in Irish and British history. How do you know so much about it? Surely not from just being a detective at Scotland Yard.'

'No, from spending much of my life here in Camden Town,' said Daniel. 'When you've been here a bit longer you'll realise that it has one of the largest populations of Irish immigrants in London.'

'Why's that?'

'Because of Euston Station. Which connects with the boat train from Liverpool. During the Famine, thousands of Irish left Ireland to come to England. Most caught the boat from Dublin to Liverpool, and those who didn't want to stay in Liverpool came to London, where it was said the streets were paved with gold. They didn't find gold, but they found other Irish who'd emigrated earlier, so they moved in. The result was it was impossible to live in this area without hearing stories of the troubles the Irish had suffered at the hands of the British, especially under Oliver Cromwell, and then the Famine.'

'The Famine was before my time, and we really didn't hear much about it in Cambridge.'

'You would have if Cambridge had been home to thousands of immigrant Irish,' said Daniel. 'The 1840s.'

'As I said, before I was born,' said Abigail.

'The potato crop failed,' said Daniel. 'Blight. There was no food. A million died in Ireland, and another million fled the country, some coming to England, thousands of others to America. The Irish blamed the absentee English landlords.'

'Surely they must have seen that they weren't responsible for the crops getting blight.'

'Yes, but the landlords were responsible for the fact that most of the cattle that grazed their Irish lands were sent to England as beef, while the Irish starved. The Irish view was that if they'd been allowed to own their own lands they could have decided what the land could be used for, crops, beef, whatever. The fact was that by the start of the century, the Irish only owned five per cent of the land, while absentee English landlords and the Crown owned the rest of it.'

'Hence the demand for home rule.' Abigail sighed. 'Own your own land and decide what you do with it.'

'Exactly,' said Daniel. 'You can see where the anger comes from that drives the Republic Brotherhood and the like. People think it's just about politics, who's in charge. But really it's about the fact that a million died and another million were forced to leave their home country for ever.'

'You sound like you're sympathetic to this Brotherhood?'

Daniel shook his head. 'I'm sympathetic to what the Irish suffered, but I could never condone violence and murder. If it turns out that the Irish Republican Brotherhood was behind the murder of Professor Pickering, I'll track them down and bring them to justice.'

'Well while you're considering that, you can go and wash your hands,' said Abigail. 'The potatoes are ready. I'll mash them and get the sausages out of the oven and serve.'

'The sausages are cooked?' queried Daniel.

'To perfection.' Abigail smiled happily.

CHAPTER TWENTY-FOUR

As Daniel and Abigail walked into the museum the next morning, they were immediately accosted by the attendant on duty at the front entrance.

'Mr Wilson, Miss Fenton, Sir Jasper said for you to go up and see him as soon as you arrived.'

Daniel frowned. 'Sir Jasper's in early,' he commented.

'Indeed, sir. And, may I say, he looked quite worried.'

'Trouble,' muttered Daniel to Abigail.

They hurried up the stairs to Sir Jasper's office and found him in his office staring worriedly at a sheet of paper.

'It's another letter,' he said.

As before, it contained just a few handwritten lines, and was brief and to the point:

We are not fools. Your trap was obvious. We warned you not to tell the police. You will pay for that. The price is now £2,000. You will leave the parcel of money as before, beneath the same bench at Clarence Gate. A further letter will tell you when.

'Can I see the previous letter?' asked Abigail.

Sir Jasper opened a drawer in his desk, took it out and gave it to her.

'It's written by a different person,' she said, showing them the differences in the handwriting. 'I'd also say that this latest letter was written by a girl. It's in a more feminine hand, but not yet fully confident. I would suggest a girl in her middle teens.'

'So, this is definitely a conspiracy, but one involving children,' mused Daniel. 'That suggests a hoax, if children are involved.'

'Not all children are innocents,' said Abigail. 'This could have been written at the direction of someone else, an adult, to disguise their handwriting. Or to make it look like a conspiracy of more than one person.'

'What shall we do?' asked Sir Jasper.

'Again, my advice, Sir Jasper, is to inform the police.'

'It didn't work last time,' said Sir Jasper sadly.

'No, and if it turns out they were watching, it will be even harder to mount a proper watch on the bench.'

'I wonder why they say they will send details of when the transaction is to take place later, rather than give the time and say now, as they did before?' mused Abigail.

'To prolong the agony,' said Daniel. 'They're playing with us.'

He tapped the letter and asked, 'May I hang on to this for the moment, Sir Jasper? We're due to meet with Inspector Feather this morning. He's coming here to talk with us to Mr Whetstone about Professor Pickering. We'll show this to the inspector and let him pass the information on to Superintendent Armstrong.'

'Thank you,' said Sir Jasper, then groaned. 'This whole business is turning into a nightmare. I can't sleep at night for wondering what dreadful thing might happen next.'

Daniel picked up the letter and put it in his pocket, then he and Abigail left Sir Jasper to his gloomy thoughts and headed back down to the main reception area.

'I suppose we just wait here for John Feather and this Mansfield Whetstone to arrive,' said Daniel.

'No,' said Abigail firmly. 'What *you* have to do is take this opportunity to dig further into the book.'

'Why?' demanded Daniel.

'I told you, for clues,' said Abigail.

'There aren't any!' insisted Daniel.

'You can't say that until you've read it.'

'I've read most of it,' said Daniel.

'I'll wait down here to look out for Inspector Feather while you retreat upstairs to our office to look at the book in peace.'

'Slave-driver,' grumbled Daniel. 'You're worse than Abberline ever was.'

Nevertheless, he headed upstairs to their office, while Abigail returned to looking at the exhibition again, in the hope of some kind of enlightenment. After half an hour of intensive examination, none was forthcoming, and she was relieved to see the arrival of John Feather.

'Morning, Miss Fenton.'

'Abigail, please.'

'Yes, sorry, force of habit.' Feather smiled. 'Where's Daniel?'

'He's upstairs in our office, reading the professor's book while we wait for Mr Whetstone to arrive,' said Abigail. 'He's hoping to find some clues in it. And there's been another letter demanding money.'

'What?'

'Daniel's got it. He's waiting to show it to you.'

'Well, I've also got something to report. My contact inside Special Branch says he's happy for us to set up a manhunt for young John Kelly. But he's not saying whether Pickering was the target, or not.'

'Hopefully, things will be moving forward,' she said. She led the way towards the winding staircase to their small office 'Let's go and update Daniel. I gather you've known him for a long time.'

'Years,' said Feather. 'I was a young copper just promoted from uniform when I joined Abberline's team at Scotland Yard. Daniel was Abberline's sergeant. I learnt everything I know about being a detective from watching the pair of them. Fred Abberline was the tops, but Daniel ran him a very close second. He had a copper's nose. Still has. He's got this sixth sense of being able to sniff out guilt. That's one of the reasons the superintendent can't stand him.'

'Why?'

'Because Armstrong doesn't have it, and never will. He doesn't understand how Daniel does what he does, all he knows is that Daniel succeeds where he fails, and that riles him.'

'You said "one of the reasons".'

Feather smiled. 'Years ago when Armstrong and Daniel were both detective sergeants, Daniel found Armstrong trying to beat a confession out of a man.'

'What?!'

'Daniel dragged Armstrong away and hit him. Almost laid him out.'

'Was the man guilty?'

'No, he turned out to be quite innocent. But Daniel said that was irrelevant. We were the protectors of the law, not abusers of it. Armstrong's never forgiven him.'

Abigail pushed open the door of their office and Daniel looked up at them from the book.

'Morning, Daniel,' said Feather.

'Good morning, John,' Daniel greeted him.

'How are you getting on with the book?' asked Feather.

Daniel gave an unhappy scowl. 'Give me Charles Dickens any time,' he said.

'I've told him about the latest letter,' said Abigail, 'and John's got news of his own.'

Feather repeated what he'd told Abigail about Special Branch and young John Kelly.

'Typical Special Branch,' grunted Daniel. 'Not just playing their cards close to their chest, but not letting on if they've got any cards in the first place.'

'Where's this latest letter?' asked Feather.

Daniel laid it on the table for him to look at.

'It doesn't say when they want the money paid over,' he mused thoughtfully. 'I wonder why?'

'If it's serious, maybe they've got something in mind to spring on us,' suggested Daniel. 'Some nasty surprise.'

Suddenly, the sound of a woman screaming echoed up the stairs from below. They stared at one another, shocked, then Daniel, Abigail and Feather ran as fast as they could out of the small office and down the stairs, towards the source of the sound.

'There!' said Daniel, pointing towards the anteroom beside the exhibition. Museum stewards were already rushing to the spot. The sound of screaming changed to loud sobbing. Daniel, Abigail and Feather rushed through an arch and found themselves in the room.

A young woman in a museum steward's uniform was kneeling by the body of a man. She looked up as people arrived, her mouth open in shock, the agonised expression on her face showing she was having difficulty understanding what was happening. Her hands and arms and the front of her uniform were drenched in blood. In her hand she held a knife. The body of a bearded man lay on his back, blood still pumping from a wound in his chest.

'I saw the knife and . . . and pulled it out,' sobbed the young woman. 'I thought I'd save him, but instead . . .' And she let out a howl of despair, the knife falling from her fingers and clattering to the stone floor.

'You take care of the body, I'll look after her,' Abigail said to Daniel. She hurried forwards, knelt down beside the sobbing young woman and put her arm around her, ignoring the blood. 'Come on,' said Abigail. 'Let's get you up and away from here.'

The young woman allowed herself to be helped to her feet by Abigail. David Ashford appeared, his face showing horror when he saw the blood-soaked man on the ground, and the young woman and her bloodstained outfit.

'Where are the stewards' private quarters?' asked Abigail.

Ashford turned to one of the female stewards standing transfixed in horror. 'Mrs Sawyer, take them to the female stewards' room,' he said hoarsely.

Feather had dropped to his knees beside the prone man and felt for a pulse in his neck, then pulled out his fob watch and held the face to the man's mouth, examining it for signs of breath. He looked at Daniel and shook his head.

'The stab was right into the heart,' he said.

'If Jenny hadn't taken the knife out . . .' began one of the stewards unhappily.

'He'd have died anyway,' said Daniel. 'All that did was open the wound so the blood could spray out. Poor girl.' He looked down at the man and wondered aloud, 'I wonder who he is?'

'He's Mansfield Whetstone,' said Feather. 'Pickering's publisher.'

CHAPTER TWENTY-FIVE

Jenny had managed to stop crying but she still shook as Abigail and Mrs Sawyer helped her out of her blood-soaked uniform. Then, while Mrs Sawyer put the uniform in a sink and went to get clean clothes for the young woman, Abigail sat down with her. Now she saw her up close she realised she was only about seventeen, little more than a girl.

'It wasn't your fault,' she stressed.

'But if I hadn't taken the knife out . . .'

'He'd have died anyway. The way the blood pumped showed the knife had gone deep into his heart—' She stopped as the girl began crying again at the vivid memory. 'I'm sorry, I didn't mean to make it worse for you.'

Mrs Sawyer returned with a clean uniform. 'It's only an old one of mine,' she said. 'But it'll do while we get yours cleaned.'

Jenny stood up and allowed the two women to dress her. 'What happens now?' she asked, her tone showing her feeling of utter helplessness.

'I'll take you home,' said Mrs Sawyer. 'Mr Ashford says we can get a cab and the museum will pay for it.'

'She'll need to talk to the police first,' said Abigail.

'No!' said the girl, frightened. 'I can't bear to talk about it. Not yet.'

'Surely, she can talk to them later,' said Mrs Sawyer. 'She's terrified. And in shock. Whatever she says won't make any sense.'

Abigail weighed this up, then said, 'I'll have a word with the police inspector and with Mr Wilson. They're both very kind and won't want her to suffer more than she has done.' She asked the girl gently, 'What's your name?'

'Jenny,' said the girl. 'Jenny Warren.'

'I'm Abigail Fenton and I'm working with Mr Wilson to investigate the . . .' She hesitated. 'What's happened here at the museum.'

'Yes,' said the girl. 'Mr Ashford sent a note round to everyone telling us about you.'

'Well, I'll see if the inspector agrees for you to talk to me later, rather than them. Would that be alright?'

Jenny nodded. 'Yes,' she said, her voice just above a whisper.

'In that case I'll accompany you, with Mrs Sawyer, to your home, and we can talk there, once you feel a bit better.'

'It still might be too soon for her,' said Mrs Sawyer doubtfully.

'It might be, but we'll see how it goes,' said Abigail.

'Alright,' said Mrs Sawyer. 'I'll make Jenny a cup of strong tea while you talk to the inspector and Mr Wilson. Tea's good for shock.'

Abigail was tempted to retort, 'Not as good as brandy,' but decided against it in case Mrs Sawyer was of the temperance persuasion. Instead, she left Jenny and Mrs Sawyer in the stewards' room while she went in search of Inspector Feather and Daniel. John Feather was directing two police constables who'd arrived in to taking statements from the people who claimed to have seen what happened but weren't able to add anything new.

'So far everyone just says they heard screams and rushed to the scene, and saw the girl crouched by the dead man,' Feather told Abigail. 'They saw her pull the knife out of his chest and the spray of blood. But that's about it. Exactly what we saw. I'm going to go back to the Yard and bring in my sergeant and a couple of detectives to take statements. The constables are doing their best, but detectives know the kind of things we're looking for.'

'Where's Daniel?' asked Abigail.

'He's taking statements, so at least we've got one detective who knows how the game works. How's the girl?'

'In a state of shock,' said Abigail. 'So, I wondered if it would be alright if I talked to her. The museum has arranged a cab to take her home. One of the other female stewards is going with her. I know you need to talk to her, but I don't think you'll get much that's useful out of her at the moment.'

Feather looked doubtful. 'She's the one most likely to have the answers,' he said. 'Who else did she see just before she discovered the body? Was there anyone around acting suspiciously? Who exactly did she see, and can she describe them?'

'I can ask her those things,' said Abigail. 'But at the moment she's still too petrified to be able to talk about it properly. Once I get her back in her home surroundings and settle her down, she might find it easier to talk.'

'Yes, I suppose so,' said Feather. 'You're right that often people only really remember details later. Very well, take her home.'

'I'll report when I get back.'

Daniel appeared and asked Abigail, 'How is she?'

Once again, Abigail described Jenny's state of shock and told Daniel that she was taking her home. When Daniel also began to express the same doubts about this as Feather had, saying they needed to talk to her while everything was still fresh in her mind, Abigail told him that Feather had given his approval.

'She's in no fit state to give proper answers at this moment. But once she's settled down in her own home, I'll talk to her.'

'You don't know what questions to ask,' said Daniel.

'John's given me some pointers. And later you'll be able to talk to her, and maybe get better answers.'

'Alright,' said Daniel. 'I suppose it makes sense.'

'How have you got on?' Feather asked him.

Daniel groaned. 'Nothing to add to what we saw ourselves.'

'Same for me,' said Feather. 'I just told Abigail, I'm heading back to the Yard to dispatch a team of detectives here to start taking statements. My sergeant's pretty good, and if there is anything extra to find, I'm sure he'll nose it out.'

'I'll get back to the girl and take her home,' said Abigail.

'Remember to write down whatever she tells you,' said Daniel. 'When we're clutching at straws the way we are now, we need everything written down so we can keep going through it.'

'You can leave that to me,' Abigail assured him.

She left the two men looking at the place where the murder had taken place. Screens had been hastily erected after Feather had given instructions that he didn't want the bloodstains or anything else removed or disturbed until his detectives had had the chance to make a proper examination of the scene.

'And I'm off to the Yard,' said Feather. 'I'll make sure Sergeant Cribbens introduces himself to you when he arrives.'

'Thanks, John,' said Daniel.

As Feather made his exit, Daniel saw David Ashford approaching.

'This is dreadful!' moaned Ashford. 'One tragedy after another! I'm beginning to wonder if this exhibition isn't cursed.'

'I wouldn't have thought of you as a man who believed in superstitions like that,' remarked Daniel.

'I'm not,' said Ashford. 'But you will admit it's been one thing after another. Two murders. The attack by those vandals from the so-called Children of Avalon. The red lead paint. The extortion letters. All in such a short space of time!'

'How many of your staff knew that Mr Whetstone was coming to the museum today?' asked Daniel.

'All of them,' said Ashford. 'I sent a note round to all the staff to ensure Whetstone was received cordially.' He looked at Daniel unhappily. 'You don't think a member of the museum staff did this?'

'I don't know,' said Daniel. 'But everything that's happened so far does suggest someone with a knowledge of the operation of the museum.'

CHAPTER TWENTY-SIX

Mrs Sawyer had returned to the British Museum, leaving Abigail with Jenny Warren in her small two-roomed flat above an ironmonger's shop in Chapel Street. Even here, at home, Abigail noticed the girl couldn't relax properly. Which was hardly surprising, she reflected; the sight she'd seen had been enough to unsettle even the toughest of people.

'I can make you a cup of tea,' suggested Abigail. 'Unless you have something stronger that you'd prefer.'

'There's some rum in the cupboard,' said Jenny. 'I don't like it much myself. It's only here because my husband, Tom, got a taste for it, being in the navy.'

'The navy?' said Abigail, pleased to find a subject to talk about away from the murder.

'Yes. He's at sea at the moment.'

'Don't you get lonely when he's away?' asked Abigail.

'I used to at first, but I got used to it.'

Abigail went to the mantelpiece above the small fireplace and looked at the photographs there. There were two, one of a young man in a sailor's uniform, standing stiffly to attention; the other of Jenny herself standing with an older man in a smart suit and hat who stood with his arm around her shoulder, both of them smiling at the camera.

'I assume this is Tom,' said Abigail.

'Yes, miss.'

'And the other one I can see is you.'

'Me with my father,' said Jenny. Abigail heard the crack in her voice and turned to see the girl wipe away tears. 'He's just died.'

'I'm sorry,' said Abigail sympathetically. 'You look very happy together.'

'We were,' said Jenny. 'My dad was the greatest man I ever knew. Clever. Kind.' She dabbed at her eyes again, then asked abruptly, 'Have you ever seen anyone who's been murdered, miss? I've seen dead people before, like my gran and others when they died, but not someone who's been murdered.'

'Sadly, yes,' said Abigail. 'Two in England and two in Egypt.'

'Is that from you being a detective?'

'No, all of them happened at a time before I began working as a detective with Mr Wilson. The two in England were also killed at a museum, the Fitzwilliam in Cambridge. The ones in Egypt happened while I was working at a dig there. I'm an archaeologist, really. It's only recently I've added being a detective to it.'

'Yes, one of the other stewards told us, the one who does the Egyptian rooms.'

Abigail sat down on a chair near to Jenny and looked at her sympathetically, but at the same time with purpose.

'Inspector Feather agreed that you could come home at once, rather than talk to him, on the understanding that you'd talk to me about what happened.'

'Yes, miss. I remember you said. And I'm very grateful. I don't know if I could have coped with his questions. Not then.'

'Can you cope with mine now?'

Jenny hesitated, then nodded. 'I'll try, miss.'

Sergeant Cribbens was sitting at a desk, puffing at his pipe with a puzzled frown on his face as he scanned the reports, when Inspector Feather walked in.

'I've got a job for you, Sergeant,' said Feather. 'There's been another murder at the British Museum.'

'Another?' gasped Cribbens. 'Who?'

'Do you remember that publisher we met? Mansfield Whetstone? Him.'

'How was he murdered? Do we know who did it?'

'The answer to do we know who did it is no, we don't. But as he was stabbed to death it seems highly likely that whoever killed Professor Pickering may have struck again. Although there is a difference: Pickering was killed with seven stab wounds, Whetstone was killed with just one, straight into the heart. So either it's a copycat crime, or our killer is becoming more efficient at wielding the knife.

'I was there when it happened, so I've already talked to most of the people who were there at the time, but so far we haven't got much to go on. No one saw the actual killing, and no one saw anything they could

183

describe as suspicious. I want you to go to the museum, taking two of the best detectives with you – and I leave it to you to choose who you take – and talk to everyone again. It doesn't matter if we end up with duplicate statements; sometimes people only remember things later.'

'Yes, sir.'

'I'll join you as soon as I've seen Superintendent Armstrong and given him my report.'

'Actually, sir, he's not in'

'Oh? Where is he?'

'His secretary says he had to go to Parliament for something. Some top level meeting.'

'In that case, I'll go and leave a note on his desk telling him about Whetstone's murder. You head for the museum and start taking statements. I'll see you there. Oh, and make a point of introducing yourself to Daniel Wilson.'

'Is that the man the superintendent doesn't like?'

'The very same.'

Cribbens looked doubtful. 'Will it go badly for me if the superintendent thinks I've been hobnobbing with someone he doesn't like?' he asked unhappily.

'As Daniel works for the British Museum and was one of the first people on the scene when the murder took place, you can't really avoid questioning him, can you?'

'No, sir,' agreed Cribbens.

'Right, off you go. Did the superintendent give any idea of when he'd be back?'

'No, sir.'

Feather sighed. 'Very well. As I said, I'll leave my report on his desk and meet you later at the British Museum.'

* * *

Daniel sat with Ashford in the man's office, going through the list of employees.

'All of these people got the note to say Mansfield Whetstone was coming today?'

'Yes,' said Ashford.

'And do you know if any of them had any prior contact with Mr Whetstone?'

'None, as far as I know,' said Ashford. 'He came here to observe the exhibition being set up, mainly to check the display of the professor's book, but he hasn't been back since.'

'And on that first visit, who did he encounter?'

'Just myself and Sir Jasper,' replied Ashford. 'We had been told what time he would be arriving, so I was in reception to greet him on his arrival and sent a message to Sir Jasper, who joined us. We showed him the exhibition, and he expressed his pleasure at it, and then he left.'

'Professor Pickering didn't join you?'

'No. He was giving a lecture that day. He used to lecture occasionally on Roman history at University College.' He gave Daniel another unhappy look. 'I do hope you're wrong about it being someone connected to the museum. I know all these people and would trust them implicitly.'

'I hope it isn't someone from the museum either, Mr Ashford, but we have to accept that possibility. By the way, how many female stewards do you have?'

'Six. You met Jenny Warren and Mrs Sawyer. There are four others and, as with most of our staff, they rotate their duties, so only two will be on duty at any one time. Why do you ask?'

'I was just curious. I hadn't been aware that museums employed female stewards.'

'We didn't ourselves, at first, but then it was drawn to our attention that we had a great many women visitors who might find themselves in need of assistance of a kind they would feel reluctant to approach a man about. The initiative has proved very successful, so much so that I believe other organisations are following suit.'

'Very commendable,' said Daniel. 'You must feel proud to be able to say that the British Museum has led the way.'

'In many things,' said Ashford. 'Our aim is to establish the British Museum as the foremost museum in the world.'

'In the world?' echoed Daniel. 'That's very ambitious.'

'Achievement is only truly rewarding if one aims high,' said Ashford.

With that sentiment ringing in his ears, Daniel made his way down the stairs to the main reception area, just as Abigail entered the museum.

'How is she?' he asked.

'Recovering,' replied Abigail. 'She's still in a bit of a state, which is understandable in view of what she experienced, but she was able to answer some questions. Sadly, she wasn't able to enlighten us with anything useful. She didn't see anyone hanging around that area before she discovered the stabbed man, she didn't notice anyone acting suspiciously and she hadn't seen Mr Whetstone before she discovered him.'

'The same response as everyone else we spoke to,' said Daniel gloomily. Then he brightened. 'Anyway, at least we now have a connection that definitely links both murders.'

'The book?'

'Exactly. The author and the publisher both stabbed to death here at the museum. The book is the key to this case, so our next port of call has to be to the publishers.'

* * *

Inspector Feather made his way down the wide staircase to main reception. He'd left a brief report about the murder of Mansfield Whetstone on Superintendent Armstrong's desk, and now he was on his way back to the British Museum to join Sergeant Cribbens and his fellow detectives in asking questions. The trouble was he already felt they'd discover nothing they didn't know already. Whoever this killer was, he was like a shadow, able to flit in and out and commit murder without anyone seeing him, or even being aware of his presence. Two murders, and no sighting of anyone by anyone. A real will o' the wisp.

As he reached the wider marbled floor of reception, a constable burst through the main doors, saw Feather, and rushed towards him.

'Inspector Feather, sir!'

'Yes, Constable?'

'There's been another stabbing.'

'I know. At the British Museum. I'm just on my way back there.'

'No, sir. This is another one. A Mr Tudder's been stabbed at Professor Pickering's house near Regent's Park.'

CHAPTER TWENTY-SEVEN

Daniel and Abigail arrived in Fitzroy Mews, the home of Whetstone and Watts publishers.

'Just a stone's throw from Regent's Park,' noted Daniel.

'We seem to be brought back to this area time and again,' Abigail observed. 'First, to the Pickerings' house, then for the abortive random demand and stake-out, and now the publishers. Pretty soon I will be able to find my way to this part of London blindfolded.'

'That is one of the beauties of London,' said Daniel. 'At first it seems overwhelming, intimidating, but once you've explored it for a bit you realise how neatly it all connects, which is why the most efficient way to travel is on foot. At least, once you're in a particular area – north-west London, for example, or the East End.'

Whetstone and Watts were identified by a shiny black door with a brass plaque next to it. Daniel pulled the brass bell handle below the plaque, and shortly the door was opened by a smartly dressed nervous woman of middle age who peered anxiously out at them.

'Good afternoon. My name is Daniel Wilson, and this is my colleague, Miss Abigail Fenton. We're from the British Museum. May we come in and talk to you?'

'Is this . . . is this about poor Mr Whetstone?' she asked.

'You've heard?' said Abigail.

'Yes,' she said, and they could see the tears in her eyes. She opened the door wider and they stepped inside, then followed her into a small reception area.

'Might we have the pleasure of knowing who we are addressing?' asked Daniel.

'Miss Roseberry,' said the woman. She was nervous, twisting her hands together, and close to tears. 'I'm . . . I was . . . Mr Whetstone's secretary.' At the mention of his name, tears welled up in her eyes and ran down her cheeks and she slumped down onto a chair. 'I'm terribly sorry,' she said, taking a handkerchief and putting it to her eyes, dabbing at her face.

'Please, no apology from you is needed,' said Daniel. 'If anything, we should apologise to you for disturbing you at this very difficult time.' He paused, and then asked, 'When did you hear the tragic news?'

'Late this morning. Mr Watts, the other partner, came in, looking ill. "Mansfield's been killed!" he said. "Just like Pickering!" I was in shock.' She looked up at them, her face pale, tears still brimming in her eyes. 'Who could have done such a wicked thing?'

'That's what the museum has asked us to find out,' said Daniel. 'We're private enquiry agents hired by Sir Jasper Stone at the museum. We were already investigating what had happened to Professor Pickering when today's tragic event happened to Mr Whetstone.'

'Perhaps it might be better if we talked to Mr Watts,' suggested Abigail. 'It would be unfair to subject you to anything at this moment.'

Miss Roseberry shook her head. 'You can't,' she said. 'He's gone.'

'Gone?'

'He rushed upstairs to his office, then came running down and said he was going away. And then he flew out of the door.'

Daniel and Abigail looked at one another, puzzled.

'You don't know where he went?'

'I assume he went home,' said Miss Roseberry.

'Do you have his address?' asked Daniel. 'We'll go and contact him there. There's no need for us to disturb you any more at this time.'

'Yes. 43 Mount Street. It's off Park Lane.'

'In Mayfair,' said Daniel. 'I know it. Thank you, Miss Roseberry. One more thing, what is Mr Watts' first name?'

'Jerrold. Jerrold Watts.'

As they left the offices, Daniel asked, 'What did you make of that?'

'Firstly, how did Mr Watts learn about the murder of Whetstone so quickly?' said Abigail. 'As far as we knew he wasn't at the museum with Mr Whetstone this morning, and there hasn't been time for the story to appear in the newspapers.'

'Yes, that was my thought,' agreed Daniel. 'And secondly, why rush off like that in such a panic?'

'Frightened?'

'Of what?'

'That he might be next.'

'Which suggests he has a good idea as to why both Pickering and Whetstone were murdered.'

'So why didn't he go to the police with that information?'

'Perhaps he did,' said Abigail.

Daniel shook his head. 'I was with John Feather all morning and there was no contact to him from Watts, nor any word from Superintendent Armstrong about Watts being in touch. Hopefully, we'll find the answer when we call him at home.'

Daniel and Abigail left Fitzroy Mews and made their way through to Euston Road, where Daniel hailed a hansom cab.

'I thought you said on foot was the best way to travel in London,' pointed out Abigail.

'Within a set district,' said Daniel. 'Mayfair is off this particular patch, and speed has suddenly become essential.'

If the houses of Regent's Park outer circle had appeared grand, they were dwarfed by the residences of Mayfair, all of which bespoke wealth. 43 Mount Street was an elegant three-storey house in this exclusive part of town.

'I hadn't realised there was so much money in publishing,' observed Abigail as they stepped down from the cab.

'Obviously more than in detective work,' added Daniel as they made their way to the ornate front door, with its tall marble columns framing a door adorned with highly polished brassware.

The door was opened by a smartly dressed lady of middle-age, and Daniel was reminded of the similarity to Miss Roseberry at the publisher's offices. Mr Watts preferred a certain type to look after him.

Once again, they went through the introductions, who they were and their reason for calling.

'Would it be possible to talk to Mr Jerrold Watts?'

'I'm sorry, sir. He's not here.'

'Not here?'

'No, sir.' Adding, 'I'm Mrs Harris, his housekeeper.'

'Was he here earlier?' asked Daniel.

'Yes, sir,' said Harris. 'It was all very strange. He rushed in, threw a few things into a small suitcase, and said he was going away for a while.'

'Did he say where?'

'No, sir. That was what was odd. Mr Watts always lets me know where he's going in case anyone needs to get in touch with him. But today . . .' She looked at them helplessly. 'Is there something wrong?'

'I'm afraid there is,' said Daniel. 'Mr Whetstone, Mr Watts' business partner, has been killed. Stabbed, I'm afraid.'

Mrs Harris stared at them, horrified. 'Killed? Mr Whetstone!'

'It's very important that we get in touch with Mr Watts,' said Daniel. 'Does he have friends or relatives he goes to stay with on a regular basis that he might have gone to?'

'Not really. He only has two relatives, a brother who lives in Canada and a sister in Harrow. To be honest, he's very much a home person. There's just him, you see. He's a bachelor and his pleasure is his library here. He's not a great socialiser.'

'Could you let us have the address of his sister? Just in case he might have been in touch with her.'

'Yes, sir. If you wait a moment, I'll get it for you.'

She disappeared inside the house.

'Surely, if he's frightened, he'd go somewhere no one knows him,' suggested Abigail. 'Or abroad.'

'True, but that depends on people's characters. Mr Watts

doesn't come across as the adventurous type, and he has a limited circle of acquaintances. I suggest we start with his sister and see if she can offer any ideas.'

'He's got a brother in Canada. He could be trying to get a boat there.'

'Unlikely,' said Daniel. 'Too much organising involved.'

Mrs Harris returned and handed them a piece of paper with an address in Harrow.

'Here you are,' she said. 'Her name's Jemima. Miss Jemima Watts.'

'So, what next?' asked Abigail as they left the house. 'Harrow?'

'Yes,' said Daniel. 'But before we traipse all the way out there with all that entails, getting a train and so forth, I think we need to alert John Feather to this development. If Watts isn't at his sister's then the police need to put a manhunt in place for him as a matter of urgency.'

'They'll need a description of him,' said Abigail. 'Can I suggest we might be able to speed things along if I went back to the publishers to see if Miss Roseberry has a photograph of Mr Watts while you go and see if you can talk to Inspector Feather.'

'Yes, good thinking,' said Daniel. 'And to avoid getting John into trouble with Armstrong by going to the Yard, I'll go back to the museum and send him a message asking him to meet us there. I can also look up trains to Harrow. By the time John arrives, you should be there with the photo of the elusive Mr Watts.'

They caught a cab from Park Lane that deposited Abigail at the offices of Whetstone and Watts, and then took Daniel on to the British Museum. As Daniel walked into the building he was hailed by the man on duty at the main reception desk.

'Mr Wilson! A telegram's just arrived for you!'

A telegram? Daniel took the buff envelope from the man and tore it open. Inside was the brief but shocking message from Inspector Feather: *Come to Pickerings'. Urgent. Tudder stabbed.*

CHAPTER TWENTY-EIGHT

Abigail watched as Miss Roseberry studied the framed photographs on the walls of her office, before pointing to one particular picture which showed a round, smartly dressed man, bald except for tufts of hair just above each ear, with a serious expression on his chubby face.

'I think this is the best image of Mr Watts,' she said.

In fact, as Abigail observed, there were only two pictures of Mr Watts: this one and one of him standing next to the large and more imposing figure of the late Mr Whetstone. All the other framed pictures adorning the walls were of Mr Whetstone with different people, mostly men.

'I get the impression that Mr Watts isn't fond of having his photograph taken,' said Abigail.

'That's true,' said Miss Roseberry. 'He's basically a very shy person. Mr Whetstone, on the other hand, was only too keen to have his photograph taken with our authors.'

'Was that because he was the senior partner?'

'In part,' said Miss Roseberry. 'But mainly it was his nature. He was ebullient, very outgoing. Gregarious with a love for life.' The memory of him brought tears to her eyes again, and she took a handkerchief from her pocket and dabbed her cheeks. 'I'm sorry,' she said. 'I still can't believe what's happened.'

'That's absolutely understandable,' said Abigail.

Miss Roseberry began to take the photograph of Watts from its wooden frame.

'You said about needing the photograph to pass on to the police. Do you believe Mr Watts is in danger?'

'We're not sure,' said Abigail. 'But we do feel it's important to find him. His housekeeper, Mrs Harris, has given us the address of his sister in Harrow, but if he's not there, or she doesn't know where he is, the sooner we can put out a search for him the better. His safety is our main concern.'

'Yes, of course,' said Miss Roseberry. She put the photograph carefully into a stiff envelope and handed it to her.

'You will take care of it?' she asked. 'As you'll have seen, we don't have many pictures of him.'

'I will guard it with my life,' Abigail assured her, slipping the envelope into her bag.

'And if you do get news of him from his sister, I'd be most grateful if you could call back and let me know. I am worried about him,' said Miss Roseberry.

'I will,' said Abigail. 'Although I'm not sure what time we will get back from Harrow.'

'It doesn't matter what time, I will be here,' said Miss Roseberry. 'I . . . I've decided that I need to send letters to our clients and other associates to let them know what has happened to Mr Whetstone. There are many of them, so it will take me some time to type them all.' She looked at Abigail in appeal. 'I feel I need to be here at this time. You do understand?'

'I do,' said Abigail.

As Miss Roseberry escorted Abigail to the door to the street, she asked hesitantly, 'Can I ask, Miss Fenton, how you got into this business? Being a private detective? It's so unusual for a woman!'

'Through Mr Wilson,' replied Abigail. 'He was formerly with Inspector Abberline's team of detectives at Scotland Yard, and when he left he became a private enquiry agent. We were involved in solving a series of murders at the Fitzwilliam Museum in Cambridge, and he invited me to work with him.'

'But isn't it dangerous?' asked Miss Roseberry, looking at Abigail with a mixture of wonder and awe.

'Everything is dangerous if you do it without proper thought,' said Abigail. 'A person can get killed crossing the road if they are careless, run down by a horse.'

'Yes, but, tracking down and facing a murderer . . . !'

'Caution is the key,' said Abigail.

With a smile of farewell, she shook hands with Miss Roseberry, but as she walked away from the publishers she reminded herself of the reality of her previous experience and told herself: *Be careful. In a murder case, no matter how cautious you are, there is always danger.*

* * *

Joshua Tudder was sitting on a chair at the kitchen table when Daniel arrived. He was bare-chested, a bloodstained shirt thrown to one side on the floor. Mrs Pickering sat on another chair and watched as a doctor finished sewing a wound in his upper arm. John Feather moved towards Daniel when he saw him arrive and steered him out into the passage.

'What happened?' Daniel asked Feather.

'It was the girl. Elsie Bowler. I'll let you talk to Tudder and Mrs Pickering once the doctor's finished with him. He shouldn't be long now.'

'But why stab Tudder?' asked Daniel.

'Tudder stepped in to defend Mrs Pickering and got the knife thrust intended for her. He's a brave man.'

They became aware of the doctor packing his case, then heading for the bathroom to wash his hands. 'He's all yours, Inspector,' said the doctor.

Feather walked to where Mrs Pickering was helping Tudder put on his shirt. 'I've told Mr Wilson the bare bones of what happened, sir, but if you're up to it, it would be helpful if you could let him know what happened,' he said.

'I'll tell it, Joshua,' said Mrs Pickering. 'At least, the first part.' She looked enquiringly at Tudder as he began to button his shirt. 'Shall I help you further?'

'No thank you, Laura,' said Tudder. 'I'm sure I can manage. You tell the investigators what occurred.'

Laura Pickering gestured for Feather and Daniel to sit down, and took a seat herself. 'The girl who called before, Elsie Bowler, arrived on our doorstep and said she wanted to see me. I told our housekeeper, Mrs Arnott, to let her in and I took her into the drawing room. Mr Tudder was here, and I asked him to excuse us while we spoke.'

Daniel looked inquisitively at Tudder, who winced at the pain in his arm as he continued buttoning his shirt, and said, 'I went into the library, which is just across the passage from the drawing room.'

'I asked the girl what she wanted,' continued Laura Pickering, 'and at first she seemed calm, but suddenly she became agitated. "I want money," she burst out. "For all the years my mother suffered." She then became very angry, accusing me of having known about my late husband's relationship with her mother, and said it was all my fault. I began to tell her that I was sympathetic and I would contact my solicitors and see if any sort of arrangement could be made, but suddenly she started raging, that wasn't good enough, and then she produced a knife and began shouting that she wanted what she was owed.'

'It was the shouting that made me come in,' said Tudder. 'I could hear the rage in her voice that was almost hysteria, and I was worried that Mrs Pickering might be in danger. When I saw the girl holding the knife I advanced towards her, asking her to give me the knife. I could tell she was in a deranged state and there was no knowing what she might do. I hoped to calm her down, but suddenly she let out a roar of anger and lunged at me. Fortunately, I managed to dodge to one side so that, although the knife struck me, it only caused a flesh wound. At the same time, I chopped down with my other hand on her hand that was holding the knife, and the weapon fell to the carpet, and I put my foot on it. At that point, she turned and ran out of the house.'

'That was a very brave action, sir,' said Daniel.

'Do you think it was she who stabbed Lance?' asked Tudder.

'It seems likely,' said Feather. 'We'll take the knife she dropped to the Yard and compare it with the wounds inflicted on your late husband, Mrs Pickering, but even if they don't correspond, that doesn't mean she didn't do it.'

Daniel and Feather left the house and waited until the housekeeper had closed the door, before Feather asked, 'What do you think?'

'I think that Joshua Tudder is a brave man, and Mrs Pickering shows great control.'

'About the girl. Do you think she did the murders?'

'Pickering, possibly. But I have my doubts. And I don't think she killed Whetstone, and I think the second murder holds the key to the whole case, especially because we've got a new lead.'

'Oh?'

'Jerrold Watts, the publishing partner of Mansfield Whetstone, has vanished,' said Daniel. 'I suspect he's done a runner because he's scared, and if that's the case it's likely he knows something about why Whetstone and Pickering were killed, so we need to find him. Abigail's gone to the publishers to get a picture of him. We've got a possible lead as to where he might have gone, but in case he's not there we need to mount a search for him . . .'

He was interrupted by a hansom cab pulling up at the kerb beside them. The door of the cab opened, and the burly figure of Superintendent Armstrong stepped down from it.

'What's going on, Inspector?' demanded Armstrong. 'I found your message on my desk when I got to my office. First this publisher . . .'

'Mansfield Whetstone,' said Feather.

'. . . stabbed to death this morning. And now Tudder stabbed.' He swung angrily towards Daniel. 'And what's he doing here?'

'As I've said before, I'm here at the request of the British Museum,' replied Daniel. 'You may not like my involvement, but

Professor Pickering and Mansfield Whetstone were both killed on their premises.'

Armstrong scowled and swung back to Feather. 'So, what's happened here?'

Feather told him, summing up the events culminating in the stabbing of Tudder and the girl fleeing.

'Well that's it, then,' said Armstrong. 'A knife attack on the widow, the same as on the professor and the publisher. Luckily for us, by doing this she's as good as confessed to both murders. All we have to do now is bring her in. Right, drop everything else and concentrate on finding this girl.'

'What about the murder of Mansfield Whetstone?' asked Daniel.

Armstrong frowned at him. 'What about it?'

'I agree that Elsie Bowler wanted to revenge against Pickering for what he did to her mother, raping her and making her pregnant all those years ago. She came to attack Mrs Pickering for the same reason, claiming that Mrs Pickering must have known what her husband had done, so she was also responsible.'

'Poppycock!' snorted Armstrong. 'Mrs Pickering is innocent here.'

'Absolutely,' said Daniel, 'but that's not how this girl sees it. But it doesn't give us a motive for why she would attack Mr Whetstone. I don't think she did that.'

'Two murders and this attack here, exactly the same, stabbing with a knife!' said Armstrong incredulously. 'It's her, Wilson. Elsie Bowler. Who cares why she did them, she's shown what she's capable of.' He turned to Feather. 'I want a manhunt for this Bowler girl put in place, Inspector.'

'Already in operation, sir,' said Feather. 'Posters with her description are being printed, and they'll be in all the next editions of the papers.'

'Good,' said Armstrong. 'I'm going in to see the widow, let her know this case has me at the helm, that no expense is being spared to catch this girl.' A thought struck him. 'You've arranged protection for the house?'

'Yes, sir. A constable will be on duty twenty-four hours a day until the girl is caught.'

'Good.' Armstrong nodded. 'I'll let the widow and the commissioner know I've authorised it. And as I said, nothing else counts. No other line of enquiry is to be pursued. Find this girl.' He glowered again at Daniel. 'As for you, Wilson, you have no place here. I shall be contacting Sir Jasper Stone and letting him know that we've solved the case, and there's no longer any need for you. I want you out. Out of the museum. Out of the way.'

Feather gave Daniel a rueful look as the superintendent headed for the house. 'Sorry, Daniel.'

'That's alright, John. But I still have doubts that Elsie Bowler's our killer. The person who killed Lance Pickering was clever in the way they went about it, the "Out of Order" notice on the door, the business of climbing over the cubicle after they'd locked it. That suggests planning. Same thing with the murder of Mansfield Whetstone. All those people in the museum this morning when he's stabbed to death, and no one sees anything. Again, that takes planning. But the attack on Mrs Pickering and Tudder by Elsie Bowler today was frenzied, mindless, frantic. Altogether different.'

'She's still a likely candidate,' said Feather.

'I agree, I'm just expressing my doubts,' said Daniel. He let out a sigh. 'Not that my concerns will stop Superintendent Armstrong from declaring the case is solved once the police have located her. Anyway, we need this search to find Jerrold Watts urgently.'

'Sorry, Daniel,' said Feather. 'I can't do it. You heard Armstrong just now. He's decided that the killer is Elsie Bowler so he's just ordered everything to be put into finding her and dropped any other line of enquiry. So, no search for John Kelly. And there'll be none for this Jerrold Watts. Armstrong wants this wrapped up, and to do that he wants Elsie Bowler brought in fast.'

'But I'm sure she didn't kill Whetstone!' exploded Daniel. 'And I don't think she killed Pickering. It's not her style. Those killings were calculated, her attack on Tudder was frantic and out of control. And what about this latest letter? We talked about a nasty surprise. Maybe the killing of Whetstone was it. And from what we know about Elsie Bowler, these letters don't sound like her.'

'I'm sorry, Daniel, those are Armstrong's orders, and I can't go against them. You know that.'

CHAPTER TWENTY-NINE

Abigail saw that Daniel was in a foul mood as soon as he walked into their small office.

'I assume it's bad news,' she said. 'I saw the message you left with John's telegram, but decided to wait for you here rather than go off chasing to the Pickerings' house. What happened? Is Joshua Tudder dead?'

'No,' said Daniel, and he outlined the events for her.

When he'd finished, Abigail asked, 'If this girl went there to attack Mrs Pickering with a knife, could she be the one who stabbed Pickering and Whetstone?'

'That's certainly Superintendent Armstrong's opinion. But I have my doubts.'

As he'd done with Feather, he expressed why he wasn't convinced that Elsie Bowler was responsible for the murder of Professor Pickering, or of Mansfield Whetstone.

'Yes, that's logical,' she agreed when he'd finished. 'But you could be wrong. Perhaps Elsie Bowler did carry out the first murder in the planned way you describe, but afterwards she felt adrift. Yes, Pickering was dead, but where was the satisfaction for her? She wanted more. But now she hasn't got Pickering to direct her anger at, so she casts around. Anyone connected. Mrs Pickering is the obvious first choice.'

'But why be so blatant about it? Why not be careful in her attack, the way she did with Pickering – if it was her who killed him.'

'Because now she wants the reason for the attack to come out. She wants the public to know about the awful way her mother was treated.'

'You're suggesting she wants to get caught so it will all come out?'

'Possibly. Have you read any of the work of Sigmund Freud?'

'This new-fangled psychiatry stuff.' He shook his head. 'No. I've heard it mentioned, but I can't see how it relates to criminal investigation.'

'That's because you haven't read it.'

'I don't have much time to read,' said Daniel, then smiled. 'I count on you to draw my attention to things I need to know.'

'And then you ignore them.'

'Not all the time,' he said defensively.

'Anyway, Freud says that in some cases the culprit's main desire is to be caught to make them feel valuable.'

Daniel looked doubtful. 'I'd have thought they wanted to be caught because they couldn't cope with the weight of their guilt.'

'Not all people who are guilty of crimes feel weighed down by any conscience over what they've done. Some are so proud they want everyone to know and admire them.'

'Yes, that's true,' admitted Daniel. 'I've met a few like that. But they're usually vain and with an inflated view of their own worth. I can't see Elsie Bowler fitting that mould.'

'You don't think she feels undervalued?'

'Yes, but that's not the same. The people you're talking about like to consider themselves as some kind of secret puppet-master, pulling the strings and manipulating things behind the scenes. Then they want their cleverness known and acknowledged. Elsie Bowler doesn't feel clever, she feels abandoned and hurt.'

'You may be right.' Abigail shrugged. She produced the photograph she'd been given by Miss Roseberry. 'Anyway, I got a picture of Mr Watts so we can pass that on to John Feather, then he can institute the search for him.'

'No, he can't,' growled Daniel. 'Armstrong's forbidden it.'

'Why?'

'Because he's convinced that it's the girl, Elsie Bowler, who is the killer, and every other avenue of investigation is to be shelved. The police have only one job as of now: to find Elsie Bowler.'

'That's why you're in such a bad mood.'

'It is. It's so short-sighted! Watts could be the key to this whole case!'

'So, what's our next move?'

'Well, since the police won't look for Watts, it's up to us to find him. And we start our search for him at his sister's in Harrow.'

Euston Station seemed to be in the same chaos as it ever was, masses of people searching for the right train, struggling to find the correct platform. The place was enveloped in low clouds of steam and smoke which drifted across the station from the trains at their platforms, filling the huge building with the intense smell of burning coal. The high ceiling of the station and the ornate stone columns that supported it were black with soot.

Daniel and Abigail found seats on the suburban train to Watford and journeyed in silence as it trundled northwards. After Wembley the landscape changed from urban to countryside, reverting back to a built-up area as they approached Harrow.

The house where Miss Jemima Watts lived was just a short walk from the station, and the woman who opened the door to them at their knock was a very different character from either Watts' housekeeper, Mrs Harris, or his secretary, Miss Roseberry. Jemima Watts was short, thin and with a sharp, fox-like face.

'Miss Jemima Watts?' asked Daniel, politely doffing his hat.

'Yes,' she said, looking at them suspiciously.

'My name is Daniel Wilson and this is Miss Abigail Fenton. We're private enquiry agents employed by Sir Jasper Stone at the British Museum to investigate recent unhappy events there, and we believe your brother may be of great help to us.'

'I've no idea where Jerrold is,' she said. 'Good day.' And she began to close the door.

Daniel slipped his boot in the gap to stop it closing. 'Please, Miss Watts—'

'Remove your boot at once or I shall call the police!' she barked angrily.

'Yes, I think that will be a good idea,' said Daniel quietly. 'In fact, I'll go and get a constable now. Miss Fenton will wait here until we return.' He began to take his boot out of the gap in the door, but before he did, said, 'The fact is, Miss Watts, we are here to offer protection to your brother. We know he is frightened, but we can prevent the same fate from falling to him that happened to the unfortunate Mr Whetstone.'

'I don't know what you're talking about!' she burst out, but they could tell she was flustered. 'You will please leave!'

'Indeed, we will. But we will return with a constable, as we promised, and he will verify as to who we are, and our role in this situation. But I must advise you, the arrival of a constable will draw attention to this house, and that is the last thing your brother wants or needs if he is to remain safe. Please tell him that. Tell your brother—'

'I told you, I haven't seen him!' she hissed angrily at them.

Daniel ignored her and continued, '—that we will return in fifteen minutes without a constable and hope he will agree to see us.'

'I tell you, he's not here!' insisted Miss Watts.

'If that is the case, then – as I say – we will return with a constable. But we are here to protect him, Miss Watts. We can ensure his safety.'

As Daniel and Abigail walked away from the house, Abigail asked, 'What makes you so sure he's in there?'

'When we were in the publisher's offices I noticed the cigar stubs in the ashtray. There was the same smell of cigars when Miss Watts opened the door. I took a guess that she wasn't the person who smoked them.'

Inspector Feather sat at his desk feeling angry, but at the same time aware there was little he could do about it. The order for the search for Elsie Bowler had gone out, as it should have done. What angered Feather was the fact that all other lines of enquiry had been abandoned. He agreed with Daniel that it was unlikely that Elsie Bowler had killed the publisher, Whetstone. He was also sure that she had no part in the blackmail letters delivered to the British Museum. Although he also had his doubts if those letters were connected to the murders.

The hope was that once Elsie Bowler was found, evidence might appear that showed the murders were not connected to her, at which time he could resume his proper investigations. But Feather was also sure that once Elsie Bowler was found, Armstrong would declare the case closed, regardless of what might be uncovered.

There was a knock at his door, which opened before he could call 'Come in'. His visitor was Walter Grafton.

'Walter,' said Feather. 'To what do I owe the pleasure?'

'I've come to see what's happening with John Kelly,' asked Grafton. 'Any sightings of him yet?'

Feather shook his head. 'The manhunt for him's been called off.'

Grafton stared at him. 'Called off!' he repeated. 'Why? On whose authority?'

'Superintendent Armstrong,' said Feather. 'He's given me orders to stop everything else and only follow one lead in the murders at the museum: a seventeen-year-old girl called Elsie Bowler. So, no manhunt for John Kelly.'

Grafton's face creased into an angry scowl. Then, without a word, he stormed out of the office, slamming the door behind him.

CHAPTER THIRTY

This time the door was opened to their knock by a short, round bald man with tufts of hair sprouting above each ear.

'Good afternoon, Mr Watts,' said Abigail, recognising him immediately from the photograph.

'You told my sister you can ensure my safety,' he said nervously.

'Indeed, we did,' said Abigail. 'This is Mr Daniel Wilson, formerly with Superintendent Abberline's squad at Scotland Yard. And I'm his partner, Abigail Fenton.'

'We know why you fled,' said Daniel. 'But we do need some more details to ensure you are given proper protection.'

Watts opened the door wider, glancing nervously over their

shoulders as he did so, looking out for potential danger.

'Come in,' he said.

The small terraced house was far different from Watts' palatial residence in Mayfair, and the stout man seemed to fill the narrow passageway as he led them to a small room at the back of the house. It was neatly if sparsely decorated, a small table and four chairs, bookcases and open shelves with small pottery ornaments.

'I am afraid I cannot offer you tea because I'm unused to making it, and my sister doesn't wish to be involved in our conversation, so she's gone to her room,' said Watts, gesturing for them to sit.

'You fled because you were concerned you might be the killer's next target,' said Daniel, seating himself at the table.

'Yes,' said Watts.

'How did you know that Mr Whetstone had been killed?' asked Daniel. 'It was too soon for it to be in the newspapers, and there was no mention of you being at the museum with Mr Whetstone.'

'No, that's true,' said Watts. 'Whetstone had said he'd go alone, but I was curious to see how it went, so I decided to go anyway. But when I got to the museum the police were there, preventing people from going in. I explained who I was to one of the constables on duty and asked what the problem was, and it was he who told me that Whetstone had been stabbed and killed. I panicked. First Pickering, now Whetstone. The connection was obvious: the book and those associated with it.'

'Why?' asked Daniel. 'Who would have a reason for killing Professor Pickering and your partner?'

'I thought it might be to do with the letters.'

'Letters?'

'After we published Lance Pickering's book on Ambrosius, we received a letter from a man who claimed that Pickering had stolen his work for his book. To be honest, every publisher and author gets this when a new book comes out, someone claims that they had the idea first, or that the author stole their work from them. Unfortunately, it often happens that many people will have the same idea at the same time, whether it's for a novel or a book of scholarship. Just look at the number of people in Shakespeare's time who claimed he stole their plots from them.'

'So, you thought this was just a coincidence?'

'Well, yes. Especially because we asked Professor Pickering about it, and about this man, and he said he'd never heard of him, or seen his work.'

'Can we see the letter?' asked Daniel.

'The letters are at the office,' said Watts.

'Letters?' asked Abigail. 'There were more than one?'

Watts nodded. 'The correspondence became angrier, the more it went on. Threatening. I said we ought to take them to the police, but Whetstone was adamant about not doing that, insisting the bad publicity would harm sales of the book.'

'Who were the letters from?'

'A man called William Jedding.'

Daniel looked thoughtfully at Abigail, then turned back to Watts and said in a serious tone, 'Mr Watts, think for a moment about how quickly we were able to track you to your sister's house. If someone is after you – and I stress *if* – they could trace you to here just as quickly. I would suggest you find refuge somewhere else. Somewhere where you're not known and where you don't know anyone. A place with which you have no connection, so no one will think of looking for you there.'

Watts looked at them helplessly. 'Where?'

'Have you ever been to Birmingham?' asked Daniel.

'No,' said Watts.

'Do you know anyone in Birmingham?'

'Not to my knowledge,' said Watts.

'Then I suggest you go there for a while until we lay our hands on the person who killed Professor Pickering and Mansfield Whetstone.'

'But I just said, I don't know anyone in Birmingham!' burst out Watts. 'I wouldn't know where to stay!'

'Leave that to me,' said Daniel. 'I'll escort you there by train and introduce you to someone who'll be able to put you up. His name's Ben Stilworthy, he's a former policeman who now runs a small bed and breakfast establishment, so you'll be perfectly safe. We'll register you under a false name as added protection. I would suggest we leave as soon as possible.'

'Absolutely!' said the nervous Watts. 'At once!'

'We'll also need a letter from you authorising us to go to your offices and collect these letters from this Mr Jedding.'

'Of course!' said Watts. 'I'll let you have that immediately. I'll also go and see my sister and explain what is happening.'

Watts went in search of a piece of paper, a pen and ink. Daniel turned to Abigail. 'Can you take charge of the letters while I escort Mr Watts to Birmingham? I feel this could be the first piece of concrete evidence we've had giving a motive for the murders.'

'Certainly.' Abigail nodded. 'Will you be back tonight?'

'I hope so,' said Daniel. 'The train service between London and Birmingham is frequent, but I'm not sure what time I'll be home.'

CHAPTER THIRTY-ONE

Abigail checked the time with the large clock that hung in the centre of the station as she got off the train at Euston. Five minutes before six. Miss Roseberry had told Abigail she would be working late typing letters to inform the firm's business associates about the tragic death of Mr Whetstone, and she seemed to be a woman of her word. Even if Miss Roseberry had had a change of heart and had left work already – which would be understandable in view of the shocking events of the day – it was just a short five-minute walk from Euston to Fitzroy Mews, so there would be no inconvenience for her. And Abigail felt it was important to get sight of these threatening letters. As

Daniel had said, it could be the first piece of concrete evidence revealing a motive for the murders.

When Abigail came out of the station she saw an omnibus waiting at a bus stop on the other side of Euston Road and she considered getting on, but then she reflected that, with the frequent stops the bus made, the slow plodding of the horse, and especially the traffic congestion there always seemed to be at the junction with Tottenham Court Road, she could walk to Fitzroy Mews quicker than the bus.

Her instinct was proved right when she arrived at Tottenham Court Road. A horse pulling a cart had collapsed in the centre of the road and lay between its shafts on the cobbled road, leaving buses, carts and hansom cabs unable to move in any direction.

Abigail arrived at the offices of Whetstone and Watts and pulled the bell. The door was opened almost immediately by Miss Roseberry.

'Miss Fenton!' cried Miss Roseberry, her manner anxious. 'Do you have news?'

'I'm pleased to tell you that we have spoken to Mr Watts, and he is well. May I come in?'

'Of course!' said Miss Roseberry. She showed Abigail through to the reception area and the two women sat. There was no disguising the relief on Miss Roseberry's face. 'I'm so grateful you returned! Thank heavens he's safe! I've been so worried! Especially after what happened to Professor Pickering and Mr Whetstone.'

'For that reason, Mr Watts has decided to take some time off and go away until things die down and return to normal.'

'You think he is in danger?'

'We hope not, but the truth is that Mr Watts feels he is. So my partner, Mr Wilson, has taken him to a place where he will be very

215

safe. In the meantime, he's asked us to look into the letters he and Mr Whetstone received from a Mr William Jedding.'

'Oh, those!' said Miss Roseberry unhappily. 'Yes, I typed the replies from Mr Whetstone.'

Abigail produced Watts' handwritten note and handed it to her. 'As you can see, he's allowing us to take possession of those letters so that we can look into this matter further.'

'You think this Mr Jedding might have been the one who . . . who harmed Mr Whetstone and the professor?'

'At the moment, we don't know. It's just an avenue we are exploring.' Then a thought struck her, and she asked, 'Did this problem arise over any other books Whetstone and Watts published by Professor Pickering?'

'Actually, the book on Ambrosius was the first book of his we published. He had been published before, but they were academic works published by UCL.'

'University College London?'

'Yes. He lectured there part-time, you see, on Roman Britain. But Mr Whetstone got the impression the professor was interested in publishing outside the academic world, hence his book on Ambrosius came to us.' She smiled and added, 'I'll go and get the letters for you.'

As Miss Roseberry left the room, Abigail smiled to herself. University College London. This was one she could follow up. Charles Winter, a friend she'd known when they had both been students at Cambridge – she at Girton and he at Trinity – was now a senior lecturer at UCL. His speciality had been Roman studies, which meant that he might well have had some sort of acquaintance with Pickering. She hadn't seen Charles for a while, but he'd always been friendly and inviting when their paths had crossed in the years since their student days. First thing tomorrow she'd call on him at UCL and ask Charles about Professor Pickering.

Daniel and Watts had changed trains at Watford, leaving the slower suburban line, and were now on the main route to Birmingham. Watts had insisted on buying seats in a first-class carriage, which had pleased Daniel, who was more used to travelling in second or third. Not only was there more space for them, but they were able to find a compartment to themselves, which meant they could talk freely.

Watts certainly seemed more relaxed now that Daniel was with him, acting as his protector.

'I know of your reputation of course, Mr Wilson,' said Watts. 'A sterling career working with Superintendent Abberline. So many successes. So many villains brought to justice. I remember the Cleveland Street scandal, in particular, because Cleveland Street is literally just around the corner from our offices at Fitzroy Mews, and there was a certain panic amongst one or two of our authors when the news about the – ah – brothel became public.' He shook his head. 'Dreadful!'

Sooner or later, everyone asked Daniel about the two most famous cases he and Abberline had worked on: the search for Jack the Ripper, and the Cleveland Street scandal, eager for inside information, morsels they could trade in gossip. Keen to divert Watts' attention back to the present case, Daniel said, 'Tell me more about these letters. The ones from Mr Jedding.'

Watts gave a little shudder at their mention. It was obviously not just a subject that was distasteful to him, but it reminded the publisher of why they were heading for Birmingham, apparently now fleeing for his life.

'The letters.' He sighed. 'To be honest, we ignored the first one, but when the second one came repeating the allegation, Whetstone replied to it saying that he had raised the matter with Professor Pickering, who had assured us that he did not know Mr Jedding, nor had he seen any of his work. That produced a further letter from Mr Jedding which was very angry indeed. In it he said he had delivered a parcel of his own manuscript personally to Professor Pickering's house, and it had been taken in by the Pickerings' housekeeper.'

'You showed this letter to Professor Pickering?' asked Daniel.

'We did,' said Watts. 'As we had done with the earlier letters. He insisted that his housekeeper did not give him any such parcel.'

'A simple matter to question the housekeeper, I would have thought,' said Daniel.

Watts looked uncomfortable. 'I did suggest that to Whetstone, but he was adamant that there would be no such questioning. It would put our relationship with Pickering at risk.'

'So, he was prepared to accept the Professor's denial at face value,' said Daniel.

'Yes,' said Watts.

'And after the professor was killed, you didn't think of showing these letters to the police?' asked Daniel. 'They surely suggest a possible motive for his murder.'

Again, Watts looked uncomfortable. 'I did suggest as such, but Whetstone was against it. He said that if word of the letters got out it could adversely affect sales. And, with the book in high demand because of the exhibition at the British Museum, it would be foolish to put such good sales at risk. The book trade can be notoriously unstable, and one never knows if a book will sell well or not.'

'You could have overridden him in the interests of justice and finding the killer,' suggested Daniel. 'The name of your firm is Whetstone and Watts. You are a partner, after all.'

'A very junior partner.' Watts sighed. 'Whetstone was the senior partner and he took the major decisions.'

'And you abided by them?'

'Yes. I did most of the selecting of which books to publish, but he was the one with the most commercial experience. So, I bowed to his judgement.'

'How did you get on with Professor Pickering?' asked Daniel.

'Well enough,' said Watts. 'We didn't really have a lot to do with one another. He dealt mostly with Whetstone.'

'So, as you are the one who selects which to publish, I assume he brought it to you first.'

'Er . . . no, actually. He gave it to Whetstone, after they'd met socially. Whetstone read it and liked it, then gave it to me for my opinion.'

'Which was favourable?'

'Oh yes. There's a great demand for anything with an Arthurian connection, especially following in the footsteps of Tennyson and the paintings of the Pre-Raphaelite Brotherhood. I agreed with Whetstone that it could be a commercial success. Especially once the British Museum decided to put on its "Age of Arthur" exhibition.' He gave a long sigh. 'How tragic that it should end up like this.'

CHAPTER THIRTY-TWO

Abigail read through the letters, Miss Roseberry watching. The first letters were upset and angry in tone, but still formally polite.

> Dear Mr Whetstone,
> I was shocked to receive your letter in which Professor Pickering claims he does not know me, nor had he ever seen any of my work. This is a blatant lie.
>
> As I said in my earlier letters, I have spent the past four years of my life researching the person of Ambrosius Aurelianus as the real-life model for King Arthur. I have visited places where he is said to have been, and have read the works of early historians,

Gildas, Bede and Nennius, as well as medieval writings of William of Malmesbury and Geoffrey of Monmouth. I also researched the persons of Rothamus and Vortimer, who have also been identified as being possible models for the person of King Arthur. Earlier this year I had finished my piece that concludes that Ambrosius Aurelianus and King Arthur were one and the same person and I was keen to get my work into the public domain. However, being just an ordinary carpenter with no contacts in the world of history scholarship, I decided to send my work to Professor Pickering, as I understood he was one of the acknowledged experts on Roman Britain, in the hope that he could recommend my work to a publisher.

I know he received my work because I delivered it personally to his house in Park Square East, Regent's Park, my parcel being taken in by his housekeeper who promised to pass it on to him.

Unfortunately, the copy I left at Professor Pickering's house was my only copy of my work, but I still have my original notes which will prove that large sections of the book you published on Ambrosius Aurelianus which Professor Pickering claims to have written were directly copied from my work.

I am a poor man and cannot afford to go to law on this, so I would ask you, as honourable gentlemen, to give me justice and put my name on this book, which Professor Pickering claims as his.

Professor Pickering may have done some research on Ambrosius, but the work linking Ambrosius with Arthur is mine.

I demand and will have justice in this matter.
Yours sincerely,
William Jedding

In the later letters, however, rage had taken over, and politeness was dropped, with overt threats: *You have stolen everything that is precious to me. You will pay the price*, and *The Angel of Vengeance will fall upon you unless you give me the credit for my work that was stolen from me.*

'"The Angel of Vengeance",' murmured Abigail.

'Yes,' said Miss Roseberry unhappily.

'The tone is very threatening,' mused Abigail. 'I can see why Mr Watts is worried. Did Mr Jedding ever call at these offices to put his allegations face-to-face?'

'Not to my knowledge,' said Miss Roseberry.

'And neither Mr Whetstone nor Mr Watts thought about showing these letters to the police?' asked Abigail. 'Jedding's address is on them, so he could have been warned.'

'No,' said Miss Roseberry. 'It was when that last one arrived, about the Angel of Vengeance, that I said to Mr Whetstone he really should show them to the police, but he dismissed the threats as having no substance. "A lunatic, Miss Roseberry," he said. "Or some charlatan trying to gull money out of us."'

'Was that also Mr Watts' opinion?'

'No. Mr Watts said they should be shown to the authorities. I heard him and Mr Whetstone having an argument about them, but Mr Whetstone insisted the bad publicity would harm the firm.' She paused, then asked, 'Do you think this Mr Jedding is the one who killed them?'

'At the moment, we don't know,' said Abigail. 'It does look probable, but we'll need to look into it further.'

'Will that involve talking to Mr Jedding?'

'I believe it will.'

'From his letters, he sounds like he might be dangerous. You will not be confronting him?'

Abigail gave a smile as she said, 'I may well wait until Mr Wilson returns before doing that. But, then, I might. I shall weigh up the situation.'

It was eight o'clock when their train pulled in to New Street Station, making Daniel determined to get Watts safely lodged at Ben Stilworthy's place as soon as possible in order for him to catch a train back to London before services stopped for the day, stranding him in Birmingham overnight.

'Fortunately, we won't need to take a cab, Ben's place is an easy walk from here,' Daniel told Watts.

Then he realised that Watts wasn't listening to him but was gazing upwards at the station's vast roof.

'Isn't it magnificent!' said Watts in a tone of reverential awe. 'Over the years I have read about this roof, but never seen it. And here I am! Do you know much about architectural engineering, Mr Wilson?'

'Not really,' admitted Daniel. 'The work of Isambard Brunel, obviously.'

'We published a book on the work of Edward Cowper, the man who designed this very roof,' said Watts. 'Birmingham New Street Station was completed in 1854, and this roof was rightly seen as the jewel in its crown. It was the largest single arched span with a glass roof in the world, until St Pancras opened in 1868. Look, can you see any supporting pillars in the middle?'

'Er, no,' said Daniel, taken aback by the fervour which Watts was lauding the structure.

'That's because there aren't any!' said Watts. 'It's 840 feet long, 211 feet wide and 80 feet high, and all the support pillars are at the side. There is nothing keeping that roof up but brilliant engineering.'

'Yes.' Daniel nodded, taking Watts' arm to steer him towards the exit. 'But we need to get on. I do have to catch a train back to London today.'

Reluctantly, Watts tore himself away from admiring the wondrous roof, but even then, as they headed for the exit, he continued to wax rhapsodic. 'Edward Cowper previously designed the Crystal Palace, and you know what a marvellous creation that was!'

'Indeed,' said Daniel. 'I assume Mr Whetstone shared your enthusiasm for Mr Cowper's work.'

'Alas, not to the same degree,' said Watts. 'The book on Cowper was one I had to fight for. Whetstone seemed doubtful if it would find a readership, but I proved him wrong. The book was one of our successes.' He gave a rueful sigh, then added, 'It's sad to say, but perhaps poor Whetstone's tragic loss may pave the way for more of the kind of books we should have been publishing. For example, I would love to do one on George Gilbert Scott. I assume you know his work?'

'The Albert Memorial,' said Daniel. 'St Pancras Railway Station.'

'Actually, that is a proper misconception,' said Watts. 'Scott designed the Midland Grand Hotel that fronts St Pancras; the actual station was designed by William Henry Barlow.'

Thank heavens I'm returning to London rather than staying with Watts at Ben's place, thought Daniel gratefully. Now, away from the terror of being in London, Watts had revealed his passion for architectural structural engineering and seemed determined to unleash his knowledge on all and sundry.

Abigail walked along Euston Road, the letters from William Jedding safely stored in her bag. Jedding's address on the letters was in Balfe Street, one of the tangle of small streets at the back of King's Cross Station, and King's Cross was just a few minutes' walk. The trouble was that Daniel had warned her about going alone in that particular area.

'It's a rookery,' he'd said. 'Not as bad as somewhere like Seven Dials or Whitechapel or Shoreditch, but that's because it's smaller. The people who live there are nearly all crooks, thieves, burglars. It's not a safe place for a woman on her own, or even accompanied by another woman, or strangers.'

According to Daniel, people took their life into their hands when they entered one of these narrow-alleyed, back-lane areas. Police constables would only enter them if ordered to do so, and then only in twos or threes. The canal that ran through the area added to the danger. 'Evidence ends up there, and that includes dead bodies.'

For a moment, as she passed Euston Station she faltered, tempted to instead turn left and walk up Eversholt Street towards Camden Town and their home. But then she steeled herself. *No*, her inner voice said. *I will not be intimidated. Daniel doesn't let himself be deterred, and if I am to be his equal partner in this, then neither shall I.*

And she continued along Euston Road, heading firmly towards King's Cross.

CHAPTER THIRTY-THREE

The face of Ben Stilworthy broke into a smile of warm welcome as he opened his front door to Daniel's knock and saw who his visitor was.

'Mr Wilson! It's a pleasure to see you again.'

'My feelings exactly.' Daniel smiled.

'Come in!' said Stilworthy, and Daniel and Watts squeezed past him into the narrow passageway.

'This is a client of mine. Mr . . . Smith,' said Daniel.

Stilworthy smiled and shook Watts' hand.

'Good afternoon to you, Mr Smith. Any client of Mr Wilson's is very welcome here.'

'He needs somewhere to stay for a few days, until a certain London issue is resolved,' said Daniel. Carefully, he added, 'I suggested Birmingham because he's not known here, and it's unlikely anyone will come calling for him.'

'I understand,' said Stilworthy. 'Come through to the kitchen. I'll put the kettle on and make a pot of tea. I'm guessing you'll be parched after your long journey.'

They followed him along the passage and into the spotlessly clean kitchen.

'Rest assured, Mr Smith, you will be perfectly safe while you're at my establishment,' said Stilworthy as he filled a kettle and put it on the hob.

'I can echo that sentiment,' added Daniel. 'Before he retired from the police force, Ben was one of their most diligent officers. Intelligent, perceptive and brave.'

Stilworthy let out a chuckle. 'Careful, Mr Wilson. You'll be giving me a swollen head.'

'This is the first time Mr Smith has ever been to Birmingham, and I believe he's particularly pleased to be here because he was able to see New Street Station.'

'And isn't it magnificent!' enthused Watts. 'That roof!'

'One of the marvels of the world!' agreed Stilworthy. 'I saw it being constructed, you know.'

Watts gazed at Stilworthy, his mouth dropping open in awe. 'You saw it being built!'

'I was only a nipper at the time,' said Stilworthy. 'Early fifties it was. The foundations had all been done, but I used to go along and watch as they started to put the roof together. The sense of excitement . . .'

'I can imagine!' burst out Watts, barely able to contain his delight. 'Mr Stilworthy, it is indeed fortunate that Mr Wilson has brought me to your place, because I would love to hear from you all about what you remember of that construction. I waxed lyrical to Mr Wilson about the roof on the way here, a veritable marvel of architectural engineering, but to hear from your own lips the story of its construction . . .'

'It will be my pleasure,' said Stilworthy. 'Ah, the kettle's boiled. I'll make the tea, then I'll take you to your room and show you the usual offices.'

'Actually, I need to get back to London tonight, so I'll pass on the tea. Thanks, Ben,' said Daniel.

'An urgent case?' asked Stilworthy. Then he added quickly, 'Not that I'm prying!'

'You never pry, that's why I know Mr Smith will be safe with you. So, I'll be off. As soon as the issue in London is resolved, I'll send you a letter, Ben.'

'And I'll let Mr Smith know the coast is clear,' said Stilworthy.

They shook hands all round, and then Daniel slipped out to head back to the station. The last words he heard as he closed the front door behind him were Watts asking how many men had worked on the roof, and how it had been put into place.

As she passed King's Cross Station, Abigail once again remembered Daniel's warnings about the area at the back of King's Cross. Squeezed between York Way and the Caledonian Road, it was notorious for prostitutes of both sexes, as well as gangs of muggers waiting for unwary travellers, especially those new to the city, just off the train and making their way from the two termini of King's Cross and St Pancras. And here she was, going right into the heart of the York Way–Caledonian Road hellhole, according to Daniel.

He will be furious when I tell him, she thought. *He'll give me a lecture on walking around London safely. It is ridiculous*, she told herself sharply. *I have walked through the backstreets of Cairo and been perfectly safe, with no fear for my safety, and yet I am made to feel ill at ease in the capital city of my own country.*

Children are born in these backstreets. They run and play. They survive. They do not all live in fear. And neither will I.

Often she'd found in the past that when she entered a new area, or a new city, it was about striding through with an air of confidence. Muggers and bandits looked for the signs of fear marking out their victims. *Well, I will not be a victim.*

She crossed a bridge that ran over the canal, the smell from it rising, filling her nostrils with a nauseating stench and she almost reached for a handkerchief to cover her nose; but then decided against it. It would mark her as weak. She'd smelt worse in the tanneries of Egypt. All she had to do was harden herself to it.

She entered the warren of backstreets and found herself looking at groups of children sitting on the pavement kerbs, playing a game with small stones. They looked at her as she passed, and she could feel their eyes on her as she continued down the street. Curtains in the windows of some of the houses twitched as she walked and she knew she was being watched because she was so obviously a stranger.

She found Balfe Street, a short, narrow road with terraced houses on either side, and despite her determination to approach this with confidence, she wavered.

Say it was this William Jedding who'd carried out the murders. How would he react if she confronted him? Might he attack her? Stab her? If it was he who'd already killed two strong men, how could she defend herself against him?

Possibly it would be better to wait until Daniel was with her, or possibly Inspector Feather and some constables.

But no, she decided. *You can still face him if you use your brain. Don't let him know the real reason you want to talk to him.*

But what reason, then?

Pretend it's about the book. Yes, that was it. Say she'd been sent by Whetstone and Watts to talk about publishing an apology for the way he'd been treated by them about Professor Pickering's book. See how he reacted when she mentioned those names. Would he invite her in? If so, she'd decline. She'd tell him that this was just an initial courtesy visit, and she would return later with the paperwork to . . . to what? To deal with giving him credit for his work and compensation. Yes, that was the way. The important thing was to see the expression in his eyes when she mentioned the names, and the book. And to watch his hands to make sure he wasn't armed when he opened the door.

Despite her determination to be full of confidence, her heart was beating wildly as she knocked at the door. *I shouldn't have come alone, I shouldn't have come alone*, she told herself. *But I have to if I'm to play my full role as Daniel's partner in this enterprise. I have to be as strong as he is.*

The woman who opened the door was in her forties and dressed in mourning black. A recent death. The expression of deep anguish and grief on the woman's face confirmed it.

'Good afternoon,' said Abigail. 'I'm very sorry to trouble you at what is obviously a difficult time, but I'm looking for William Jedding.'

The woman's face tightened, and tears sprang into her eyes.

'Who are you?' she demanded angrily. 'And if you say it's a difficult time, you must know why. So why are you coming here asking for my husband when you know he's dead!'

Abigail gave her a look of deep apology. 'I am sincerely sorry, Mrs Jedding,' she said. 'But I did not know your husband had passed away. I saw the black of mourning, but never thought it was for him. When did he—?'

'I don't want to talk to you!' she burst out. 'And I don't have to talk to you! Go away and leave me in peace!'

With that, she slammed the door.

Abigail stood looking at the closed door and wondered whether to knock at it again, but the expression on the woman's face, and the tone of her voice, had been very firm. There were no answers there.

She looked along the road and saw a shop at the corner. As she approached it, she saw that the pavement outside was laden with broken bits of bric-a-brac, chairs with wooden slats missing, chipped items of crockery, rusted tools. A rag-and-bone shop, the detritus of society thrown away and discarded, gathered up by the rag-and-bone man on his cart, and assembled for sale. Here, even the poorest could buy a chair or a stool or a teapot.

The owner of the shop seemed to be moving his stock from the pavement to safety inside the shop, so it was obviously approaching closing time.

'Good afternoon,' said Abigail. 'I'm sorry to trouble you. My name's Abigail Fenton and I've been employed by the British Museum to investigate the recent deaths there.'

'Oh aye! The murders! Grisly, eh!'

'Indeed,' said Abigail. 'The thing is, I wanted to talk a William Jedding because someone said he might have information that might be of use, but I've just learnt that he's passed away.'

The man gave a sad nod. 'Last Monday, it was.'

Last Monday. The same day that Pickering was attacked and killed.

'Poor old William,' continued the man. 'Topped himself, didn't he.'

'Suicide?'

'Terrible, it was. He loaded stones into his pockets, then threw himself in Battlebridge Basin.'

'Battlebridge Basin?' queried Abigail.

'Just up the canal. The water's so murky at that point it's a wonder they found him. They wouldn't have if someone hadn't seen him throw himself in.' He shook his head. 'Terrible way to go, drowning in all that muck.'

'Last Monday, you said. Do you know what time of day it happened?' asked Abigail.

'Late afternoon, from what I can gather.'

'Does anyone know why he did it? Killed himself, I mean.'

The man looked at her, puzzled. 'I thought you said you was from the British Museum.'

'I am,' said Abigail.

'Then you oughta know it was that exhibition there what killed him. With that book. William told me what happened, how he did all that work on it and that bloke stole it from him, and there the book was, with all William's work, there for all to see, but without his name on it.' He shook his head. 'Criminal, it was. If you ask me, the bloke what got killed got what he deserved.'

Daniel sat in the compartment, glad he'd managed to catch one of the last trains back to London. The thought of an evening in the company of Jerrold Watts and Ben Stilworthy swapping memories of the construction of New Street Station filled him with dread and a feeling of gratitude he was able to escape. But there was something nagging him about Watts. For all his nervousness and claims of being in fear of his life, there was something that jarred.

Daniel ran over their conversation during the train journey in his mind and realised what it was: Watts had positively disliked his partner, Whetstone. Daniel wondered if Abigail had picked up any gossip from Miss Roseberry about the two men's relationship when she went to get the letters. Had she even managed to get hold of the letters? If so, he was looking forward to reading them, seeing if they would contain the motive for the murder of Pickering and Whetstone. If they did, the next move was to confront this Mr Jedding.

He couldn't resist a small smile at the thought that Abigail would be waiting for him at home. Sometimes he wondered how he'd managed to be so lucky as to find her and to have her as his – what? Wife? Partner? Lover? It didn't matter. The happy fact was that they were together, and he was determined that this was a relationship he wanted to last. Which meant that he had to do something about moving on from the house in Plender Street.

He should have talked about it to Abigail before, once she'd said she'd be moving in with him. But once she'd begun decorating the house, hanging pictures, adding cushions and changing it from the austere, almost monastic place it had been, turning it from a house into a home, he'd been so happy with her in the refurbished surroundings he'd let it slide. But the fact was that Abigail had been used to such things as piped plumbing: an indoor toilet and a bathroom with hot and cold water on tap. Daniel's house in Camden Town still had an earth closet in a privy outside. And bathing meant filling up a large copper in the scullery with water from the cold tap and lighting a fire under it, then drawing the hot water off and emptying it by means of a bucket into a tin bath, brought in from where it hung in the backyard and putting it in front of the coal-fired kitchen range so the bather wouldn't catch cold.

And emptying the bath afterwards was equally laborious, filling buckets with the waste water and emptying them on the small patch of soil in the backyard.

Not that his house was any different from most of the others in Camden Town; most had an outside privy and no piped water inside the house. But Abigail deserved better. Perhaps they could even take on a house which had this new electric lighting system instead of gaslights.

We have to move, he decided. A better house in a better part of town. It was time for a change.

CHAPTER THIRTY-FOUR

As Abigail put her key into the lock to let herself in, a voice behind her called, 'Excuse me!'

She turned and saw the small thin newspaper reporter, Ned Carson, approaching her. As before, he had a beaming grin on his face.

'We met with Mr Wilson at the museum a few days ago.'

'Yes,' said Abigail. 'I remember.'

'I've since learnt your name is Abigail Fenton and you're working with Daniel Wilson on the murders at the British Museum. Strange he didn't mention it. Why?'

'You'd have to ask that question of Mr Wilson,' said Abigail.

'Yes, that's what I was hoping to do,' said Carson. 'That's why I called.' He smiled again. 'I notice you have a key to his house.'

'Mr Wilson is not at home at the moment and he asked me if I'd look in and check on things for him,' said Abigail.

'You mean he's away?'

'I do.'

'Do you know when he'll be back?'

'I'm not sure. But when he returns, I'll let him know you called and you wish to speak to him.'

'Will you be here when he returns?' asked Carson. 'At home?'

'Why do you want to know that?' demanded Abigail.

'The personal aspect.' Carson smiled. 'It's what our readers like.'

'I wish you good evening, Mr Carson,' said Abigail curtly. And she shut the door.

It felt very late for Daniel when he finally arrived home. It had been a long day with lots of action and stress, made worse by the seemingly endless train journey to and from Birmingham. And he realised, as he opened the front door, that he was starving. He should have got some food from one of the stands at Euston, but he had seen the way some of it was produced. He'd been doubtful about the provenance of some of the food ever since he'd seen a rat being skinned by one of the purveyors.

'I'm home!' he called, shutting the door and heading for the back kitchen, and as he did so a delicious aroma came to greet him, along with Abigail, who threw her arms around him and hugged him close.

'You managed to catch the last train.'

'I'd have walked home if I'd missed it,' said Daniel, hugging her tightly back and kissing her. He sniffed and smiled. 'I can't believe it,' he said, 'but my nose tells me there's a delicious smell coming from the kitchen. You don't mean you . . .'

'I do! I went round to Royal College Street and got pie and mash for us both. With parsley sauce. I put them in the oven to keep hot.' She smiled. 'This had better be as good as you say it is.'

As far as Daniel was concerned, it was as good as ever, although he felt he saw doubt rather than enjoyment in Abigail's face as she ate.

'It takes getting used to,' he said.

'And I'm sure I'll get used to it,' she said. 'How did you get on in Birmingham?'

'There isn't much to tell,' he said. 'Watts is safe at Ben Stilworthy's. How about you?' Daniel asked. 'Did you get the letters?'

'I did.'

She took them out of the drawer she'd put them in and gave them to him. As he ate, Daniel read them through, his face clouded. 'Definite threats,' he said. 'We need to talk to him.'

'I've already done that,' said Abigail.

He stared at her, stunned. 'What?' he said.

'Although he wasn't there. In fact, he's dead. He killed himself the afternoon that Pickering was stabbed. Threw himself in the Battlebridge Basin.'

Daniel stared at her, then tapped the address on the letter. 'You went to Balfe Street?'

'Yes.'

'On your own?'

Here it comes, she thought. *The lecture.*

'You know what I've told you about that area!' he snapped. 'It's a hellhole! And to go there unaccompanied to face a man who was quite possibly a murderer!'

'I could have handled myself.'

'Beating him with a shovel you just happen to have to hand?' demanded Daniel angrily. 'This wasn't some Egyptian labourer trying to molest you, it would have been a possible killer! A murderer, desperate to protect himself from arrest!'

'He wasn't. I told you, the man killed himself.'

'But you weren't to know that when you knocked at his door!'

She looked at him, resolute. She'd been practising what to say to him about this subject since she'd returned from Balfe Street, wondering how to broach it without hurting his feelings, and she knew – for her own sake as well as his – it had to be said. It was something that couldn't be put off.

'Daniel,' she said, 'you know I love you. Very, very much.'

He nodded, a puzzled expression on his face and also slightly suspicious about where this was going. 'Yes,' he said.

'And I know you love me and want to protect me.'

'I do,' he said.

'But all this talk of places I should fear to go is making me nervous of setting foot almost anywhere.'

He looked at her, unhappy. 'I'm sorry,' he said. 'That's the last thing I would ever want.'

'I know,' she said. 'Daniel, I am not a young girl any more. I have been looking after myself, and my sister, Bella, since our parents died. I have made my own way in the world. I have been to places that some consider to be dangerous, and I have travelled there alone, as a woman, and been safe. Mainly because I had the confidence to do it. Where I have encountered danger I have

238

handled it, sometimes by confronting it, sometimes by worming my way out of a situation. But it has never stopped me from pushing on, testing myself. I know you mean best when you warn me of which places to avoid, and I promise you I would never willingly put myself in danger. But I am used to viewing myself as a strong person. Someone who does not hide from what life has to throw at me. And I want to carry on being that person. But with you.'

Daniel sat looking at her, and for a moment she wondered how he was going to respond. Finally, after what seemed like an agonising eternity, he got up and moved towards her, his arms held out.

'My darling Abigail,' he said. 'I can only apologise. You are quite right. My love for you, which I intended to be protective, has been smothering. Can you forgive me?'

She got up, moved into his arms and hugged him close, his face on hers. 'There is nothing to forgive,' she whispered. 'It's not your fault. I've allowed it to happen. But thank you for hearing me out, and for you being the way you are and the way you responded. I love the feeling that you want to protect me. I, in turn, want to protect you.' She hugged him tightly again. 'Now we've got that out of the way, can I tell you the whole thing of how it went?'

He hugged her back, then released her with a kiss. 'Of course. And I promise, no interruptions.'

They both returned to finish their meals as Abigail told him about her encounter with Mrs Jedding, and then her visit to the rag-and-bone shop at the end of the street and how she'd learnt about Jedding's suicide.

'Afterwards I thought about it. The letters show that William

Jedding was absolutely bereft when Pickering stole his work on Ambrosius and published as his own. He had no recourse against what Pickering had done, he couldn't sue Pickering because he had no money – and what court would find in favour of a well-intentioned carpenter against the word of a historian of Dr Pickering's lofty reputation. Pickering coming to the museum to present Jedding's work as his own was the final straw. So Jedding kills Pickering. But then guilt overcomes him. He can't live with what he's done. So that same day, he kills himself.'

Daniel looked doubtful. 'What about the murder of Mansfield Whetstone?' he asked.

'Someone very close to Jedding did that. Someone so enraged by the unfairness of what Pickering had done to Jedding, and furious at Jedding then killing himself, then takes revenge on the other person to blame for the situation, the man who published the book: Mansfield Whetstone. Which means whoever this is, must have been aware of the letters between Jedding and Whetstone.'

'So, the graffiti, "Who killed Ambrosius". . . ?'

'By Ambrosius he means, of course, Jedding, and the people who killed him are Pickering and Whetstone. Both are now dead, so the next stage will be to expose that Pickering stole Jedding's work, but the concern is that to ensure that gets the most publicity, he'll carry out another murder to accompany it.'

'Actually, I had another thought on the train on the way back,' said Daniel. 'Might it have been Watts who killed Whetstone?'

Abigail looked at him, bewildered. 'Why on earth would he do such a thing?'

'From the things Watts talked about on his way to Birmingham, it was pretty obvious that he resented Whetstone. Whetstone treated him as a dogsbody. And I'm fairly sure that Watts knew that Pickering was lying, that he had stolen Jedding's work. And by keeping quiet and going along with it, Watts was being forced to be complicit in a fraud. It must have hurt him deeply. It makes even more sense now you've told me about Jedding killing himself. Watts could well have felt guilty over Jedding's death, and he'd been forced to play a part in that death by Whetstone bullying him. Watts knows when Whetstone is going to the British Museum, so he follows him and kills him. We know Watts was there around the time that Whetstone was murdered.'

'He kills his own partner?'

'With the outcome that he is now the *senior* partner. At last he can get out from under Whetstone's dominance.'

'But why run away to his sister's and say he was in fear of his life?'

'A smokescreen,' said Daniel. 'It makes him look innocent, and a potential victim.'

'It's very convoluted,' said Abigail.

'These murders have been carried out with great thought and planning,' Daniel pointed out.

Abigail thought this over, then nodded. 'It's possible,' she said. 'By the way, I got an interesting piece of information from Miss Roseberry at Whetstone and Watts. Professor Pickering lectured part-time on Roman history at University College London.'

'Yes, David Ashford told me the same, but how does that relate to the case?' asked Daniel.

'Because if he stole this William Jedding's work and published it as his own, he may well have done the same with the work of some of his students.'

'How can we find out?'

'I know a senior lecturer at the UCL whose speciality is Roman studies.'

'Oh?'

'His name's Charles Winter. I knew him when I was at Girton; he was at Trinity at the same time, and our paths have crossed a few times since.'

'How crossed?' asked Daniel with a frown.

Abigail laughed. 'Daniel, are you jealous?'

'No,' replied Daniel quickly. Too quickly. 'Possibly,' he admitted shamefacedly.

'There was never anything between us in that way,' she said. 'We were just interested in the same subject, and he was an intelligent and nice person.'

'Nicer than me?'

'No, but more intelligent.' She laughed as she saw the look of indignation on his face 'I'm joking, you idiot! Anyway, I thought I'd call on Charles at UCL tomorrow morning. It's just around the corner from the museum.'

'Yes, I know,' said Daniel. 'Do you want me to come along?'

'No need,' said Abigail. 'It'd be better if you go to the museum and see if anything happened there today after the murder of Whetstone.'

'Yes, good idea,' said Daniel. He paused, then asked, 'Is he handsome, this Charles Winter?'

'Like a Greek god!' enthused Abigail. She gave a happy sigh. 'Kind, caring, highly intelligent and beautiful to look at. He's every woman's dream, except for one thing.'

'What's that?'

She hesitated, then said: 'He prefers men.'

'He's homosexual?' said Daniel.

'Illegal, I know. But there it is.' She sighed. 'Poor Charles.'

Later, cuddled up in bed, she said, 'By the way, that odious man, Ned Carson, called this evening and caught me letting myself into the house with a key.'

Immediately, Daniel looked wary. 'What did he want?' he asked.

'To talk to you,' he said. 'I told him you were away. But he asked me if I'd be here when you got home.'

'The slimy rat!' snarled Daniel.

'I said nothing more, just shut the door on him.'

'That'll be enough for someone like Carson. Be prepared for a story to appear. Something like "Ripper Tec's Secret Love-Nest".'

Abigail laughed.

'It's not a laughing matter,' snapped Daniel. 'He'll ferret out your name and publish it.'

'He already knows it,' said Abigail. 'He's resourceful, I'll give him that.' And she chuckled again.

'What's so funny?' demanded Daniel. 'He's going to be slandering your reputation.'

'I'm just thinking of Bella's reaction when she reads the story.' Abigail smiled. 'I really will be a fallen woman in her eyes!'

'Fortunately, that rag only circulates in London,' said Daniel.

'Oh, I'm sure Bella has friends in London who'll be only too happy to make sure she sees a copy,' said Abigail.

'You're not angry?' demanded Daniel. 'I'm furious! I'm going to see Carson tomorrow and threaten to punch his face in if he prints anything about us.'

'Thus confirming it's true,' said Abigail. She shook her head. 'Why give him the satisfaction? Ignore him.'

'But what about what people will think of you? Sir Jasper Stone?'

'If they ask, we'll tell them you're going to make an honest woman of me.'

Daniel stared at her. 'You . . . you'll marry me?'

'Ah, I didn't say *when*,' she said. 'Perhaps in ten years or so, if you haven't tired of me . . .'

'I'll never tire of you,' said Daniel.

'. . . and I still find you a passable companion,' finished Abigail.

'Actually,' he said, 'I did some thinking on the train on the way back from Birmingham.'

'Whenever you say "actually" in that way, it usually means something with serious implications,' said Abigail.

'Well, this may fit that. I think we need to move house.'

'Why?' she said. 'What's wrong with it?'

'The outdoor privy. No bath.'

'There's the tin bath.'

'And all that entails,' said Daniel. 'We need a proper bathroom. With inside sanitation.'

'Because of me,' she said.

'Not necessarily,' said Daniel. 'I've been thinking about it for myself.'

'Oh, come on, Daniel!' You've been living in this house for fourteen years.'

'And it took you moving in to make me see it for what it is. Uncomfortable. Fine for a man who was hardly ever here and used it as basically a place to lay his head . . .'

'And cook on his own coal-fired kitchen range.' Abigail smiled.

'Yes, well, maybe we need one of those new gas ovens, with a gas hob.'

'Daniel, this is so radical!' said Abigail. 'But rest assured, there's no hurry to move on my part. This house will always be where we began our life together, so it has a special place. And I have lived in harder circumstances than this.'

'You're about to say, "When I was in Egypt",' said Daniel.

She hesitated. 'Well, I was. But then I thought, I'd rather kiss you and make love to you.'

He smiled. 'That gets my vote every time.' And they kissed, at first tenderly, gently caressing, then deeply and passionately.

CHAPTER THIRTY-FIVE

As they left the house next morning, Daniel announced, 'I think, after the busy day we had yesterday, we'll treat ourselves to a cab. We can't have you calling on your highly intelligent and extremely handsome old friend looking crumpled through being crushed by the crowds on an early morning omnibus or sweating from a fast-paced walk.'

'Remember what the poet said: "horses sweat, men perspire, women merely glow",' said Abigail.

'Which poet was that?' asked Daniel.

'I can't remember, but I doubt if it was Shakespeare,' said Abigail.

They hailed a cab in Camden High Street and settled back to the rhythm of the horse's *clip-clop* as they journeyed, planning their day.

'I'll see you at the museum after I've met with Charles,' said Abigail. 'What do you plan to do?'

'I thought I'd see Sir Jasper and explain to him why, despite Superintendent Armstrong's insistence that this Elsie Bowler is the killer, we don't agree. Otherwise, once the board learn the superintendent's view, they'll pressurise Sir Jasper into terminating our employment.' He scowled. 'It's not just the money we'd lose, it's the fact that the real killer will get away with it that upsets me.'

'Let's recap on our suspects,' said Abigail. 'Top of the list?'

'Possibly William Jedding for the murder of Pickering, and someone close to him for the murder of Whetstone.'

'Agreed,' said Abigail. 'Mr Ashford?'

Daniel shook his head. 'No, I don't feel it.'

'John Kelly Junior and the Irish Republican Brotherhood?'

'Possibly for the stabbing of Pickering, but not for Whetstone. And as I'm convinced that the murders of Pickering and Whetstone were connected, I think we can discount the Brotherhood.'

'You said last night you thought Mr Watts was a serious suspect.'

'Last night I was tired and my brain was clutching at straws. I can't see Watts as the killer.'

'Elsie Bowler?'

'Absolutely not. And I shall tell Sir Jasper why.'

The cab pulled to a halt and the driver called out, 'University College!'

Daniel helped Abigail down from the cab and paid the driver.

'I'll walk from here,' he told Abigail. 'I'll see you later.'

Daniel walked off, and Abigail headed for the massive white building that housed UCL's history department. Abigail had always held a regard for UCL. It may not have had the long history of the universities of Cambridge or Oxford, having only been established in 1826, but it was the first to have a secular policy and to admit students from any religion, or even none. It also claimed to have been the first university of Britain to admit women as students, although there was some argument about that in academic circles.

Truth be told, her particular affection for UCL was because of the Petrie Museum of Egyptian Archaeology, established just two years before, which had one of the world's leading collections of Egyptian artefacts. Sadly, she'd only managed to make one visit to view the collection a year after it had opened, and that had been the last time she'd met Charles Winter. She chuckled to herself at the thought of Daniel being jealous of Charles. She was also slightly surprised, thinking of Daniel as a man of great confidence, independent of spirit. She hadn't thought of him as being jealous. Although she had seen signs of it during their early acquaintance in Cambridge. But then, that had been understandable; she had to admit she'd treated him abominably. And, if their situations were reversed and she felt that Daniel was showing too much affection and interest towards another woman who was beautiful, intelligent and kind, she, too, would feel a pang of jealousy.

I'd punch her in the face, she decided.

She tracked Charles down to his office, where he was busy marking students' papers. 'Abigail! This is a pleasure!'

'No lectures?'

Charles looked at the clock. 'Not yet,' he said. 'Students are notoriously late arrivals, so I've got an hour before the horde arrive. What brings you to London? I thought you were either a fixture in Cambridge, or busy digging up half of the Middle East.' Then he remembered. 'No, wait, you were up at Hadrian's Wall recently. I read about it in one of the journals. Where were you at?'

'Most of my time was spent at Housesteads. The Clayton family have done wonderful work in clearing the later buildings from the land and getting down to the remains of the actual Roman fort. I was engaged in excavating the underground heating system, the hypocaust. Absolutely fascinating! It just brought home to me what marvels of engineering were lost after the Romans left.'

'Proper sanitation,' said Winter. 'Decent roads. And it's taken nearly two thousand years to rediscover those techniques! The stupidity of the human race never fails to amaze me. So, is it your Roman work that's brought you here, or have you come to see the recent additions to the Petrie Collection?'

'Neither. I've recently taken on a new addition to my work as a historian.'

'Oh? This sounds intriguing. What kind of addition?'

'Detective.'

Winter laughed. 'Oh, really, Abigail! Let me guess, Scotland Yard have got hold of you to help them out.'

'Not Scotland Yard, but one of their former detectives. Daniel Wilson, he used to be part of Inspector Abberline's team.'

'Abberline! The Ripper case!' He frowned, curious. 'You're not serious.'

'Have you ever known me to joke, Charles?'

'No, that's why I'm puzzled. You, and a Scotland Yard detective.'

'Former detective. He's a private enquiry agent now, and he brings me in on cases with a historical perspective. For example, at the moment we've been hired by the British Museum to look into the killings there. Professor Pickering, and his publisher, Mansfield Whetstone.'

'A tragedy.' Winter sighed. 'I didn't know Whetstone, but Pickering used to lecture here, you know, on Roman Britain.'

'Yes, so his publisher told us. Which is why I wanted to talk to you. Were there any problems while he was here?'

'Problems?' asked Winter.

'With using some of his students' work for his own, for example.'

Winter regarded her cagily. 'I'm guessing that something has prompted this question?'

'Yes,' said Abigail. 'We've been informed that someone claimed that Pickering stole his research on Ambrosius Aurelianus and used it in his own book.'

'There's often an exchange of research between scholars,' said Winter guardedly.

'This was done without Pickering giving credit to the original researcher,' said Abigail.

'This original research, was it done as part of a thesis, or a history degree?'

Abigail shook her head. 'It was done by a keen amateur historian, a carpenter. According to what we've been told he sent his work to Pickering to ask for his help in getting it published. Instead, Pickering used it in his own book and claimed it as his own.'

'That's a very serious allegation,' said Winter.

'It is,' said Abigail. 'He was only able to get away with it because he took the work from someone with no reputation or published credits. Which is why I thought of his having access to unpublished research by students.'

Winter was thoughtfully quiet for a while, then he said, 'There was an instance last year. A student called Winston Adams claimed that Pickering had stolen his work on the sacking of Anglesey by Suetonius Paulinus in AD61.'

'The destruction of the Druids and the sacred oak groves.' Abigail nodded.

'And not just the Druids,' said Winter. 'At that time Anglesey was the last refuge for rebel Celtic warriors from Gaul and all over the Empire. The massacre of every man, woman and child on the island was intended to eradicate the Druids' power and complete the domination of Britannia.'

'Except that Boudicca rose in the east at the same time,' added Abigail.

Winter gave an apologetic smile. 'I'm sorry,' he said. 'I keep forgetting that Roman Britain was another of your areas of scholarship.'

'Tell me about this Winston Adams.'

'He'd been to Anglesey and carried out an archaeological dig there and discovered some rare artefacts, both Celtic and Roman, and he wrote a very long and detailed study of them as part of his coursework.'

'Pickering was his tutor?'

'Just for this one piece of work. He was only a part-time lecturer here. Anyway, three months later, Adams complained to the college authorities that his work had been published in a magazine under Pickering's name. Pickering, of course, refuted the charge and insisted that he had already been doing his own work on the massacre on Anglesey, but Adams persisted. And, what was more, he produced his own original essay and showed that certain sections of the article that Pickering claimed was his contained word for word sections from Adams' essay.'

'So, he had stolen it.'

'We preferred the term "assimilated".'

'Whatever term you used, the fact is that this student was able to prove that Pickering had plagiarised his work.'

'Yes, that did appear to be the case.'

'So, what was the outcome?'

'It was decided that possibly it was time for the professor to relinquish his tenure at the university.'

'He was sacked.'

'He retired.'

'Was this instance with Adams the only one?'

Winter hesitated, then said, 'After word spread about Adams' claim, other students came forward and claimed they'd had the same experience.'

'Why hadn't they spoken about it before?'

'Because they said that Pickering bullied them into keeping quiet. He said he would destroy their chances of getting a good degree. So, they kept quiet.'

'But he didn't attempt to bully Adams that way?'

'Apparently, he did, but Adams' uncle is some very high-powered lawyer, and Adams threatened to sue Pickering and the college.'

'And so, Pickering took the easy way out to save his skin.' Abigail scowled. 'The man was a rat.'

'He was a noted a historian,' pointed out Winter.

'Who apparently based much of his published work that gave him that reputation on the hard work of others who were too powerless to protest.'

'Yes, well, he's dead now,' said Winter. 'And his faults die with him.'

'Not all,' said Abigail grimly. 'There are people out there who've been hurt and abused by him and who want revenge.'

When he arrived at the museum, Daniel made straight for Sir Jasper's office, determined to press his case for himself and Abigail to be allowed to continue their investigations, but before he could begin to present their evidence, he stopped, seeing the extremely worried look on Sir Jasper's face. At first, he thought Sir Jasper might be worried because he was about to tell Daniel the difficult decision that the board were discharging them; but instead Sir Jasper held out a sheet of paper to Daniel.

'Another letter arrived this morning,' he said.

As before, the letter demanded money, but this time it wanted the money left at Paddington Station, although there was no date or time for the money to be left, just the same message as before that *We will contact you and tell you when to leave the money.*

'I've compared the writing to the two previous letters,' said Sir Jasper. 'It's different. So, either the extortioner is disguising their handwriting, or this gang is larger than we at first thought.'

As Daniel looked at it, a flash of recognition clicked in his mind. 'I'll be back in a moment, Sir Jasper,' he said. 'I need to check this against something.'

He picked up the letter and hurried out of the room, He rushed up the stairs to their small office, opened his desk drawer and took out a sheet of paper, which he compared with the letter. His face lit up in triumph.

'Got him!'

CHAPTER THIRTY-SIX

Superintendent Armstrong sat at his desk composing the speech he was going to give to the reporters and journalists once the girl, Elsie Bowler, was in custody. A dangerous killer brought to book on his watch. The newspapers would lap it up. Two prominent figures, a learned professor and a publisher, stabbed to death at the British Museum. A leading artist stabbed. And by a seventeen-year-old girl. She was a lunatic, obviously, and that fact alone would strike fear into the papers' readers: that someone like that could be roaming the capital, killing leading figures in society indiscriminately! But Superintendent Armstrong was the public's saviour. The man who brought in the Lunatic Girl Killer. No, it needed a better name than that. Something snappier. Something the public would remember. Which was why Jack the Ripper had resonated so well, a great name. He smiled smugly as he reminisced that was one thing Abberline and Wilson had never been able to do, bring the Ripper to justice. But he would do it with the Lunatic Girl Killer, once they'd laid their hands on her.

There was a sharp knocking at his door, then John Feather came in.

'Yes?' barked Armstrong. 'What is it?'

'Those anonymous threatening letters, sir,' he announced. 'The ones demanding money from the museum.'

'Yes?' queried Armstrong.

'We've got him. He's in custody at Covent Garden police station. Do you want to question him, or shall I?'

'Damn right I want to!' exclaimed Armstrong, getting to his feet. Then he stopped, wary. 'How sure are you he's the right one?'

'One hundred per cent,' said Feather. Then, as Armstrong strode to the coat hook to put on his overcoat, he added carefully, 'There's one thing, sir. It was Daniel Wilson who identified him.'

Armstrong swung round and stared at him, shocked. 'Wilson!'

'Yes, sir. I've had to bring him and Miss Fenton in to help with the questioning because it's their evidence that will convict him.'

Armstrong's face became suffused with anger. 'How come they did it and not you?' he demanded hotly.

'Because they had something in the suspect's handwriting.'

'So, they were concealing evidence!' snapped Armstrong. 'We can charge them!'

'No, sir,' said Feather. 'At that time, it wasn't evidence in this case, or the murders. It was from another investigation.'

Armstrong stood, his hand still holding the coat hook where his overcoat hung, a man in turmoil.

'This suspect, can he be linked to the murders? The stabbings?'

'Wilson doesn't think so, sir. And nor do I. It's just the sending of the threatening letters to the British Museum.'

'Then you deal with it, Inspector.' Armstrong returned to his desk and sat down.

'Yes, sir,' said Feather.

'But we get the credit for it!' barked Armstrong. 'We arrested him! Wilson didn't!'

'Wilson can't arrest anyone, sir, except to make a citizen's arrest,' pointed out Feather.

'Yes, I know that!' said Armstrong irritably. 'I just want to establish that if the story comes out in the press – and I say "if" because in my opinion there's no need for this to be of any interest at all, it'll only muddy the waters of the real case, the fact that this girl Elsie Bowler is our killer – that if it comes out in the press, the Metropolitan police get the credit, not Wilson and this Fenton woman.'

'I'll see what I can do, sir, but Daniel's very popular with some members of the press.'

'Yes, damn him! And we ought to investigate that! Is there corruption there, do you think? Wilson paying bribes to them to get publicity?'

'I don't think so, sir. I've never heard of anything like that.'

'No, you may not, but someone might. He's a wrong 'un, Inspector, posing as some kind of people's hero, and one day I'm going to prove that!'

'Yes, sir. I'll report back to you after we've questioned the prisoner.'

'We?' barked Armstrong sharply.

'As I said, sir, Wilson and Miss Fenton will be taking part in the questioning.'

'But they're civilians!'

'In view of the fact that it's their evidence, and they brought it to us, and they've met the accused before, there's not much of a way round that if we're to get a conviction.'

Armstrong scowled and glared at Feather for what seemed like a long time, before he waved a hand in dismissal.

'Go,' he ordered. 'But this is a small story. It doesn't deserve any press coverage. Remember that.'

Edward Chapman sat at the table in the interview room at Praed Street police station, doing his best to look defiant, but the way his eyes darted from Inspector Feather and Daniel facing him from the other side of the table, Abigail sitting just a short distance behind them, and two uniformed constables standing guard who surveyed him with grim expressions, betrayed his nervousness.

Feather pushed the first letter across the table to him. 'Have you ever seen this letter before?' he asked.

Chapman didn't even look at it. They saw him gulp nervously, then he shook his head and said, 'No.'

Feather didn't show any emotions at this reply. He took the second letter and passed that across to Chapman.

'Have you ever seen *this* letter before?' he asked.

Again, Chapman shook his head. 'No.'

Feather slid the latest letter, the one that had been received just that morning at the museum, across the table to in front of Chapman.

'Have you ever seen *this* letter before?' he asked.

This time, Chapman gave a nervous swallow before giving a stuttering 'N-n . . . no.'

Feather then produced the list of names of the members of the Order of the Children of Avalon that Daniel had given him, the list that Chapman had written out.

'Have you ever seen this list of names before?' asked Feather.

This time, Chapman nodded. 'Yes,' he said. And now his old defiance came back as he glared angrily at Daniel. '*He* made me write it.'

'The writing on this list and the writing of the previous letter I showed you, the latest letter received by the British Museum, are identical,' said Feather. 'You wrote this latest letter.'

'No!' said Chapman.

'Yes,' said Feather. 'You got two other people to write the first two letters, but you wrote this one. And this one followed the murder of Mr Mansfield Whetstone, and it suggests that the writer is responsible for that murder.' He looked intently at Chapman. 'You are the writer. This is an admission that you were behind the murder of Mansfield Whetstone. And the first letter is a confession that the writer of it was behind the murder of Professor Lance Pickering. As I said, we believe you got someone else to write the other two letters and we are confident that we can prove and charge them, but you are the person behind these letters, and therefore responsible for the murders of—'

'No!' burst out Chapman. 'No! This was nothing to do with the murders!' He pointed a finger angrily at Daniel. 'It was his fault! The letters were just a prank to get back at him for the way he treated me! Like a criminal! And calling in my parents! My father has cut my allowance!'

'So, you admit sending the letters?' said Feather.

'Yes, but it was just a harmless joke!' protested Chapman. 'No one was hurt by them!'

'You demanded money.'

'But we didn't collect it! It was to teach him a lesson for ruining my life!'

'As I understand it, he apprehended you and your companion when you came to the British Museum to mount an attack on the exhibition. An attack that you and your companion planned, that was nothing to do with Mr Wilson here, except that he stopped you. But then, instead of giving you to the constables, he arranged for you to be released without charge. He saved you from jail. How is that ruining your life?'

'Like I say, he brought in my parents and my father has cut my allowance! He made my life a misery!'

'No, *you* made your life a misery the moment you decided to attack the exhibition,' said Feather. 'You've made it far, far worse by sending these threatening letters to the museum.'

'They were a joke!' repeated Chapman urgently. 'They didn't do any damage. They didn't harm anyone!'

'They took vital manpower away from the investigation into the murders in order to stake out the place allocated for the delivery of the money. They harmed the murder investigation. They brought fear to the museum and the people who worked here, all of them wondering if they might be the next victim. Because that is what these letters are saying.' He fixed Chapman with a grim stare. 'Edward Chapman, I am charging you with demanding money by menaces, and also with interfering with the police in the course of their duty. This time you will stand trial, and you will go to prison.'

'No, please!' begged Chapman, and he burst into tears.

'Who did you persuade to write the other letters?' demanded Feather.

'My . . . my younger sister and my cousin,' sobbed Chapman. 'They thought it was for a joke I was playing on someone.'

'Their names?' asked Feather.

'Millicent's my sister. She's only fourteen. And my cousin, George Fell.'

Feather wrote down the names, then nodded at the constables.

'Take him to the cells,' he said.

CHAPTER THIRTY-SEVEN

As Daniel and Abigail left the police station, they found Joe Dalton waiting for them on the pavement.

'Daniel! Abigail!'

'Joe!' Daniel smiled. 'Are we to believe this is a coincidence?'

Dalton chuckled. 'If you believe that, then I've got plenty of things I think I can sell you. Like Buckingham Palace.'

'Let me guess, a little bird's told you that someone's been brought in.'

Dalton nodded. 'Related to the events at the British Museum. Is it the murderer?'

'No,' said Daniel.

'In that case it must be the threatening letters.'

'You know about them?' said Abigail, surprised.

'I wouldn't be much good at my job if I didn't,' said Dalton.

'Joe has contacts inside the police,' explained Daniel.

'Inspector Feather?' asked Abigail.

'No no,' said Dalton. 'John Feather's too . . . what can I say?'

'Honest?' hazarded Daniel with a smile.

'Let's say he does everything by the book.'

'Joe has contacts with constables all over London.'

'Who are always grateful for a small remuneration in exchange for information,' said Dalton.

'But you haven't written anything about the letters before,' said Abigail. 'At least, I'm sure we would have known if anything had appeared in the newspapers.'

'I thought it might be counterproductive,' said Dalton.

'What do you know?' asked Daniel.

'I know there was a stake-out with the police waiting to pick up anyone who turned up to collect a ransom of £1,000. And that no one turned up. Which suggested it was a hoax. So that's why I kept a lid on it for the moment. I thought there might be a bigger story. And it looks like I might be right. I got a message today telling me that an arrest was made of a young man called Edward Chapman. And I remembered that was the name of one of the young men who did the damage that day when I was at the museum.'

'We never told you his name,' said Abigail.

'You didn't need to,' said Dalton.

'Someone inside the museum,' said Daniel.

Dalton smiled again. 'It's always useful to have good contacts. So, the story?'

'You might want to talk to John Feather,' suggested Daniel.

'And I will,' said Dalton. 'But it would be useful to get the story from you before I do.' He smiled. 'Remember, Daniel, you owe me for not writing about those two young toffs who did the damage at the museum. Mr Chapman and his pal.'

'Payback?' enquired Daniel.

'I call it fair's fair,' said Dalton. 'And there's no reason anyone should know it came from you. John Feather knows I have my snouts inside the force. He'll guess my information came from them. At least, that's what I'll tell him.'

'I can't do that to John,' said Daniel. 'He's an honest copper. But what I will do is give you the story as we know it, but I'll tell him I did that. Then it's up to him what he says to you.'

'Was Armstrong in on the bust?' asked Dalton.

Daniel shook his head.

'So, it wasn't connected with the murders,' said Dalton.

'Inspector Feather deserves the credit for this,' said Daniel. 'He was the officer in charge.'

'So why are you two here?'

'Let's say we had information that was of help to Inspector Feather.'

'These threatening letters were sent by this Edward Chapman?'

'That's the allegation. It will be up to the trial to say whether he's guilty or not.'

'And how was he caught? Because my information says no one turned up to collect the ransom money.'

'Good dogged police work on the part of Inspector Feather,' said Daniel.

'And a tip-off from Daniel Wilson and Miss Abigail Fenton,' said

Dalton. 'How did you do it? How did you work out it was Chapman?'

'Let's just say information came to us,' said Daniel. 'Just like it comes to you. But, like you, we can't reveal our sources.'

'Fair enough,' said Dalton. 'Will it annoy Superintendent Armstrong if I mention you in the article?'

'That depends on what you say about us,' said Daniel.

Dalton grinned. 'Thanks,' he said.

'What will he say about us?' asked Abigail as Dalton walked jauntily away.

'Something calculated to annoy Armstrong,' replied Daniel. 'Joe doesn't like him, and he knows the superintendent doesn't like me. But Joe's a fair man. He'll make sure that John Feather gets the proper credit.'

'So,' said Abigail, 'with one crime officially solved – the extortion demands – what's our next move?'

'Jedding,' said Daniel. 'With what you got from your friend Charles, it's obvious that Pickering did steal Jedding's work. The question is: did Jedding kill Pickering and then kill himself in a fit of remorse? In which case, who killed Whetstone on his behalf? Or did Jedding *not* kill Pickering, in which case who did – and again, did they do it in revenge for what Jedding had suffered at the hands of Pickering and Whetstone?'

'It's the timing of Jedding's suicide that's the puzzle,' said Abigail. 'He killed himself shortly after Pickering was stabbed to death, which does tend to suggest he did it because of guilt.'

'So, we find out who felt so strongly about the way Jedding had been treated that they killed Whetstone. Which means we go back to Balfe Street and see if we can persuade Mrs Jedding to let us know who was closest to her late husband.'

'She wasn't very forthcoming when I saw her,' said Abigail. 'In fact, she refused to talk about him and slammed the door in my face.'

'Maybe we'll have better luck this time,' said Daniel.

Abigail had to admit that she felt reassured on her return to Balfe Street to have Daniel with her. He exuded a confident strength as he walked through the narrow streets, and although the curtains twitched as they did before, at the sight of him the children playing in the street scattered and disappeared.

'They know I'm a copper,' said Daniel. 'Even though I'm not, they can sense the walk and look.'

This time there was no answer at the Jeddings' house to Daniel's knock. Daniel tried knocking at the houses on either side, but again there was no response.

'Like I said, they think I'm a copper,' said Daniel.

'The man at the rag-and-bone shop at the end of the street was approachable,' suggested Abigail.

'Let's hope he's still of the same opinion' said Daniel.

They made their way to the rag-and-bone shop and found the owner sitting on a chair outside his shop.

'Good afternoon,' said Abigail.

'Afternoon,' said the man. 'Back again, eh?' He looked at Daniel. 'And this time with company. Copper?'

'Not any longer,' said Daniel. 'Private investigator, along with this lady.'

'Investigating the murders at the British Museum.' The man nodded.

'You've heard about the second one,' said Daniel.

The man shrugged. 'You'd be surprised how fast word spreads. Another stabbing, they say.'

'And they'd be right,' said Daniel. He looked up at the sigh above the door. 'Am I addressing Mr Flood?'

265

'Billy Flood,' said the man. 'That's me, and proud to put my name over this shop. People round here know me for a fair and honest man to deal with.' He looked at Abigail. 'Last time you were asking about poor old William Jedding.'

'This time we're looking for Mrs Jedding,' said Abigail. 'But there's no answer at her house.'

'That because she's away,' said Flood.

'Away?'

'She got fed up with all the looks she was getting over poor old William topping himself the way he did. The shame of it. So she took herself off.'

'Do you know where?' asked Daniel.

Flood looked at him and said warily, 'I might. But I'm a trader. Information is the same as any other commodity.'

Daniel took a coin from his pocket and held it concealed in his fist.

'And what's the price?' he asked.

Flood studied him, then said, 'Let's say I hope that's something better than a shilling you're holding.'

Daniel opened his hand to reveal a florin, a two-shilling piece. The man reached for it, but Daniel closed his hand again and said, 'I need something better than a promise first.'

'The Isle of Dogs,' said Flood. 'She's got a cousin there.' He gestured at Daniel's closed hand. 'That'll get you her name and address.'

Daniel handed the florin over. The man pocketed it then said, 'Daisy Rennie. 12 East Ferry Road. Close to the football ground. Do you know it?'

'The Athletic Ground,' replied Daniel. 'Home of Millwall Athletic. Formerly Millwall Rovers.'

'Football fan,' said Flood with a smile.

'Not necessarily. Let's just say when I was in the force we spent many a time at most of London's football grounds, so I got to know most of them.'

'Football and money, Inspector,' said Flood. 'It can be a deadly combination.'

'Like I said before, I'm not on the force any more. Not an inspector.'

'But you were,' said Flood. 'Inspector Wilson. I remember you. Your picture was in the papers when you was part of old Fred Abberline's squad, especially around the time of the Ripper. Never caught him, did you.'

'Not for want of trying,' said Daniel. He tipped his hat. 'Thank you for the trade, Mr Flood. I hope it doesn't turn out to be a fool's errand.'

'I only pass on what I hear. I can't guarantee it.'

'And where did you hear this piece of information?'

Flood looked at him, shocked. 'More info for the same money?'

'Just a piece of added insurance,' said Daniel. 'I'd hate to go all the way to the Isle of Dogs and find out I'd been had. If that happened, I'd be in a very bad mood.'

Flood shifted uneasily on his chair, then said reluctantly, 'Kathleen Purvis. Lives next door to the Jeddings. She told me.'

'Thank you,' said Daniel. 'By the way, what's Mrs Jedding's first name?'

'Peg,' said Flood.

As they walked away from Flood and his shop, Abigail asked, 'Are we going to check out his information with this Kathleen Purvis?'

'No,' said Daniel. 'She didn't answer the door when we

knocked there before, and I've been watching, no one's gone into her house. Tomorrow we'll go to the Isle of Dogs. And if it does turn out to be a waste of time, then we'll talk to Kathleen Purvis. And I'll have words with Mr Flood again.'

CHAPTER THIRTY-EIGHT

The next morning as Daniel and Abigail left their house to make their way to the Isle of Dogs, they were startled to see the figure of Ned Carson loitering by the kerb outside. He moved towards them as the front door opened, waving a copy of a newspaper.

'Can I have a word, Mr Wilson?' he called.

Daniel murmured to Abigail, 'Better leave this to me.'

'I can handle myself,' insisted Abigail.

'Please,' said Daniel. 'I promise I won't lose my temper and do something we'll regret.'

'Promise?' she asked.

'I promise,' he said. He smiled. 'In fact, looking at your face at this moment, I think there's more chance of you inflicting damage on him than me. It's lucky there isn't a shovel nearby.'

Abigail nodded, then walked back into the house, leaving Daniel to turn and face Carson.

'I see Joe Dalton's got a piece in the paper where he quotes you, and your friend Miss Fenton,' said Carson, tapping the copy of the *Telegraph*.

'And Inspector Feather,' said Daniel.

'True. But what he doesn't say is what the relationship is between you and Miss Fenton.'

'Why should he?'

'Yes, well, that's not his style, I suppose.'

'But it is yours.'

'The people who read the *People's Voice* like the personal angle. Now, I can understand you may not want your personal life all over the papers. Nor that of Miss Fenton. So, I was wondering if there was room for some sort of cooperation between us.'

Daniel said nothing, just watched Carson and waited. This was exactly what he'd been expecting.

'You see, this is a big case. Two murders at the British Museum, one after the other. Sounds like a bastion of the Empire is under threat. Is there a bigger story here? Now I don't know, but I'm sure that you do.' He tapped the copy of the *Telegraph* again. 'You've been helpful to Joe Dalton, so why not be helpful to me? After all, me and him are in the same business, informing the public. And that way I won't feel the need to mention about your private arrangements. You and Miss Fenton aren't married, I believe.'

Daniel felt the urge to punch Carson, wipe the smirk off his face, but he bore in mind what Abigail had said to him. Ignore it. Instead, forcing himself to remain calm and polite, he said, 'I believe you're mistaken on quite a few points, Mr Carson. One is that I would give you any information in exchange for you not writing about my private life. That would be responding to threats and blackmail, which – as you know – would be condoning a criminal offence.'

'Now, look!' exclaimed Carson defensively. 'I never said anything about blackmail!'

'The second mistake is to suggest that you and Joe Dalton are in the same line of business. You're not. He is a news reporter. You peddle gossip and innuendo for the titillation of your alleged readers. I'm always prepared to talk to a proper reporter. I'm not prepared to talk to you. Good day.'

Daniel turned on his heel. Behind him, Carson shouted, 'You'll regret this, Wilson! I'll ruin you! And your woman!'

Angered by the reference to Abigail, Daniel spun round and was about to lunge at Carson, when he stopped himself. That would just give Carson the perfect story. Instead, he said, 'Be careful, Mr Carson. Bad deeds having a habit of returning to haunt you. I believe in India they call it karma.'

The door of the house opened, and Abigail appeared.

'Well done!' she congratulated him warmly.

'I still wanted to punch him when he talked about you.'

'Yes, but you didn't. And that's what matters.'

Their journey by rail to the Isle of Dogs entailed a change at Fenchurch Street on to the London and Blackwall Railway to Millwall Docks Station.

'Looking at the names of the stations we'll be going through, many of them seem to be associated with docks,' observed Abigail. 'West India Dock. East India Dock.'

'That's because the Isle of Dogs is at the very heart of London's dockland. Ships from all over the world come up the Thames to it. It's a perfect docking place for large ships because it's surrounded on three sides by the Thames. It's one of the largest loops in the river.'

Abigail took in the passing views as the train trundled on, crossing the river and then making its way south. As Daniel had said, the area was dominated by docks and wharves, with ships of sail and also of steam moored in massive numbers.

'This line is mainly used for goods,' added Daniel. 'All that cargo being unloaded and then onto goods trains heading for London, and every other place in Britain.' He leant forward and pointed. 'We're not far from Millwall Docks now, and we'll be passing the football ground soon.'

'How do you know so much about football?'

'What do you mean?'

'You know where Millwall football club play, but it's not as if it's local to you.'

'We always kept a watch when there was a big football match on,' said Daniel. 'Pickpocketing's rife when you get a large crowd, and at Millwall games can get a crowd of ten thousand. Sometimes more. Lots of illegal business happening on the fringes which needed an eye kept on them. Also, football supporters are very tribal, so sometimes there could be trouble between rival fans. But I'm sure you know about that, being a Cambridge student.'

Abigail looked at him, puzzled. 'The social aspects of football supporters was not something we studied at Girton.'

'I'm talking about sporting rivalry,' said Daniel. 'The annual Boat Race between Oxford and Cambridge has always been an absolute nightmare for the police, with gangs of rival students, usually drunk, rioting in the streets, attacking each other and generally causing mayhem.'

'I can assure you I have never rioted in my life,' said Abigail. 'And to be honest, although – as a Cambridge graduate – I'm always interested in the outcome of the Boat Race, it doesn't rate as of that great an importance.'

'Well that's the difference between you and a football club supporter. Most football clubs have come about through the people who live and work in a particular area playing for their firm's football team. Millwall, for example, was formed by workers at the Morton's Canning and Preserves factory in Millwall in 1885. Woolwich Arsenal, as the name suggests, was made up of munitions workers at Woolwich Royal Arsenal. As a result, these teams have fierce local loyalty; it's not just a football team, it's their workmates out there on that pitch playing for their reputation. That's why things get so heated. Unlike the students on Boat Race night, who are just out to cause mayhem.'

'I think you're being unfair,' said Abigail. 'Students work very hard. The Boat Race and similar events are their chance to let off steam.'

'By attacking police officers who try and keep order and protect property, and in return have their helmets stolen?'

'We're talking about a minority of students who engage in that kind of behaviour,' said Abigail. 'I'm glad to say I never encountered any when I was at Cambridge.'

'That's because you were at Girton, a women's college, and without exception the hooligans I'm talking about were male. And nearly all of them from upper class families who are supposed to represent proper social behaviour, but who turn a blind eye to their delinquent sons' behaviour and excuse it – as you say – as "letting off steam". In my book it's still causing criminal damage and assault.'

Abigail laughed. 'I do love it when you get on your high horse.' She chuckled. 'You sound like one of these radical politicians. I'm surprised you don't stand for Parliament.'

'No, thank you,' said Daniel. 'My experiences with politicians have not endeared me to them. I'm always reminded of the saying that you can tell when a politician's lying because their lips move.'

Feather answered the call from the superintendent, and as soon as he entered Armstrong's office he knew that whatever he had been summoned for did not bode well. The superintendent was banging one of his fists angrily on his desk as he read a newspaper spread out before him.

'You sent for me, sir?' said Feather.

'This is a disgrace!' growled Armstrong.

'What is, sir?' asked Feather.

'This story in the *Telegraph* about Chapman and the threatening letters. Have you read it?'

Feather frowned. 'Yes, sir. I thought it was pretty accurate, sir. For a newspaper, anyway.'

'Yes, but where's my name!'

'With respect, sir, you said you didn't want to be involved in the arrest.'

'That's irrelevant! I'm the superintendent in charge! Did you even tell this reporter' – he searched for the byline – 'this Joe Dalton, that?'

'Of course, sir. I stressed that everything that happened on this case is directed by you.'

'You're mentioned. And so are Wilson and the Fenton woman, God blast them!'

'I don't think they can be blamed, sir. Dalton was given the facts of the case—'

'And he chose deliberately not to mention that I'm in charge of it! Well, I want to see this Dalton character and put him straight about a few things. Wilson is no longer part of this department, and as far as I'm concerned he's not part of this investigation!'

'Is that wise, sir?' asked Feather warily.

'Why not?' demanded Armstrong. 'You obviously didn't make the case for my name to be included strongly enough, so it's up to me to straighten him out.'

'If you recall, sir, you did have a confrontation with Dalton before.'

Armstrong frowned. 'When?'

'The robbery at the jeweller's in Piccadilly a year ago. The one where we arrested the manager of the store, following your orders . . .'

'Was that Dalton?!' shouted Armstrong, furious. 'I couldn't remember his name, just that he was disrespectful in the extreme towards me!'

'The manager was innocent,' pointed out Feather.

'I was acting on information received,' snarled Armstrong.

'From the real culprit,' said Feather.

'What are you getting at, Inspector?' demanded Armstrong.

'I'm just saying that you were misled, sir. But unfortunately, the manager of the jeweller's was a cousin of Dalton's . . .'

'Exactly! He got personal to get back at me! He humiliated me!'

'I'm just saying, sir, that in view of that, it might be advisable not to confront Dalton about the fact he didn't include your name in his report about this matter. He might not take it well.'

'I know how to deal with the press, Inspector!' snapped Armstrong.

They were interrupted by the door opening and a uniformed messenger stumbling in, causing Armstrong to turn and shout angrily at the man, 'What do you mean by bursting in like that without knocking?!'

'I'm sorry, sir,' apologised the messenger, 'but I've got an urgent message for Inspector Feather.'

Feather held out his hand and the messenger handed him a note. Feather read it, then handed it to the superintendent.

'Looks like we've found her,' he said.

Armstrong read the brief note: *Missing girl Elsie Bowler with mudlarks. Observation being kept north bank by Waterloo Bridge. Danl Verity. PC 49.*

The superintendent gave a smile of grim satisfaction. 'Right! Let's go and get her! Then we'll see what Mr Joe Dalton and the other so-called reporters will be forced to put in their papers.' He gave Feather a wolfish smile. 'They won't be able to ignore me now!'

CHAPTER THIRTY-NINE

The address they'd been given for Daisy Rennie was just a short walk along East Ferry Road from the railway station. A knock at the door was answered by an elderly woman wearing an apron splashed with flour.

'Excuse the mess,' she said, 'but today's my day for making bread.'

'Daisy Rennie?' asked Daniel.

'That's me. Who might you be?'

'My name's Daniel Wilson and this is Miss Abigail Fenton.'

The woman sniffed warily at them. 'You're not coming round bringing the Word of God, are you?' she asked suspiciously. 'Only you look like the same as the ones we had round here yesterday. Like I say, today's my day for bread-making and I ain't got time to be saved.'

'No,' Daniel assured her. 'We've been sent here by Kathleen Purvis, Peg Jedding's neighbour in Balfe Street, with a message for her. Is she available?'

Daisy Rennie shook her head. 'Sorry,' she said. 'She was, but she took off. Said seeing all the activity round here at the docks, and especially all the water, made her think of poor William.' She looked at them suspiciously again and asked, 'You know what I'm talking about?'

'Sadly, we do,' said Daniel. 'Where did she take off to, do you know?'

'Southend,' said Daisy. 'She said she wanted to be far away from everyone. She's got an old friend of hers who lives there.'

'Do you know the name and address of this friend?'

Daisy Rennie frowned, giving it thought. 'Her first name's Rose, but I don't recall her second name. All Peg said was she's got a shop that sells lace on the front near the pier.'

Daniel doffed his hat. 'Thank you,' he said.

As he and Abigail walked away, she asked, 'So, what next? Southend?'

'No,' said Daniel. 'We're being given the runaround. They're protecting her.'

'What do we do?' asked Abigail.

'When we came up against something like this when I was on the force, we'd get heavy,' said Daniel. 'Send in uniforms to start rousting people, and sooner or later people would talk. But we can't do that, and Armstrong won't support anything like that, not while he's got this bee in his bonnet about Elsie Bowler. No, our next port of call is a return visit to Billy Flood, the rag-and-bone man. We've been led a dance for my two shillings, and I'm a man who likes to get value for his money.'

Feather and Armstrong arrived at Waterloo Bridge to find Constable Verity waiting for them.

'Where is she, Constable?' demanded Armstrong.

'Along the riverbank, sir,' Verity replied, gesturing along the Embankment.

'You left her unobserved?' growled Armstrong angrily.

'No, sir. Constable Wickford is keeping an eye on her.'

'Good thinking, Constable,' said Feather. He turned to Armstrong. 'I suggest we move forward carefully, sir. Too many of us at once might scare her into running off.'

'She's on a muddy riverbank, where can she go?' demanded Armstrong.

'She could throw herself into the river,' said Feather. 'Or run into one of the sewer openings. The mudlarks tend to operate near where the sewers empty into the Thames because that's where the richest pickings are.'

Armstrong hesitated, then nodded. 'Very well,' he said. 'You and I will go forward, Inspector. We're in plain clothes so that shouldn't scare her. We're just two gentlemen out for a walk, taking in the sights of the river.' He turned to Constable Verity and ordered, 'I want you ready to get down and grab her when I give the shout.'

'In the mud, sir?' asked Verity doubtfully.

'Of course in the mud,' snapped Armstrong. 'That's where she is.'

'But I could get stuck,' Verity pointed out. 'The kids don't sink down deep because they're small and light.'

'This girl is a murderer, Constable,' said Armstrong sternly. 'And you won't be alone. There'll be other constables to pull you out once we've got her.'

'Yes, sir,' said Verity, still obviously unhappy at the prospect of getting caught in the mud.

Armstrong and Feather set off along the Embankment towards where Constable Wickford was waiting.

'Constable Verity's got a point, sir,' said Feather. 'He is rather heavy, and Thames mud is notorious. In parts it's like quicksand, pulling people down and holding them so it's difficult to get out of.'

'All that matters is laying hands on that girl,' said Armstrong curtly.

'Yes, sir,' said Feather.

Feather and Armstrong arrived beside Constable Wickford, who saluted smartly.

'Don't salute, you fool!' hissed Armstrong. 'We don't want to alarm her.'

'Sorry, sir,' said Wickford.

Armstrong leant on the granite wall and looked down. With the tide out, an area of mud had been exposed and about ten children of different ages were scavenging, the level of mud halfway between their ankles and their knees as they dug with their hands, searching for anything of value. The youngest looked about six, the oldest, seventeen. They scavenged for coins that had been thrown in the river, old nails and other bits of metal, items of clothing, even lumps of coal, washed up after falling from a barge. Everything they found went into a sack to be sorted out later, the money to be kept, the metal and coal sold on to a rag-and-bone man. And, indeed, there were bones, mostly of small animals, but there were human bones, too, as the corpses of people who'd fallen – or thrown themselves – into the river broke down and their bones were washed along with the rest of the river's detritus.

'Which one is she?' asked Armstrong.

The constable gestured towards a thin girl who was taller than most of the other children. She was pale, and her clothes were smeared with mud, which also matted her long hair and streaked her face.

'That's her, sir,' he whispered.

'How can you be sure?' demanded Armstrong. 'She could be anybody.'

'Constable Verity says so. He knows one of the rag-and-bone men who buys the stuff the kids collect. His name's Sammy and he's got an old van in the Adelphi and it was Sammy who found out who the girl was.'

'How?'

'One of the kids found out her name and told Sammy. Sammy likes to know who's who. Sometimes it's worth money if he finds a runaway who someone's looking for.'

Armstrong looked down at the girl, who seemed too intent on clawing her hands through the thick mud to take heed that she was being watched. He turned to Feather and said, 'Right, go and tell Verity to get down there with the other constables and bring her in. And remind them she's dangerous. She might still have that knife on her.'

Feather nodded and returned to where Verity was waiting with two other constables, still looking miserable at the prospect of going onto the mud.

'Alright, Constable. Down you go and bring her in. And watch out, she had a knife on her.'

Verity nodded. 'Yes, sir.'

He jerked his hands towards the steps beside the bridge, and the other two constables followed him down them as he made his way to the muddy riverbank below. As the constables slowly began to walk along the mud, sinking up to their ankles at each step, Feather returned to where Armstrong and Constable Wickford were standing, looking down at the children. Suddenly one of the small boys spotted the three police constables making their way unsteadily towards them.

'Coppers!' he shouted.

Immediately, the other children scooped up the sacks containing their meagre findings and began to flee in the opposite direction.

'Get to the other steps!' Armstrong yelled at Wickford, and the constable broke into a run, heading towards the next set of steps.

'They're heading for the sewer outlet!' shouted Feather.

Verity and the other two constables were still some distance from the children and getting more bogged down in the mud. One of the constables had sunk in up to his knees.

'Stop her!' screamed Armstrong frantically.

The children were making their way as fast as they could, but still sinking in the mud as they moved, and were now directly beneath where Feather and Armstrong were standing. Elsie Bowler suddenly abandoned the sack she was carrying and began to head out towards where the water was deeper.

She's going to drown herself! Feather realised with a shock.

He threw off his overcoat, slung a leg over the thick balustrade and then launched himself down, reaching out his hands as he did so. He crashed into the mud, sinking into the stinking ooze, but one of his hands managed to grab hold of Elsie's skirt. She turned and lashed out at him, but he clung on desperately.

CHAPTER FORTY

There were problems with the trains on their journey back to central London, so their return took a lot longer than their outward trip.

'And all for nothing.' Abigail sighed as they walked from Gospel Oak railway station down Camden Street towards their house in Plender Street.

'Yes and no,' said Daniel. 'The fact that everyone is protecting Peg Jedding suggests she knows something, so it's important we get hold of her.'

'What might she know?'

'I'm not sure. Maybe she's got papers that William Jedding wrote which might give us the name of whoever was closest to him when he was writing his book on Ambrosius. Because I'm sure that whoever killed Whetstone did it in revenge for what happened to Jedding. We need to find that name.'

'Could it be Peg Jedding herself?'

'Possibly. You've met her. Would you think she's a likely suspect for a murderer?'

'It's hard to say,' admitted Abigail. 'She was certainly seriously upset when I saw her, but that was only for a few seconds before she shut the door on me.'

They turned into Plender Street and Abigail stopped suddenly.

'Not again!' she groaned.

Daniel saw what had brought her to an abrupt halt: a man was waiting outside their house. Then his face broke into a grin.

'It's alright,' he said. 'It's not Carson. It's John Feather.' As they headed towards the detective, Daniel added, puzzled, 'But it's very rare for him to call like this. Something must have happened.'

Daniel greeted the inspector. 'John! This is rare! I hope you haven't been waiting long.'

'No, I just got here,' said Feather. He gestured to the house. 'Can we talk inside?'

'Of course.' Daniel unlocked the door and they went in.

'I'll fix us a pot of tea,' said Abigail. 'You look as if you could use one, John, and so could we.'

'That'll be perfect,' said Feather.

They went through to the kitchen, and Feather sat down while Abigail set to work making up the fire in the range and filling a kettle with water.

'What's happened?' asked Daniel. 'It's got to be important to bring you here.'

'I've come to alert you about a story that's going to appear in the papers first thing tomorrow. The killer has been caught.'

Daniel frowned. 'When?' he asked. 'Who? And how?'

'Elsie Bowler,' replied Feather. 'She was nabbed working among the mudlarks by the Embankment.'

'But she didn't kill Whetstone!' said Daniel. 'And I'm not sure she killed Pickering.'

'That's not how the superintendent sees it,' said Feather. 'Three stabbings. We know she stabbed Tudder. We know she was angry at Pickering for the way he treated her mother. So, according to Armstrong, that's enough. He's giving a speech about it to the gentlemen of the press at Scotland Yard as we speak.'

'It won't wash at her trial,' insisted Daniel.

'It won't come to trial,' said Feather. 'She's unfit to plead. And that part is true, because I sat in with Armstrong when we interviewed her. Her mind's gone. She rambles about nothing.'

'Where is she?'

'She's been taken to the Royal Bethlem Hospital for the Insane. And she's going to be there for life, by the look of it.'

'So, Armstrong gets his result. A killer arrested on his watch. Praise all round. And no trial.'

'That's about the size of it,' said Feather.

'Do you think she's guilty, John?'

'Of stabbing Tudder, absolutely. Of the murders, no. But it doesn't matter what I think.'

'It means the murderer is still out there.'

'Not according to Superintendent Armstrong.'

'Do you think they press will believe him?'

'There may be a few dissenting voices, but I think they'll accept what he says. "Murderer Caught" makes a better headline than "Murderer Still At Large".'

'You're not attending this press conference?' asked Abigail.

'No,' said Feather. 'I had to go home and change my clothes. I was the one who jumped into the mud and caught her, so the superintendent said he'd look after it.'

'He doesn't want to share the glory,' said Abigail disapprovingly.

'Frankly, there's not a lot of glory here,' said Feather. 'If he's right, we've caught some poor brain-addled girl. If he's wrong, the murderer's still out there.'

'Can we go to see Elsie Bowler at Bethlem?' asked Daniel.

'I don't see why not,' said Feather. 'Armstrong hasn't said you can't. In fact, I get the impression he'd be pleased for you to see her just to rub your nose in the fact that it was he who got her and solved the crime, not you.'

Daniel sighed. 'All in all, it seems a disappointing day for all of us.'

'Why? What happened to you?'

'We went all the way to the Isle of Dogs in search for Mrs Jedding, and she wasn't there.'

'What made you think she might be?' asked Feather.

'It's a long and annoying story,' said Daniel. 'Have you eaten?'

'No,' said Feather. 'And there won't be anything at home, either,' he added gloomily. 'Ellen and the kids are at her sister's this evening.'

'I'm not starting to cook a meal now,' said Abigail firmly. 'It's too late.'

'I wasn't going to suggest you do,' said Daniel.

'Even if you do it, it'll still take a while before we get to eat,' pointed out Abigail.

'I know,' said Daniel. He turned to Feather. 'Do you like pie and mash?'

'With parsley sauce?'

'Of course! It wouldn't be the same without it.'

Feather beamed. 'I love pie and mash!'

Daniel looked at Abigail, who gave a sigh of defeat.

Superintendent Armstrong stood at the table in front of a gathering of journalists in a room at Scotland Yard specially set aside for such occasions. All of the national newspapers were represented, along with most of the local London ones, like the *St Pancras Chronicle* and the *Bloomsbury Gazette*. Sergeant Crews from the uniformed division sat next to the superintendent, not because he'd been involved in the capture of Elsie Bowler but because he cut a fine figure in his sergeant's uniform, and he was also someone that Armstrong could count on to remain silent during the press conference and not be lulled into answering any questions.

Armstrong surveyed the assembled reporters, each of whom had a notepad and pencil in front of him, with an air of great confidence. This was his moment. 'I am pleased to tell you,' he began, 'that today we have arrested the person responsible for the two recent terrible murders at the British Museum, those of Professor Lance Pickering and his publisher, Mr Mansfield Whetstone. Their murderer we identified as a young girl called Elsie Bowler. Elsie Bowler bore a deep personal grudge against Professor Pickering, a grudge which we believe was a fantasy of her own making. It was that which drove her to stab Professor Pickering with a knife. She then, for reasons of her own, proceeded to target those close to Professor Pickering. These included the senior publisher of the firm that published the professor's most recent book, Mr Mansfield Whetstone, and also another close acquaintance of the professor's. For reasons of discretion, we are keeping the identity of this third victim confidential. Fortunately for him he did not die, although he was stabbed by this Elsie Bowler. The fact that both Mr Whetstone and this other gentleman were very closely connected to Professor Pickering backs up the fact that this girl was the culprit.

'It became obvious after we apprehended this girl that she was deranged and of unsound mind. If you recall, I said after the murder of Professor Pickering that it was my belief we were dealing with a lunatic of some sort, and this opinion has now been borne out. She has been taken to the Bethlem Royal Hospital where she is being kept under close guard.

'This has been a difficult case, not least because it has generated various theories among the public as to the reasons for the murders. But the reality is that this case was solved by dogged determination and applied procedural investigative work by the professionals of the Metropolitan police alone, not by any private enquiry agents or other amateurs.' He gave a smile of great pride to the assembly and announced, 'I am now ready to answer questions about this case.'

A man in the second row stood up. 'Joe Dalton, the *Daily Telegraph*, Superintendent,' he introduced himself.

Immediately, Armstrong was on his guard. Dalton, the man who'd cut him out of his report on the successful arrest of that Chapman character. The man who'd attacked him in the press over that robbery at the jeweller's.

'I understand that the actual arrest was made by Inspector Feather, who jumped into the Thames to apprehend the girl. Is that correct?'

Damn him! Where did Dalton get his information from? The superintendent had been told that Dalton had various constables on his payroll who fed him with information. Well, if he found out who'd passed on this story, that person would be in serious trouble.

'Inspector Feather did what he did acting on my orders,' retorted Armstrong stiffly. 'I was on the scene with him and in charge the whole time.'

'But leaping into the Thames in pursuit of a murderess, possibly armed, suggests an act of great courage. Will he be getting an award of some sort for his act?'

'The tide was out when Inspector Feather went after the girl. He was in no danger at all.'

Eager to move on, he pointed to a small man at the back holding his hand up.

'Thank you, Superintendent. We understand that the girl is too ill to stand trial?'

'That is correct,' said Armstrong. 'That is the verdict of the physician at Bethlem Royal Hospital.'

'Which is rather convenient for you,' said the man. 'You've got an arrest with no way for anyone to check if the arrest is sound. I understand that this girl is seventeen and a vagrant with no living relatives. Are you sure that this isn't an arrest of convenience, putting the blame on some poor unfortunate—'

Armstrong exploded with fury. 'How dare you!' he roared. 'Who are you?'

'Ned Carson from the *People's Voice*.'

'The *People's Voice*!' shouted Armstrong. 'That's not even a real newspaper!' He gestured angrily at the constables standing at the side. 'Who let this imposter in? Throw him out at once!'

As Carson was lifted from his chair by two constables and hustled towards the door, the small man called out, 'What are you hiding, Superintendent?', before being pushed out of the room.

Armstrong, struggling to contain his rage, turned to the assembled reporters again, ready to have the lot of them thrown out, but the next to stand was a tall man he recognised as friendly towards him. At least, he'd shown that to be the case so far. But what sort of question did he have ready now?

'Edgar White of the *St Pancras Chronicle*,' said the tall man. 'I'd like to say on behalf of the gentlemen of the press, despite the last comment, that we congratulate you, Superintendent, on bringing this case to a successful conclusion. It is gratifying to know that after the dreadful fear that has hovered over us all, this city is safe once more.'

With that, White began to applaud, and was joined by others who also clapped. Not by everyone, Armstrong noted. That Dalton character, for one. But most of the others joined in, and Armstrong smiled and made a small bow.

His triumph was complete.

CHAPTER FORTY-ONE

Daniel and Abigail read the newspaper reports of Superintendent Armstrong's speech as they journeyed in a hansom cab towards St George's Field in Southwark.

'According to *The Times*, he made a point of stressing that this case was solved by the police alone without – and I quote – "assistance from any outside agencies such as private enquiry agents",' said Abigail. 'He's having a go at us.'

'No, he's having a go at me,' said Daniel. 'He doesn't know you well enough to want to score points off you. But he will in time, I'm sure.' He smiled. 'Joe Dalton doesn't say anything about that, and he makes the point that it was John Feather who leapt into the Thames to catch the girl. Armstrong won't like that.' He looked out of the window as the cab crossed Blackfriars Bridge. 'We're nearly there. Have you been to Bethlem Hospital before?'

'No,' said Abigail, her tone deeply disapproving. 'But I know its reputation. Bedlam. A place where the poor unfortunates are paraded as entertainment for paying visitors. Those that are lucky enough to have some sort of freedom to move around, while other poor wretches are kept chained and naked, and again, are gawped at by idiots for their so-called fun.'

'That's how it used to be,' said Daniel. 'Sadly, we often had cause to visit the hospital to try and talk to people whose names had been suggested as suspects, especially in some of the more lurid cases we investigated.'

'The Jack the Ripper case?'

'Exactly,' said Daniel. 'There were claims that some of the patients had been allowed out and had committed the crimes while they were away; other suggestions were that patients were taken from the hospital specifically to commit the crimes, then returned afterwards.'

'And did you find any evidence to support those allegations?'

'None, but they had to be looked into.'

'So, you experienced Bethlem at close hand.'

'I did,' said Daniel.

'And was it as bad as people said?'

Daniel hesitated before answering. 'Let's say it wasn't the happiest of places, but I was told conditions had improved following the Parliamentary enquiry into it. And during our Ripper investigations, a new director was put in charge who I believe has changed the tone of the hospital completely.'

'Who's that?'

'Dr T. B. Hyslop. Unlike many of his predecessors, he's a fully qualified medical man whose speciality is psychiatric disorders. Certainly, in the six years since he's taken over there has been a change in the regime. Before, many of the warders – and that's what they were – were cruel in their treatment of the patients. They treated them badly and made money from them and their relatives. Under Dr Hyslop, the staff are now considered as nurses and expected to act that way.'

'This Dr Hyslop sounds a remarkable man,' said Abigail.

'He is,' said Daniel. 'Although I haven't seen him for some time. The last time was three years ago, when Abberline and I were both still at Scotland Yard and we received information that a doctor at the hospital was carrying out illegal abortions, and that two women had died at his hands.'

'And had they?'

'No. The women had died, but not at the doctor's hands. He was innocent of being involved in abortions. It turned out the allegation was a smear against him by a former mistress of his who was angry because the doctor had decided not to marry her. The abortionist who carried out the operations in which the women died was someone not associated with the hospital.'

'But still a doctor?'

'No. It was a woman who was also a midwife. The sad aspect of it was that she was not doing it for profit, she genuinely wanted to help women who found themselves in a distressing situation.'

As they drew nearer to the hospital, Daniel reflected that the hospital's history was as chaotic as the conditions which had dominated until the arrival of Dr Hyslop. It had the proud boast of being the oldest psychiatric hospital in Europe, long before the word 'psychiatry' had even entered common usage. From its early days as a 'home for lunatics' way back in the mists of time – it was said to have been founded in the thirteenth century during the reign of Henry III – its original name of the Bethlehem Royal Hospital had soon been shortened to Bethlem, and then to Bedlam as a tone of derision. It had moved locations in London many times, its last siting before the current one at St Georges Fields in Southwark, south of the river, having been at Moorfields, not far from Moorgate. But until the arrival of Dr Hyslop, the medical regimes had remained much the same: those deemed mad incarcerated and left to rot away from respectable society, although 'respectable society' took enjoyment in the entertainments the chained-up unfortunates offered for an outing.

Abigail sat, stunned at the sight of the hospital as they drove down the driveway towards the main building.

'It's enormous!' she said. 'I hadn't realised the building was this huge! It's almost as big as the Houses of Parliament!'

'It wouldn't surprise me to discover it's larger,' said Daniel.

The cab pulled up at the ornate main entrance, and Daniel led the way in.

'I can assure you, you'll be safe,' Daniel told Abigail. 'The really dangerous patients are kept in secure cells.'

He went to the main reception desk, where he presented his card. 'I'd be grateful if you'd tell Dr Hyslop that Daniel Wilson and Miss Abigail Fenton are here, and we'd be grateful if he could spare us a few moments,' said Daniel. 'It concerns Elsie Bowler.'

The receptionist sent a messenger off into the innards of the building. The messenger returned a few moments later.

'Dr Hyslop will see you,' he told them. 'Please follow me.'

Dr Hyslop's office was in the first corridor near to the main entrance, and he rose from behind his desk as the messenger ushered Daniel and Abigail in.

'Inspector Wilson,' he said, reaching out to shake Daniel's hand.

'Just plain Mr Wilson these days, Doctor,' said Daniel. 'I left Scotland Yard and work now as a private enquiry agent. Although I do still work in association with some of my old colleagues who are still at the Yard. Like Inspector Feather, who told us that Elsie Bowler was here in your care.'

'Ah yes, the poor girl,' said Hyslop.

Daniel gestured towards Abigail. 'Allow me to introduce you to Miss Abigail Fenton, my partner in the case we are currently working on.'

'If it concerns Elsie, then it must be the murders at the British Museum,' said Hyslop.

'Indeed,' said Daniel. 'I believe that Superintendent Armstrong of Scotland Yard considers her to be the person responsible for both murders.'

'That is his opinion,' said Hyslop carefully.

'And yours?' asked Daniel.

Hyslop thought his answer over, then replied, 'Unfortunately, as you are not police officers officially engaged in the case, nor relatives of the girl, I'm afraid I can't really discuss her with you.'

'I understand your situation, Doctor,' said Daniel. He produced the card of authority that Sir Jasper Stone had given him and passed it to Hyslop. 'However, you'll see that we have been officially employed in this matter by the British Museum, and we are here with the knowledge and recommendation of Inspector Feather.'

Hyslop examined the card, then turned to Abigail. 'Do you have similar evidence of authority, Miss Fenton?'

'I do,' said Abigail, and she handed him the card Sir Jasper had given her. He studied it, then returned it to her.

'Thank you,' he said, visibly relaxing. 'It's part of the new staff disciplines I am introducing to the hospital to avoid some of the unfortunate events of the past. And if I am to make sure that others obey the rules, then I have to set an example myself.'

'No more free access to patients for all and sundry,' said Abigail.

'I see you are aware of the hospital's previous unfortunate reputation,' said Hyslop.

'Would it be possible for us to talk to Elsie?' asked Daniel.

'I don't see why not,' said Hyslop. 'Although it may not be productive. She hasn't said much since she arrived.'

'Her manner?' asked Daniel.

'I would say docile,' said Hyslop. 'If there was any anger in her, it seems to have disappeared. But we have kept her apart from the other patients as a precaution for reasons of safety.' He rose from his desk. 'If you'll follow me, I'll take you to her.'

He led the way along a corridor, then down another. They passed various people sitting on chairs or benches in the corridors, many of them with vacant expressions on their faces. Others appeared who were in states of agitation, one in particular who scurried to Hyslop in a nervous state. 'Doctor, you have to get me out of here!' he whispered urgently. 'I have something of great importance to tell the Queen. It's a matter of life or death!'

'Indeed, James, and you will,' said Hyslop gently. 'Let me deal with these people first and then I'll come and talk to you about it and we'll make the arrangements.'

As Hyslop walked on, Daniel and Abigail in his wake, Abigail asked, 'What was that about the Queen? What arrangements need to be made?'

'Sadly, none. By the time I next see James he will have forgotten our conversation, or that he asked to be released to talk to Her Majesty.'

He arrived at a door, selected a key from a large keyring, and unlocked it.

A small girl, painfully thin, sat on the floor pressed into the corner of the room, even though there was a bed and a cushioned chair there. The girl wore a simple shift made of a rough material.

'Elsie,' said Dr Hyslop, crouching down beside the girl. 'These people have come to talk to you. I promise you they won't harm you. Would you come and sit on the bed while they talk?'

Obediently, the girl pushed herself up off the floor, walked to the bed and sat down. Dr Hyslop nodded for Daniel and Abigail to proceed.

'Elsie,' said Daniel gently, 'my name is Daniel, and this is Abigail. As Dr Hyslop says, I promise you we mean you no harm. We just want to hear from you about what happened at the British Museum.'

Elsie mumbled something brief and inaudible, then looked blankly at them. Daniel looked enquiringly at Hyslop.

'She said she's never been to the British Museum,' said Hyslop.

Daniel nodded, then turned back to the girl again. 'You stabbed a man,' he said.

'Yes,' they heard her whisper. 'At the rich man's house.' She dropped her head and began to cry.

'There, there, Elsie,' said Hyslop. 'It's alright. We're here to help you.'

Elsie lifted her head. 'They said I stabbed the other men, but I didn't. I went there to do the woman, the rich man's wife, because she was protecting him and what he done to my mum.' Her head dropped again, and she said, 'I was angry. I shouldn't have done it to her. It wasn't her fault.'

'The man you stabbed?' asked Abigail.

'He got in the way. I didn't mean to stick him.'

As they walked along the corridor away from Elsie Bowler's room, Daniel asked, 'What do you think, Doctor?'

Hyslop was silent for a moment, then he said, 'From what I understand of the two murders, they took a certain amount of planning and calculated intelligence in order to carry them out without detection. All I can say is that Elsie Bowler, in her present state, does not appear capable of organising or carrying out the acts in that way. However, I stress again, in her *present* state.'

'You think she might have been capable before?'

Again, Hyslop hesitated, then said, 'It appears unlikely, but one can never be sure when the state of mind is precarious. For now, I am satisfied that she is in the right place, where she can hopefully gain some respite from the ordeals she has endured. A trial and possible imprisonment would serve no good purpose, either to her or to society.'

Later, as Daniel and Abigail made the return journey in another hansom cab, Abigail said thoughtfully, 'He doesn't think she did it.'

'No,' said Daniel. 'Instead, he's elected to give her protection at Bethlem.'

'I think Dr Hyslop is a wonderful man,' said Abigail. 'To have changed a place like Bethlem so radically. To turn it from a place of horrors to a sanctuary. An asylum in the true sense of the word.'

'Indeed,' said Daniel. 'But the problem is, the murderer is still out there.'

CHAPTER FORTY-TWO

Sir Jasper was reading the day's newspapers when Daniel and Abigail entered his office on their return to the museum.

'You have seen the statement by Superintendent Armstrong?' he asked.

'We have, Sir Jasper,' said Daniel.

'But you're still not convinced that this girl, Bowler, is the one who killed Professor Pickering and Mansfield Whetstone?'

'We're not. And neither are Inspector Feather and Dr Hyslop at the Bethlem Hospital, although Dr Hyslop will not say so publicly. But we accept that, in view of the announcement Superintendent Armstrong has given to the press, you won't be able to keep us on investigating. As far as the general public are concerned, the case is closed.'

Sir Jasper sighed. 'Sadly, I feel that will also be the view of the board of trustees.' He hesitated, then looked at them questioningly. 'How close do you think you really are to identifying the real murderer?'

'I believe we are very close,' said Daniel. 'We're convinced the murderer is someone who was close to William Jedding. With or without the board's approval, we'd like to press on. We are aware there will be no further payment, but . . .'

Sir Jasper held up a hand to stop him.

'I shall tell the board that you will need a couple of days to bring things to a proper conclusion. Completing your reports for the board, wrapping things up, that sort of thing. It's only a couple more days . . .'

'But very gratefully accepted, Sir Jasper,' said Daniel. 'And very much appreciated.'

As they left Sir Jasper's office and headed down to the main reception, Abigail asked, 'What next?'

'I need to have words with Billy Flood,' said Daniel determinedly. 'And I think this time I'll see him on my own, if you don't mind.'

'You think I'll be in the way? Because I'm a woman?' demanded Abigail.

'No. But he needs to feel the full extent of my wrath over leading us a dance.'

'I can cope with that,' said Abigail.

'Not if it goes wrong,' said Daniel.

'What do you mean?'

'I believe that Mr Flood is more than just a harmless rag-and-bone man. I suspect he's at the hub of something more financially profitable. Which could mean he has protection.'

'What makes you say that? You only met him the once.'

Daniel tapped his nose. 'This,' he said. 'My copper's nose. I told you once before, I can smell what lies beneath the surface. Before I was prepared to give him the benefit of the doubt. But with the clock ticking, that has gone.'

'You again!' Billy Flood scowled as Daniel walked into his shop.

'Me again,' confirmed Daniel. 'You must have known I'd be calling back.'

'Why's that?'

'Because of that address you sold me. Which was a dud.'

'I was given that in good faith!' protested Flood.

'No, you were told to give that address if anyone came asking for Peg Jedding,' snapped Daniel. 'I decided to take a chance, just in case.'

'Look, Inspector . . .'

'I've already told you, I'm not in the force any more.'

'Exactly! And you have no authority any more, so if you don't like it you can sling your hook! And don't think about roughing me up, with one whistle I can have my protection here.'

'I wouldn't think of roughing you up,' said Daniel carefully. 'There's no need for me to do that. If I want to get my own back on you I'd do it differently. Once a copper, always a copper. Which means I've got friends on the force, and at top level, not local beat coppers who take a few shillings to turn a blind eye. You know I was on Abberline's squad, so you know I've got the ears of some good detectives. People who'd be interested in your shop.'

'What do you mean?!' demanded Flood.

'You don't make a living from buying and selling old rags and broken chairs. I can smell a fence when I meet one. Proceeds of crime, they call it. I was prepared to turn a blind eye if the trade you gave me had been good. But it wasn't. So be prepared for Scotland Yard to start turning your shop over regularly. You won't know when. It might be every day, it might be every week. But it makes it difficult to move stolen goods if you don't know when you're going to get raided.' As Flood opened his mouth to protest again, Daniel held up his hand and showed Flood the police whistle he was holding. 'Just in case you're thinking of calling your protection and dumping me in the canal to keep my mouth shut, this is an old memento. You surely didn't think I'd come alone this time around? One blast on this and you'll be swarming with coppers.'

Flood glared at him, then said sullenly, 'I don't know where Peg is. Her family have spirited her away.'

'So, who else was close to Jedding? Who did he talk to about the book he was writing? The one that got stolen?'

'He talked to me about it,' said Flood.

'So, tell me about Ambrosius,' said Daniel.

Flood frowned. 'Who?'

Daniel fixed him with a stony stare. 'Regular visits from the Yard. And I'm not joking.'

Flood hesitated, then he said, 'Peg wouldn't be any use to you. She told me she couldn't understand what William was talking about half the time about this book of his. Over her head, she said. You'd need to talk to the kids, his son and daughter. They were the ones he talked to about it most.'

'Where will I find them?'

'His daughter's moved away, but his son's still around.'

'What's his son's name?'

'Percy.'

'And where will I find Percy? And I've already coughed up once for dud information, so let's say this is already paid for.'

'You're a bastard, you know that!' grunted Flood.

'I am,' agreed Daniel. 'And you wouldn't like to find out just how big a bastard I can be. So again: where will I find Percy?'

Flood scowled, then said, 'The best place is the Wagon and Horses in York Way.'

'I know it,' said Daniel. 'How will I recognise him?'

'Short and thin with a face like a fox. He usually wears a sailor's jacket.'

'Thank you,' said Daniel. 'One more thing, if I find you've tipped him the wink to do a disappearing act before I get there, I'll be back.'

With that, Daniel walked away.

CHAPTER FORTY-THREE

Percy Jedding was in his early twenties and seemed very much at home in the Wagon and Horses. He fitted Flood's description perfectly, short and thin with a fox-like face, and a sailor's jacket. Daniel plonked himself down at the table where Jedding sat on his own and fixed the young man with a hard stare.

'Percy Jedding?' he said.

'No,' said Percy.

'That's funny, you fit the description I was given perfectly.'

Percy scowled. 'Copper?' he asked.

'Private detective,' said Daniel. 'I'm working for the British Museum, trying to find out who killed Professor Pickering.'

Percy spat on the floor at the name. 'Who cares who killed him! I'm glad someone did.'

'He stole your dad's work, I know, and one of the reasons I'm here is because I want your dad to get the proper credit he deserved.'

'Oh? How?'

'If I can talk to someone who he might have talked to as he wrote his book, someone who knew what he was doing, they might have papers or letters that prove he was the real author of the book that came out.'

Percy shook his head. 'I don't know about that. Dad talked about it to me, but half the time I didn't pay a lot of attention. It didn't interest me. My sister Jenny's the one you want to talk to. She was the one who knew what dad was doing. She used to take him his lunch when he was at work and he'd tell her all about the latest stuff he'd found out about what he was working on. She was the one he told everything to about this book of his.'

'And where will I find her?'

Percy looked at him, puzzled. 'Why, at the British Museum, of course. That's where she works. I told you she used to take him his lunch at work, well that's how she got the job at the museum. He was doing some work there and one day when she took him his lunch she heard someone say there was a vacancy coming up, so she applied. She's smart like that, is our Jenny.'

Daniel frowned. 'I'm sorry, but I haven't come across a Jenny Jedding while I've been at the museum.'

'That's cos her name ain't Jedding no more, not since she got married to her husband, Tom, last year. It's Jenny Warren now.'

* * *

'Miss Fenton!'

Abigail saw the figure of Jenny Warren approaching. The girl looked nervous, which was understandable in view of what she'd been through.

'Yes, Jenny. And please, call me Abigail.'

Jenny shook her head. 'No, miss, I couldn't. It wouldn't be proper.'

Abigail gave an inward sigh at this, reflecting that people would never better themselves, no matter how good they were, so long as they remained in thrall to these supposed levels of society. The trouble was, though, she had to admit, if everyone threw off these conventions it could lead to anarchy.

'I was wondering, miss, if there was any news. About . . . about the murder? The one I saw. I know the police say the person who did them has been caught, that girl, Elsie Bowler, but . . .'

And she gulped and gave a shudder. *Poor girl*, thought Abigail. *She's not convinced, she's worried the killer might still be out there and coming after her next. Maybe I can tell her something that might ease her fears, give her a clue that we might be on the trail of the real killer.*

'Actually, Mr Wilson and I feel the same way, that the police might be on the wrong track, but we think we're close to finding out who the real culprit is,' she said.

'Oh?' asked Jenny.

'Yes. It's possible that the murders were done as an act of revenge because of the wrong that had been done to someone.'

'Who?' asked Jenny, and Abigail could see the tension in the girl's face.

'A man called William Jedding. It seems that Professor Pickering may well have stolen the material for his book on Ambrosius from this Mr Jedding.'

Jenny gaped at her, startled. 'How do you know this, miss?' she asked.

'Mr Wilson and I have seen the letters from Mr Jedding complaining to the publishers that Pickering stole his work. In fact, I went to Mr Jedding's home to try and talk to him, but sadly, it seems, he killed himself. We think it may have killed himself because of guilt, because it's likely that he was the one who killed the professor. But the second murder, it couldn't have been Jedding who killed the publisher, Mr Whetstone, because he was dead by then. We think it's someone who was close to Mr Jedding who did the second murder, revenge on Mr Whetstone for being in league with Professor Pickering. In fact, that's where Mr Wilson is at the moment. He's gone to see Mr Jedding's family to see if they can throw any light on who it might be. To see if there was anyone he was particularly close to.'

Jenny stared at Abigail, a stunned look on her face. Then she swallowed hard and nodded.

'Yes,' she said hoarsely. 'That makes sense. And that's what it all means.'

'What?' asked Abigail, puzzled. '"What it all means"?'

Jenny swallowed hard again, then said in barely a whisper, 'I found something. I need to show it to you.'

'What?' asked Abigail.

The girl shook her head. 'I need to show it to you,' she repeated. 'It proves what you just said. About Mr Jedding.'

Immediately, Abigail was alert. At last! Proof! 'Where is it?' she asked.

'I've got it hidden,' said Jenny. 'You'll have to come with me.'

'Where?'

'Here, in the museum,' said Jenny. She looked nervously

around. 'But don't tell anyone else. Not till I've shown it to you.'

Abigail nodded. 'Lead on,' she said.

Ned Carson kept back on the stairs that led down to the basement and the conveniences, and watched as the Fenton woman and the girl went through the door marked 'Storeroom. Staff Only'. Something was up, but what? He knew he'd been on to a winner when he made his decision: forget Daniel Wilson, follow the Fenton woman. Wilson's lover.

The girl was wearing the uniform of one of the stewards. Carson had been intrigued when he'd seen the Fenton woman and the girl walk together down the stairs that led to the conveniences. There could be a simple reason for it, one of them needing to use the toilet, but why did they go down there together? And now, instead, they'd gone into the storeroom. What on earth were they up to?

Rather than be caught hanging around outside the conveniences, he went back up the stairs and into the main reception area, keeping an eye on the stairs. It was ten minutes before the girl reappeared, and now she was alone. Where was the Fenton woman?

He was tempted to go and engage the girl in conversation, genial chat, and see what turned up. But he noticed there was a tenseness about her. She was looking this way and that, watchful. Any attempt to chat to her would be rebuffed. But there was definitely something going on.

He watched the girl walk to the main reception desk, where she waited until the man on duty's attention was diverted by a patron asking a question before slipping an envelope on the desk. Then she darted away, heading back towards the stairs that led down to the basement.

Carson sidled to the reception desk and took a look at the envelope. It was addressed to Mr Daniel Wilson.

He was tempted to snaffle it and take a look at the contents, but saw the envelope was stuck down. But he was sure that whatever it was, was to do with the young woman and Abigail Fenton. What was it? Some love tryst? Two women together? And where did Wilson fit in?

He made for the stairs where the girl had disappeared and began to make his way carefully down towards the basement.

There was no one around. He waited for ten minutes, but no one appeared from the ladies' convenience, nor the storeroom. Finally, he went to the storeroom door, opened it, and peered in. There were shelves loaded with bottles of brooms, dustpans, cleaning fluid, towels, unmarked boxes, but no sign of people.

He noticed a door at the far end of the storeroom and saw beside it a stack of oil lamps and boxes of candles, along with boxes of matches. He made his way to the door and quietly opened it. Immediately, his nostrils were assailed by the smell of damp. Stairs led down into the gloom, and then into darkness.

He stood listening and was fairly sure he could hear voices echoing somewhere in the distance.

So that's where they were. But what was going on?

CHAPTER FORTY-FOUR

Daniel was haunted by a chill of fear as he hurried back to the British Museum. The additional information he'd learnt from Jenny's brother confirmed it: the killer was Jenny Warren. William Jedding had shared everything about the book he was writing on Ambrosius with her, and she had shared his excitement in it. It was through her father that she'd got the job at the British Museum. When he was working on the rafters she used to bring him his lunch and sit with him, so she'd been there when word of the vacancy had arisen.

The man Jenny had married, Tom Warren, was a sailor, currently away at sea, so she was on her own most of the time in their small flat. No one to be made suspicious by her actions.

The sick feeling hit Daniel again at the thought that Abigail had been alone with the girl in her flat, questioning her. Even now, Abigail might be at risk if Jenny felt that Abigail and he might be getting close to the truth.

The first person he saw as he hurried into the building was Mrs Sawyer, the woman who'd looked after Jenny after the murder of Whetstone.

'Mrs Sawyer!' he called.

'Mr Wilson?' she queried.

'Where's Jenny Warren?'

Mrs Sawyer frowned.

'Actually, I don't know. Normally her station is the Greek and Roman rooms, but I went along there just now, just to check on her after what she'd gone through, but she wasn't there. Perhaps she's gone for a break, or something.'

Daniel thanked her, then hurried up to the small office he and Abigail shared. There was no sign of Abigail.

Fighting back a feeling of panic, Daniel ran from room to room, but there was still no sign of Abigail, not had anyone seen her. It was at his last port of call, the exit at the rear of the building, that the guard on duty nodded.

'Yes, I saw her. She was with young Jenny Warren, that poor thing.'

'Which way were they going?'

The man frowned. 'I'm not sure. A member of the public came up and started asking me about the opening times, so that kind of took up my attention.'

'Did they go outside?'

'They may have done. I'm not sure.'

With fear and panic definitely mounting, Daniel rushed to the main reception desk. 'Excuse me . . .' he began.

The face of the man behind the desk lit up as he saw Daniel. 'Ah, Mr Wilson!' he said. 'A message was left for you.'

'A message?'

'Yes. An envelope with your name on it.' He rummaged around in the drawer of the table, produced the envelope and handed it to Daniel.

The writing was unfamiliar, and Daniel felt a savage rush of disappointment; he'd hoped it might have been from Abigail. He opened the envelope, and as he read the letter inside he felt sick. It was from Jenny Warren.

Mr Wilson,

You know who I am and why I did it. I want my father's reputation made good. I am holding your friend. I want a statement put on the front page of tomorrow's Times *and another big national newspaper saying that William Jedding was the one who did all that work on Ambrosius, and Pickering stole it.*

Put a copy of those two papers in every room in the museum. If the statement isn't in them, I'll kill her.

Daniel raced up the stairs to Ashford's office and found the manager at work on his ledgers.

'Mr Ashford!' said Daniel.

Ashford was immediately alerted by the urgent tone in Daniel's voice, took the note that Daniel thrust at him and read it.

'My God!' he exclaimed. 'Who . . . ?'

'Jenny Warren,' said Daniel.

'Jenny Warren?!' repeated Ashford, shocked. 'But . . . but . . .'

'We need to take this to Sir Jasper. Is he in?'

'Yes,' said Ashford.

Daniel took the note back from him. 'There's no time to lose if we're going to keep Miss Fenton alive,' he said. 'We're going to need his help with *The Times*. And I'll need your information as to the layout of the museum.'

'In what way?' asked Ashford.

'Jenny Warren has got a hiding place somewhere here. We need to find out where it is.'

'I'll bring the plans of the museum,' said Ashford. 'You go on to tell Sir Jasper. I'll collect the plans and see you in his office.'

Daniel hurried on to Sir Jasper's office, this time doing without the protocol of checking with his secretary. Sir Jasper was reading a newspaper when Daniel rapped urgently at his door and rushed in.

'Jenny Warren is the person who killed Whetstone, Sir Jasper!' said Daniel.

'But . . . but she was the one who found him!' said Sir Jasper.

'That was her being very clever. A case of hiding in plain sight,' said Daniel. He handed him Jenny's note. 'She may also be the one who killed Professor Pickering, although that may have been her father, William Jedding. She's now taken Miss Fenton hostage and is threatening to kill her unless we put this announcement in tomorrow's *Times* and another major newspaper. I have a contact at the *Daily Telegraph* who I'm sure will help, but I don't know anybody at *The Times*.'

'I know the editor quite well,' said Sir Jasper. 'In fact, we were at school together and I used to help him with his revisions for exams, so I'm sure he'll come through for us.'

The door opened and Ashford entered, holding rolls of building plans in cradled in his arms.

'I have the plans,' he said.

'I've told Mr Ashford about the letter and the threat to Miss Fenton,' said Daniel to Sir Jasper.

Ashford put the rolls of plans down on a table. Sir Jasper tapped the note from Jenny. 'This business of her wanting a copy of the newspapers put in every room.'

'She's obviously hiding somewhere in the museum,' said Daniel. 'Just as she did before, when she carried out that attack and painted "Who killed Ambrosius?" on the wall by the exhibition. We need to find out where her hiding place is, which is why I asked Mr Ashford for the plans of the museum.'

'Wouldn't it be better to wait and see what happens tomorrow morning?' asked Sir Jasper. 'If we put guards everywhere we can catch her when she appears to look at the newspapers.'

'If that's what she's really planning to do,' said Daniel. 'There's also the possibility that this is a ploy and she'll leave the museum before tomorrow morning, satisfied that her father's reputation is going to be salvaged.'

'And you're worried what might happen to Miss Fenton if she does that,' said Ashford.

'Exactly,' said Daniel. 'The only clue we've got as to where she might be hiding is the fact that she used to bring her father lunch when he was working here.' He turned to Ashford. 'So, if you can find out what he was working on, it may help us narrow down the places she'd be familiar with and where she might have her hiding place.'

'What was his name again?' asked Ashford.

'William Jedding. He was a carpenter.'

Ashford's face creased into a thoughtful frown. 'Jedding. Jedding,' he muttered. Then his face brightened. 'Yes! I remember him! An excellent worker!'

'What was he working on?' asked Daniel.

'Some rafters in the roof were in need of repair. It was quite a complicated job, so he was here for quite a time. Two months, as I recall.'

Daniel groaned. 'The place where he and Jenny used to have lunch can't have been in the roof, there's no space there. Every part of the roof is covered in skylights to let light in, and there's only about a foot of space between the ceilings and the roof. And the walls between the rooms are solid, no hidden places there.'

'As I remember, the builders and carpenters kept their tools and equipment in the old tunnels beneath the Reading Room,' said Ashford. 'It was the best way to make sure the museum was kept open to the public while the work was being carried out. That's where they used to go for their breaks.' He began to unroll one of the plans. 'Unfortunately, the plans don't show the whole network of tunnels.'

'How big are these tunnels? How far do they stretch?'

Ashford gave a heavy sigh and said, 'Miles.'

'Miles?' echoed Daniel, stunned.

Ashford nodded. 'It might appear that there are just a few small tunnels going off from the basement, but when the Reading Room in the Great Court was being constructed in the late 1850s and they dug down to put in the foundations, they uncovered a whole network of tunnels. Obviously, I wasn't here myself then, but I heard about it from the people who were here at the time, and also, I've seen the documents that supported the discovery.

'Remember, London is two thousand years old, and in that time, buildings were often constructed on top of existing buildings and even roadways, especially Roman, so those older buildings and roadways became a network of tunnels. Also, there are rivers running beneath London, like the Fleet and the Tyburn, and many others, which were once open rivers but were built over and now run through tunnels.

'Then there were the catacombs, burial places and tunnels that were dug so that people could get away if threatened during all of the many civil wars that have happened over the centuries. Some of the tunnels will be dead ends, some will have crumbled, but some will link with others that can go as far as the very outskirts of the city. And if you come across one of the underground rivers it could take you all the way to the Thames.

'Dangerous, of course. And you'd need light of some sort to be able to see. But for those fleeing for their lives, it was a risk worth taking.'

'Our only hope is that Jenny hasn't taken Abigail too far down these tunnels, but has stayed within touching distance of the basement,' said Daniel. He turned to Ashford. 'Can you show me the way into these tunnels?'

'Certainly,' said Ashford. 'At the back of the storeroom in the basement between the gentlemen's and ladies' conveniences is a door that goes down some steps. But you'll need a lamp.'

'Of course!' groaned Daniel as realisation struck him. 'That's where she or Jedding hid when Pickering was killed. And I'm now starting to think it was Jenny Warren who killed Pickering,

318

not her father.' He stood up. 'I'm going to see my contact at the *Telegraph* and get the announcement in tomorrow's paper. Then I'm going to Scotland Yard to enlist Inspector Feather's help in searching the tunnels.'

'If she is in the tunnels and she hears you coming, she might kill Miss Fenton before fleeing,' said Ashford.

'It's a chance we have to take,' said Daniel. 'If we don't, Abigail could well die down there anyway.'

Carson made his way slowly along the narrow tunnel using one of the oil lamps to show him the way. Every now and then he heard a rustling that startled him, until he realised it was rats. Of course this place, with its smell of underground rivers, would be crawling with them.

Was he in the right tunnel? There seemed to be a maze of them. He was following what he was sure were voices, but they still seemed to be muffled and distant. They were hiding, that was sure. No, not *they*; the girl was hiding.

A thrill went through him. Wilson had said he wasn't a real reporter. Well, this would show him! At last, he had a *real* story. In some way it was definitely connected to the murders. Whoever the girl was, she was involved. An accomplice of the murderer, most likely. The mystery was why she'd brought the Fenton woman down here? Maybe she'd taken the Fenton woman prisoner. Possibly a hostage. Was that what had been in the note she'd left for Wilson at the main reception? A ransom note?

Where were they? This was to be the story he'd been waiting for all his life, and he didn't want to miss a word. The *People's Voice* had been a good vehicle for him, but the story he'd produce now would push him into the top ranks of *real* reporters. Those people like Joe Dalton who'd spent years sneering at him – behind his back, admittedly, but he knew what they felt about him and the *Voice* – would have to change their tune.

CHAPTER FORTY-FIVE

Daniel leapt down from the hansom cab and ran into the building on Fleet Street that housed the offices of the *Daily Telegraph*, driven by the thought of Abigail being held prisoner by Jenny Warren.

'Is Joe Dalton in?' he asked the receptionist.

She consulted her list and said, 'Yes, he's in today. His office is—'

'I know where his office is,' said Daniel.

He ran up the stairs to the second floor and found Dalton at his desk in the large, open room where the reporters wrote their copy. Dalton was scribbling away when he saw Daniel approach.

'Daniel!'

'I worried you might be out somewhere,' said Daniel.

'I'm still dealing with the aftermath of Armstrong's announcement,' said Joe. 'I don't know if you saw what Ned Carson wrote in his rag?'

'I don't give the *People's Voice* house-room,' said Daniel.

'Well, his take on the superintendent's speech may interest you,' said Joe. He located a copy of the *People's Voice* from a pile of newspapers on his desk and handed it to Daniel. 'Page three,' he said.

Daniel turned to page three and saw the headline: *What are the Police Hiding?*

Eager to tell Dalton his reason for his visit, Daniel scanned the report quickly, but then read it again. Fortunately, as with most pieces in the *Voice*, it was short:

Yesterday we were told by Superintendent Armstrong of the Scotland Yard with the greatest confidence that the recent murders at the British Museum had been solved. They were committed, according to this smug oaf, by a seventeen-year-old vagabond orphan girl who was taken prisoner while digging for bones and coins in the mud of the Thames along with other mudlarks. We were told that she is insane, too mad to stand trial. How very convenient. This way the brave superintendent solves two notorious murders without fear of his investigative powers being questioned.

Today the Voice *sends out a warning to all other mudlarks and those other poor orphaned souls with no one to look after them: Superintendent Armstrong is after you. The next time a major crime is committed, you, too, may find yourself picked up and locked away in Bedlam. Case solved.*

The Voice *asks: What are the police hiding?*

'Carson's usual line,' said Dalton. 'Attack the police.'

'In this case he's right,' said Daniel.

He told Dalton about the note from Jenny Warren, the threat to kill Abigail, and Jenny's demand for an announcement to be put on the front page of the newspapers about her father being the true author of the book on Ambrosius.

'If she's got Abigail, trust me, I'll make sure our editor puts it on the front page. But how sure are you that this Warren girl will keep her word and let Abigail go?'

'I'm not,' admitted Daniel. 'That's why I'm going to go looking for her. I'm fairly sure she's holding Abigail prisoner somewhere in the old tunnels under the Reading Room in the museum.'

'On your own?'

'If I have to, but I'm going to Scotland Yard next to try and get help from John Feather.'

'I thought you were barred from the Yard.'

'I am, but Armstrong isn't going to stop me asking.'

'John Feather's a good man, but he's answerable to Armstrong. If Armstrong says no . . .' He thought for a moment, then said, 'How about if I come to the Yard with you? I can go and see John Feather and tell him you're outside, waiting for him, and it's urgent.'

'Thanks, Joe, but I think you doing the story for your front page for tomorrow's early edition has greater priority. And I need to get a move on to search for Jenny Warren and Abigail, so I guess I'm going to have to take my chance about running into Armstrong.'

'In that case, once I've put my story in and know it's got the editor's approval, I'll make for the Yard and seek out John Feather. If he's still there I'll know you never got past Armstrong and I'll fill him in.'

'Thanks, Joe. One thing, the *Telegraph* won't be the only one with the story on its front page. Jenny Warren insisted it went in *The Times*. Sir Jasper Stone's arranging that.'

'Fair enough,' said Dalton. 'But when this is over and you've got Abigail back, you'll tell me the whole story?'

'I will,' promised Daniel. 'And thanks for saying "when", not "if" we get her back.'

'I know you, Daniel. I've seen the way you are with her. If there's anyone can save her, it's you.'

Daniel left the *Telegraph* offices with Dalton's last words echoing in his mind. In spite of what Dalton had said, he knew that saving Abigail was still an 'if' – and a very, very big if at that.

Carson had found them. He'd located the voices, mainly one voice, that of the girl, and followed the course of the tunnel until he saw the glow from a lamp coming from a deep recess at one side. He turned out the lamp he carried and edged nearer, desperate not to make a noise.

'This is where me and Dad used to come for lunch,' he heard the girl say, and Fenton respond with, 'It's a long way. There were other places a lot nearer.'

'Me and Dad didn't mind,' said the girl. 'We preferred to be away from the others. They didn't talk about the things we were interested in. Here, we could talk about things without the others listening. Mainly it was about his book and Ambrosius.'

Carefully, Carson sat down. Rats scurried around him, but he did his best to ignore them. Ignore the rats and they'd ignore him, that's what an old sailor had once told him. Whether it was true or not, this story was too big for him to be scared off by a few rats.

He noticed that a glimmer of light shone near him where there was a crack in the tunnel wall. He put his eye to the crack and peered in at the scene. The girl was sitting on a heap of stone. The Fenton woman was sitting on the ground, her hands tied together at the wrists, the other end of the rope looped through an old iron ring set into the wall of the recess. Carson strained his ears and listened.

For Abigail, the rocky floor of the recess was uncomfortable, but she knew her only way out of this situation was to sit and listen, let the girl talk; but she couldn't take her eyes off the knife that Jenny held in her lap.

'The book that Dad wrote about Ambrosius was what made his life worth living,' said Jenny. 'Life's hard when you're poor and you're living in an area like the back of King's Cross, and you see all the rich people and those who've got everything when life's a struggle, like it was for Dad. Mum had her own problems, but different ones. She was never well. Depressed. It got worse after the babies died. She had Percy first, then me, then later she had three more, but one was stillborn and the other two both died at birth. It sort of finished her. She had no zest for life. Not like Dad. He wanted to *do* things. He was a good carpenter, one of the best, but he wanted to do something different, something that lasted.

'He was always searching through rubbish, looking for things that might be useful, and one day he found this book. It was about King Arthur, and it had stuff in it by these old writers from long ago. People with funny names.'

'Gildas,' said Abigail. 'The Venerable Bede. Nennius.'

'That's them,' said Jenny. 'And there was one bit in it that said about this bloke, Ambrosius, and one of them said he was the real

Arthur. And that got Dad thinking. We'd always been told that King Arthur was a story, not real. But Dad wondered: say he was based on someone real? And he started to go looking for stories about this Ambrosius character. He started looking in the British Museum, in the Reading Room, and then he started looking in second-hand bookshops. He used to get all excited when he found something about him, this Ambrosius. Then one day he said to me, "I'm going to write a book about him, Jenny. About how this Ambrosius and King Arthur were one and the same. And it'll be published, and my name will be on it."

'I was the one he talked to about it because there was no one else he could talk about it to. Mum had her own problems, and she didn't care about this Ambrosius, or King Arthur. And as for books of any sort, she can't read, so she wasn't interested. Same with Percy. He can read, but only just. He's not interested. But me, I always loved books and reading. I take after Dad, see.

'When Dad found something new and wrote about it, he used to give it to me to read. Mainly so I could check the spelling and put it in the right grammar, that sort of thing. Dad was clever, but spelling and stuff wasn't what he was best at. So, I knew every part of that book as he wrote it.

'About a year ago he said he'd finished it. Everything he wanted to say about Ambrosius being King Arthur was there, all the proof taken from these old writers you said: the Battle of Badon, the knights in armour which was Ambrosius and his troop of cavalry – everything. The trouble was, he didn't know what to do with it, how to go about getting it published. You see, he was just a carpenter from the lowest level of society, living by the canal at the back of King's Cross. He was worried that no one would take him seriously, these big publishers and the toffs who run everything. So, he thought about finding someone who'd back him. He said that was the way it was done in the old days; people like Shakespeare found a rich patron who'd help him put his plays on, or someone like Geoffrey Chaucer would find a well-known bloke with connections who'd persuade a publisher to print his *Canterbury Tales*.

'Dad had done a lot of reading, including some articles in magazines, and he found some by this Professor Pickering who'd written about Ambrosius. Not as well as Dad had done, nor as much, but for Dad it meant that there was this proper professor who would know what he was writing about, and he was sure would help to get Dad's book into print. So, Dad took a chance. He found out where the professor lived and took his book round to his house, along with a letter which I helped him write, and handed it in to the professor's housekeeper. And then he waited.

'Nothing happened. He never got a reply. I was a bit worried when after three months he still hadn't heard, but he said that was the way it was when you were dealing with top people like the professor. They were very busy with their own work and stuff like Dad's had to be fitted in.

'When months went by and he still hadn't heard he wrote again, but got no reply. And then, suddenly he hears about this book on Ambrosius coming out by this same professor. He's shocked. We're both shocked, but he says, "Let's not make judgement until we've seen it."

'So, he got a copy of the book, and he read it. Then he gave it to me to read. I can still see him sitting in our kitchen, tears rolling down his cheeks as I read it. It was his book. My dad's. Every word. Some parts had been changed round, but only a bit.

'We told Percy about it, and he said we should sue and make lots of money. That's all he was interested in, he wasn't really bothered about what Dad was suffering. But we knew we couldn't sue. For one thing, Dad hadn't made a copy of his book, the one he sent to Professor Pickering was the only copy. Next, who'd believe him: a carpenter from one of the poorest areas of London against the word of some high-up professor. So, Dad wrote to the publisher telling them what had happened and asking for it to be put right.'

'I've seen the letters,' said Abigail.

'Then you'll know what that crook Whetstone said in reply,' said Jenny bitterly.

'He was acting on what Professor Pickering told him.'

Jenny shook her head. 'He must have known. He was just as bad.'

'Not as bad,' said Abigail. 'The professor was the real crook. Whetstone was protecting his investment, the publication of the book.'

'Money!' snorted Jenny derisively. 'That's all either of them was interested in. Not Dad. Dad wasn't interested in money. All he wanted was to be known as the person who made the connection between King Arthur and Ambrosius. To be accepted!' Slowly, she calmed down, then resumed, 'Anyway, what Pickering and Whetstone did destroyed Dad. They took his life away. He carried on with the carpentry because he had to put food on the table, but it was like he was dead already. The exhibition coming to the museum with Dad's book as the centrepiece – under that lousy professor's name – was the last straw for me. When I knew he was coming I decided there was only one thing to do to make things right and that was to kill him. So I did. I planned it all out and did it.

'It felt great. Straight after I'd done it I went to where Dad was working and told him what I'd done, that I'd avenged the wrong that had been done to him. To us.'

Her head dropped, and Abigail realised that Jenny was crying, great heaving sobs. When she raised her head and looked at Abigail, her expression angry, even in the dim light Abigail could see the wetness on her cheeks.

'I thought he'd be pleased. He wasn't. He stared at me in shock and said "No, no, no." And then he started crying. I'd never seen him cry as bad as that before. Not even when he realised his work had been stolen. Nor when the babies were born and died. This time . . . he just wept. And then he put his coat on and went out.

'I should have followed him, but I didn't know what to do, so I left him alone, thinking we'd talk later and it would be alright. But it wasn't.' She started to cry again, and through her tears she said, 'He killed himself that same day. Because of what I'd done.'

'No,' said Abigail, 'because of what Pickering had done.'

'Yes!' burst out Jenny, suddenly shouting out loud. 'Yes! That's what I saw afterwards. It was Pickering, and that publisher, Whetstone! I did what I did because of them and what they did to Dad. They'd killed Dad. Pickering had paid, but that still left that rat Whetstone. And then we were told that he was coming to the museum. It was as if God was sending him to me for punishment.'

'You killed him.'

'I did. And this time I made sure I did it with one stab of the knife. Not like with Pickering. I thought I'd caught Pickering unawares, but he tried to fight me off, so I stuck him and stuck him until I was sure he was dead.' She stopped, suddenly alert. 'What was that?' she said.

'I didn't hear anything,' said Abigail.

'Ssshhh!' whispered Jenny sharply. She stood up.

Ned Carson put his eye to the crack in the wall and saw the girl get up, and saw that she was holding a knife. A bolt of fear went through him and he started to move back.

'There it is again!' he heard the girl say.

Carson ran. It was one thing to track them to this place, it was another to face a murderer armed with a knife in these tunnels. He abandoned his unlit oil lamp and ran by the dim glow coming from the recess in the tunnel. He could hear the girl behind him, her feet scrabbling on the gravel and rocks.

He ran blindly, then stopped as he hit darkness. He felt sick with fear, but forced himself to edge forward, hands held in front of him searching the darkness for sudden walls. Which way? Was he in the tunnel that would lead him back the way he'd come? He couldn't tell. The blessing was that there was no light coming after him, so no oil lamp. Had the girl given up? Maybe she'd decided to go in a different direction, find an escape route that would take her to one of the old underground rivers. He'd heard about the rivers that ran beneath London.

Perhaps his best course of action would be to find a recess to hide in. Just wait and let the girl go, then make his way back to the museum when he was sure it was safe for him to move. If he could find his way there, that was. Without a lamp or a candle to light his way, he was blind. His only way was to work along the tunnel by feel, letting his hands be his eyes.

He began to edge forward, stretching out his hands until they touched rock. Slowly, he shuffled forward, his hands touching the rocky surface. A sound just behind him made him stop. Then he heard the girl say, 'I learnt to see in the dark when I was down here.'

The next second a savage pain ripped into his back, then another, and another, and finally he felt the knife blade slice into the flesh of his neck, and then he felt himself tumbling into an even thicker blackness than before.

CHAPTER FORTY-SIX

As Daniel walked into the main reception area of Scotland Yard, his heart sank as he saw the burly figure of Superintendent Armstrong heading towards the door.

'What are you doing here?' demanded Armstrong. 'You're banned from here. Now get out before I have you arrested!'

'I'm here because I know who killed Professor Pickering and Mansfield Whetstone.'

'So do I,' growled Armstrong. 'That mad girl in Bedlam.'

'No,' said Daniel. 'A man called William Jedding and his daughter, Jenny Warren. We have her written confession to the crime.'

Armstrong stared at Daniel, then spluttered 'This is madness! Nonsense!'

'It's absolutely true,' said Daniel firmly.

'Where is it?' snapped Armstrong. He held out his hand. 'Where's this supposed confession?'

'Sir Jasper Stone has it at the British Museum. You can see it when we go there.'

Armstrong looked at Daniel, still obviously bewildered by this turn of events. 'Why should I go there?'

'It doesn't have to be you, it can be Inspector Feather and a few men, but right now we need Scotland Yard's assistance to arrest this girl.'

'Why?'

'Because she's holding Miss Fenton hostage in the tunnels beneath the British Museum and has threatened to kill her. As she's already killed, I don't believe it's an idle threat.'

Armstrong stared at Daniel, and Daniel could see the superintendent's mind was in turmoil.

'Superintendent, I know you don't like me, but ask yourself: have I ever lied to you or tried to deceive you? Miss Fenton is in mortal danger, and we have the chance of bringing a murderer to justice. If we act fast.'

Armstrong hesitated, then said, 'Let's go and see Inspector Feather.'

Jenny walked back into the small recess, wiping the knife on her dress.

'That's it,' she said. 'That's another one gone. They'll hang me for sure now if they catch me.'

'Not necessarily,' said Abigail. 'The girl who stabbed Mrs Pickering's artist friend, her name's Elsie Bowler, and she's also the

333

one who was arrested and charged with the murders of Professor Pickering and Mr Whetstone.'

'Yeah, I know. I saw it in the papers,' grunted Jenny. 'That fool of a police superintendent.'

Abigail looked at her in surprise.

'But you asked me if there was any news—' she began.

'Because you're cleverer than that police superintendent. I couldn't see you believing the story. I needed to know if I was in the clear. And once you said what you said, I knew I wasn't.'

'The thing is that Elsie Bowler is in Bethlem Hospital,' said Abigail. 'They say she's lost her mind. She'll never stand trial. They won't hang her. They'll say the same of you. You were driven insane by grief because of what happened to your father. You won't hang. Mr Wilson and I will see you get a proper lawyer to put your case . . .'

'Mr Wilson and you!' spat Jenny, her face contorted with anger. 'It's because of you I'm in this spot! If you'd left it alone that mad girl would have got the blame for the killings!' She glared at Abigail, her expression full of defiant determination. 'I'm not going to spend the rest of my life in no madhouse, either. I'm gonna make sure your Wilson does what I told him and puts that piece about my dad being the real writer of that book about Ambrosius in the papers for everyone to see, then I'm off. I'll disappear and start life new as someone else. Somewhere far away. A different country.'

'What about your husband?' asked Abigail. 'Your family?'

'What about them!' snapped Jenny. 'Tom's away most of the time, he won't notice. And as for Ma and Percy, we had nothing in common any more once Dad died. Even before that.' She advanced towards Abigail, the knife pointed at her. 'Trouble is, you're a loose end I can't leave behind. You know everything there is, and I can't have that hanging over me.'

'You can't kill me!' appealed Abigail. 'I can help you! I know people. Influential people.'

'So what? Like I say, I ain't gonna spend the rest of my life in a madhouse. And you've only got yourself to blame, really. If you'd left it alone, we wouldn't be here. So, you've got to be shut up, and the only way for that to happen is for you to die.'

The police van pulled up outside the museum and the party strode purposefully across the concourse led by Superintendent Armstrong, with Daniel, Inspector Feather, Sergeant Cribbens and two uniformed constables following. Sir Jasper Stone and David Ashford were waiting anxiously in the reception area for them and hurried towards them as they walked through the main doors.

'Can I see the letter from this girl?' demanded Armstrong.

Sir Jasper took it from his pocket and handed it to the superintendent, who read it through.

'That's good enough,' he said. 'Where's this way in to the tunnels?'

'I'll show you,' said Daniel.

'There are oil lamps and candles in the storeroom,' said Ashford. 'But it is a maze down there, with tunnels going off in different directions. There's a fork in two directions shortly after you go down.'

'In that case, Inspector Feather and Sergeant Cribbens will go down one. Wilson and I will search the other. The two constables will wait by the entrance, ready to come if we call.' He looked questioningly at Daniel. 'That alright, Wilson?'

'That's fine by me,' said Daniel.

Armstrong turned to Sir Jasper. 'I need to inform you that Inspector Feather and I are both armed, Sir Jasper. This is in view of the fact that we are dealing with a very dangerous person, who I believe must be unstable. Anyone who kills two people in the way she did has got to be unbalanced.'

'This way,' said Daniel.

He led the party down the stairs to the basement, and into the storeroom. Daniel, Armstrong, Feather and Cribbens each took an oil lamp, lit it, and went through the rear door to the entrance to the tunnels.

'Damp,' said Armstrong, sniffing.

'Underground rivers, sir,' said Cribbens. 'My uncle was a Thames waterman and he told me about them.'

'I suggest we maintain silence, so we can listen out for the girl,' said Daniel.

Armstrong nodded, and the four men began their search, moving at a careful pace over the uneven ground. As Ashford had told them, they soon arrived at a fork where the tunnel split in two directions. Daniel stood and strained his ears, but couldn't pick up any sounds in either of the tunnels. It was Armstrong who took the decision, heading determinedly down one of the tunnels. Daniel followed the superintendent, while John Feather and Sergeant Cribbens went in the other direction.

'There's lots of nooks and crannies along here,' whispered Cribbens.

John Feather put his finger to his lips to urge his sergeant to keep silent. Even a whisper could get picked up by their quarry and warn her. But it was true about the nooks and crannies and recesses at intervals along this section of the tunnel. They could see scraps of paper and stubs of candles in many of them, but they looked to be left over from some time before and not recent.

Feather pulled the pistol from his pocket. If they were suddenly attacked, he didn't want the gun getting caught up in the cloth of his coat and losing valuable seconds. The fact was that he and Cribbens were holding oil lamps which illuminated them and showed any hidden assailant where they were. In contrast, Jenny Warren seemed to be hiding in the safety of the darkness. She could be anywhere, especially as some of the recesses seemed to be quite deep, offering a hiding place.

He strained his ears, listening for voices, but heard none.

What had the girl done with Abigail? There was a sick feeling deep in his stomach at the thought that she could already be dead.

Armstrong continued to lead the way, moving slowly, lamp held high, casting an eerie glow on the floor of the tunnel ahead of them. In the darkness around them, he and Daniel heard the scuttling of rats, which kept well out of the lamplight. Daniel calculated they'd been walking for about fifteen minutes. At their speed he guessed they'd travelled about a quarter of a mile, but there was still no sign of Jenny Warren or Abigail.

Suddenly Armstrong stopped and gestured ahead. Daniel looked past him, and when he saw the crumpled figure lying in the dim light of their oil lamps he felt sick. He pushed past Armstrong and ran to the still figure, and as he neared it he felt a surge of relief when he saw it was the body of a man. He was lying face down. Daniel lifted his head and recognised the dead man as Ned Carson.

'Carson,' grunted Armstrong. 'That man's been the bane of my life.'

'He's not going to be anyone's bane any more,' said Daniel. 'But what was he doing down here?'

'Anyway, we're on the right track,' said Armstrong, pointing to the vicious open wound in Carson's throat.

If she's done this to Carson, what's happened to Abigail? Daniel asked himself, petrified at the thought that Abigail had met the same fate.

Daniel moved forward, keeping the lead, but this time he moved slower, eyes and ears alert. Suddenly, he thought he heard a movement behind him. It could be rats, but . . .

He turned and saw the figure of Jenny, her face contorted with anger, leaping towards Armstrong, who was just behind him, the knife pointing straight at the superintendent's back. Daniel pushed Armstrong to one side and thrust his lamp at Jenny, but her speed kept her moving forward, and suddenly Daniel felt a savage stabbing pain in his chest. The next second he was falling backwards, and everything began to go black. The last thing he heard was an explosion as a gunshot rang out, the sound filling the tunnel.

CHAPTER FORTY-SEVEN

Daniel woke, his eyelids flickering. His head felt fuzzy, as if there was a fog in his brain. There was a dull pain in his chest.

'Daniel!'

He forced his eyes open and looked towards the sound of her voice. Abigail's. Was he hallucinating?

No. She was there, sitting beside the bed, looking anxiously at him. Where was he?

A hospital room. A private room.

'Abigail.' At least, that's what he tried to say, but his tongue felt enormous in his mouth.

'Thank God! You've been unconscious for two days.'

'How did you . . . ?' he stumbled.

'John Feather and his sergeant found me.' She reached out and took one of his hands in both of hers, holding it tightly, and as his eyes adjusted he saw the traces of wet on her cheeks. Tears.

She released his hand and stood up. 'I'll go and tell a nurse you're awake. Are you in pain?'

'Yes. No.' He still felt befuddled.

'They've kept you dosed up with laudanum,' said Abigail. 'I'll be back in just a moment.'

She hurried away from his bed. Daniel looked around the room. He'd never been in a private room in a hospital before, only in the public wards. Sir Jasper and the British Museum were paying for it, he guessed.

He wondered how badly he'd been hurt. He remembered being stabbed, the pain in his chest. Not in his heart, obviously, or he'd be dead. Had the knife penetrated his lung? He took a breath in and let it slowly out again. No sharp pain. He took a bigger breath, and this time felt a dull ache, a throbbing inside his chest. But no sharp pain. Was that a good sign?

A movement at the door caught his attention, and he saw that Abigail had returned with a nurse and a doctor, a bearded man in his forties.

'If you'll excuse me, Miss Fenton, I'll need to examine Mr Wilson,' said the doctor.

'I'll wait in the corridor,' said Abigail.

She left and pulled the door shut behind her.

'You have a rare ministering angel there, Mr Wilson,' said the doctor as he pulled the bedclothes down and began to undo the bandage around Daniel's chest. 'She's been by your bedside since you were brought in two days ago.'

Yes, thought Daniel. *She's rare indeed.*

'Where am I?' stumbled Daniel, his voice hoarse and croaky.

'You're at Charing Cross Hospital.'

'How . . . how badly am I injured?'

'You were lucky,' said the doctor. 'The person who did it missed your vital organs, thanks to the blade being deflected by your ribs. But the knife still went in quite deep, and your flesh needed some sewing together. With plenty of rest you should make a good recovery.' With the nurse supporting Daniel, the doctor peeled the bandage away, then removed the gauze beneath. Daniel looked down at the gash, which had been sewn up and was surrounded by a large bruise coloured yellow and purple.

'It looks poisoned,' said Daniel.

'On the contrary, this is an anti-poison. We've treated the wound with carbolic acid, a compound of coal tar, which acts as an antiseptic. More people used to die during surgery from infection than from the surgery itself, but thanks to the work of Joseph Lister those deaths from infections have been seriously reduced. It's thanks to Dr Lister you'll be making a full recovery.'

'And thanks to you,' added Daniel.

'We all play a part,' said the doctor. 'We'll put some more carbolic acid on, to make sure, and clean you up, and then Miss Fenton can come back in.'

It was some hours later. Daniel had drifted off to sleep under the effects of more laudanum, waking to find Abigail still beside his bed.

'You should go home and rest,' he said, pushing himself up to a sitting position in the bed.

'I will, now I know you're going to be alright,' she said. 'But I wanted to be here when you woke.'

'Thank you,' said Daniel. He took a sip of water, his tongue feeling less like a dry sponge in his mouth. 'What happened to Jenny Warren?'

'Superintendent Armstrong shot her. She's dead.'

'She killed that reporter, Ned Carson. She must have found him down there.'

'She did,' said Abigail. 'I think he must have followed her, trying to get a story.'

'But she didn't kill you.'

'No,' said Abigail. 'She said she was going to. Then she appeared to change her mind. I don't know why.' She looked at the clock. 'It's six o'clock. I shall go home now, but I'll return tomorrow morning.'

'I love you, Abigail Fenton,' said Daniel.

'Then don't ever do that to me again,' said Abigail.

'Do what?'

'Nearly get yourself killed.'

As she stood up, Daniel said, 'Can you send a telegram to Ben Stilworthy, the man whose bed and breakfast place in Birmingham Jerrold Watts is staying at, telling him that it's safe for Mr Smith to return to London.'

'Of course. What's his address?'

Daniel told her, and she wrote it down.

'Consider it done,' she said. She leant down and kissed him. 'Sleep well tonight, my love.'

Evening came, and Daniel was just preparing to slide down in the bed and drift off to sleep – the drowsiness an effect of the laudanum he was being given, he suspected – when the bulky figure of Superintendent Armstrong entered his room. He stood in the doorway, surveying Daniel for a moment, then he walked in and stood by the bed.

'You're awake,' he said.

'I am,' said Daniel.

'They thought you might not make it when you first came in.'

'I didn't know much about it,' admitted Daniel.

There was pause, then Armstrong grunted, 'I've come to thank you. You saved my life. If you hadn't pushed me aside it would have been me who'd got stabbed. I owe you my life.'

'If you hadn't shot her, she might well have stabbed me again,' said Daniel. 'So I'd say we're equal.'

'No, you don't, Wilson,' growled Armstrong. 'You took the knife that was meant for me.'

Daniel hesitated as he wondered how to respond. Then he said, 'Yes, I did.'

'And you were right about the killings. It wasn't that mad girl.'

'No,' said Daniel.

This time it was the superintendent's turn to hesitate before speaking. 'You were right, and I was wrong. I respect you for that. It doesn't mean I have to like you, but I respect that.'

'Thank you,' said Daniel.

'The big thing is, you saved my life at the risk to your own. For that, I'll always owe you one. So, this is to say you're not barred from the Yard.'

'Thank you,' said Daniel again.

'Just so long as you don't take advantage of it,' added Armstrong. 'I don't want you cluttering up Inspector Feather's office and taking up his time. He's a good copper, but he's got a soft spot for you.'

'He's a *very* good copper,' said Daniel. 'The best there is on your squad.'

'Even better than me?' demanded Armstrong.

Daniel forced a smile. 'I'm hardly likely to say in case I get barred again.'

For a moment Daniel thought Armstrong was going to respond with a snarled insult, but instead he was sure he saw the corner of the superintendent's mouth twitch, almost a smile.

'Get back on your feet soon, Wilson.'

Daniel's first visitor the next morning was John Feather.

'How are you?' he asked, coming in and settling himself down on the chair beside Daniel's bed. Daniel noticed he was holding a paper bag.

'Recovering,' said Daniel. 'I'm hoping they'll kick me out today.'

'I wouldn't rush it,' cautioned Feather. 'By all accounts, the stab wound was pretty deep. You were lucky.'

'I was lucky Armstrong was carrying a revolver,' said Daniel.

'He's not as bad as you think,' said Feather. 'He's going to have to make a statement to the press about Jenny Warren being the real killer.'

'Any bets he blames you and his staff for wrongfully identifying Elsie Bowler?' asked Daniel.

'He's the boss.' Feather shrugged.

'He came to see me last night,' said Daniel. 'He told me I'm no longer barred from the Yard.'

'Quite right. Let's face it, you saved his life.'

Daniel nodded at the paper bag. 'I've been told that visitors bring patients nice things when they're in hospital. Grapes. Sweets. That sort of thing.'

'Yes, I've heard that, too,' said Feather. 'And that was my intention, so grapes it was. But as I sat on the bus coming here

I thought, "Maybe the hospital don't want Daniel eating things while he's recovering. Especially with pips in them." And it seemed a pity to waste them.'

'You ate my grapes?' said Daniel, scandalised.

'Technically speaking, they weren't your grapes,' said Feather. 'I bought them, so they were mine. But you can have them.'

He handed over the bag. Daniel opened it and looked in. There were five grapes left.

Daniel sighed. 'I suppose it's the thought that counts.'

After Feather left, one of the nurses brought Daniel some newspapers to read. Daniel had hoped that Abigail would have put in an appearance, but he guessed that something must have detained her. She arrived with the answer shortly before eleven.

'I'm sorry I'm later than expected, but I went to the museum first to tell Sir Jasper how you're doing. And also, to thank him for paying your hospital bills.'

'I thought it must be him,' said Daniel.

'He said he felt it was the least the museum could do, and it had the full support of the board.'

'Only after he'd nagged them, I expect,' said Daniel.

'And this arrived at the museum this morning.' Abigail produced a telegram and passed it to Daniel. 'It's a response from Mr Watts to the one I sent yesterday to your friend Ben Stilworthy.'

Daniel read it. *Returning to London. Will see you on my return. Will be republishing Ambrosius book as 'By William Jedding; edited by Professor Lance Pickering'. Yours, Jerrold Watts.*

'Well!' exclaimed Daniel. 'Well done to Mr Watts. Vindication and justice for William Jedding at last.'

'A pity he couldn't live to see it,' said Abigail. She sat down on the bed and took Daniel's hand in hers. 'Yes,' she said.

'What was the question?' asked Daniel.

'The one you asked me some time ago. Would I marry you. The answer's yes.' She squeezed his hand. 'When I thought I'd lost you after you were stabbed, I felt absolutely bereft. I know it won't change things between us, I don't think I can love you any more than I already do, but I don't want us to be separated again.'

'You mean you won't be going off on any more archaeological digs?' asked Daniel, surprised.

'Well, yes, I will, of course. That's what I do,' said Abigail.

'So, what do you mean about not being separated?'

'To be honest, I'm not sure,' admitted Abigail. 'It's about *feeling* separated. If we're married I don't think I'll have that feeling.'

'*If*?' queried Daniel.

'Of course I meant "when".'

'When?' asked Daniel.

Abigail thought about it. 'Not immediately,' she said.

Daniel laughed. 'You're having second thoughts already?'

'No, absolutely not,' said Abigail. 'But there are things to think about. Practical things.'

'Like what?'

'Like finding a house for us that's both of ours, as you talked about. I'd like to do that first.'

Daniel smiled. 'So would I,' he said.

Jim Eldridge was born in central London towards the end of World War II, and was blown up (but survived) during attacks by V2 rockets on the Euston/Kings Cross area of London where he lived. He left school at sixteen and did a variety of jobs, before training as a teacher. In 1971 he sold his first sitcom (starring Arthur Lowe) to the BBC and had his first book commissioned. Since then he has had over 100 books published, with sales of over three million copies. He lives in Kent with his wife.

jimeldridge.com

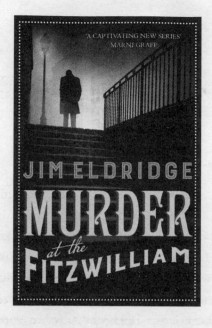

1894. Daniel Wilson made his name investigating the case of Jack the Ripper alongside the formidable Inspector Abberline. Now working as a private enquiry agent, Wilson's reputation precedes him, making him the natural first choice for the Fitzwilliam Museum in Cambridge, which finds itself in need of urgent – and discreet – assistance.

The museum will soon unveil its new Egyptian collection, but strange occurrences have followed the exhibits to Britain: a dead body inhabits a previously empty sarcophagus, a mummified bodyguard is on the loose and ancient bandages are props in another grisly murder. Aided by the talented resident archaeologist, Abigail Fenton, can Wilson unravel the mystery before the museum's public launch?

MURDER AT THE ASHMOLEAN

1895. A senior executive at the Ashmolean Museum in Oxford is found in his office with a bullet hole between his eyes, a pistol discarded close by. The death has officially been ruled as suicide by local police, but with an apparent lack of motive for such action, the museum's administrator, Gladstone Marriott, suspects foul play. With his cast-iron reputation for shrewdness, formed during his time investigating the case of Jack the Ripper alongside Inspector Abberline, private enquiry agent Daniel Wilson is a natural choice to discreetly explore the situation, ably assisted by his partner, archaeologist-cum-detective Abigail Fenton.

Yet their enquiries are hindered from the start by an interfering lone agent from Special Branch, ever secretive and intimidating in his methods. With rumours of political ructions from South Africa, mislaid artefacts and a lost Shakespeare play, Wilson and Fenton soon find themselves tangled in bureaucracy. Making unlikely alliances, the pair face players who live by a different set of rules and will need their intellect and ingenuity to reveal the identity of a killer.

To discover more great books and to
place an order visit our website at
allisonandbusby.com

Don't forget to sign up to our free newsletter at
allisonandbusby.com/newsletter
for latest releases, events and exclusive offers

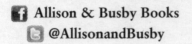 **Allison & Busby Books**
@AllisonandBusby

You can also call us on
020 3950 7834
for orders, queries
and reading recommendations